MAX COSSACK

Where There Is No Man

Song *It Ain't Gamblin' When You Know You're Gonna Lose*, Words and Music by
Joseph Vass
Copyright © 2017 Joseph Vass All Right Reserved. Included by Permission.

Song *Come Soon, Little Stranger*, Words and Music by Joseph Vass
Copyright © 2020 Joseph Vass All Right Reserved. Included by Permission.

Previous novels by Max Cossack in this series, in chronological order:
1. *Khaybar, Minnesota*
2. *Zarah's Fire*
3. *Simple Grifts   A Comedy of Social Justice*
4. *Low Tech Killers*

Other books published by VWAM include these by Susan Vass:
Ammo Grrrll Hits The Target (Volume 1)
Ammo Grrrll Aims True (Volume 2)
Ammo Grrrll Returns Fire (Volume 3)
Ammo Grrrll Is Home On The Range (Volume 4)
Ammo Grrrll Is A Straight Shooter (Volume 5)

What Readers Say

about Max Cossack's consensus 5-Star Debut Novel "Khaybar, Minnesota"

"The most realistic thriller Ever."

"Frighteningly possible story, well told."

"A fast-paced pleasurable read."

"A great read, a great story and (unfortunately) extremely topical."

"You won't be able to put it down."

"Tremendous first novel."

"An entertaining tale which I enjoyed enough to read twice."

"Great read! Hard to believe this is the first book by this author. He hit all the high notes with a timely, believable plot, interesting characters and authentic dialog…Get this book, you won't be disappointed."

ACKNOWLEDGEMENT

Sincere appreciation to Lt. Col. Ernest "Tony" Peluso (Ret.) for his technical advice on matters of war. Any factual errors are solely the author's.

DEDICATION

To All Those Who Have Served
In Our American Armed Forces,
Past and Present

EPIGRAPH

בְּמָקוֹם שֶׁאֵין אֲנָשִׁים ,הִשְׁתַּדֵּל לִהְיוֹת אִישׁ

In a place where there is no man, you be the man

Talmud, Pirkei Avot, 2:6

PART

ONE

1 Sam Breaks The First Rule

Sam Lapidos was about to ask a witness a question to which Sam did not already know the answer.

Back when Sam was a rookie allowed to prosecute only misdemeanors, Sam's mentor Preston Wilcox had used letters of fire to burn his "don't ask unless you already know" commandment into a stone tablet, then handed the tablet down to Sam from Preston's towering Mount Sinai of trial experience.

Preston had already racked up 27 murder convictions, well on his way to a career total of 33, one of them posthumous, after a stroke keeled Preston over in the middle of his devastating final argument. Preston loved to put killers away, and the jury verdict would have thrilled Preston if he could have stuck around to hear it.

Now here Sam stood in court, about to bounce Preston's stone tablet down onto the institutional gray courtroom carpet.

Or maybe not. Truth was, he hadn't quite talked himself into it.

Judge Moore prompted, "Counselor?" and Sam realized everyone in the courtroom was staring at him. He'd been standing motionless behind his defendant's table for something like half a minute.

Sam had asked Letitia Crump to read aloud from her handwritten letter describing the death of Andre Otis. She shifted her considerable bulk in the witness chair and burbled out a visible sigh. She lifted the paper and held it an odd angle above eye level. She contorted her face into a *Now What?* pout and furrowed her brow and stared at the thing like she'd never seen it before.

Which Sam suspected she hadn't.

Sam had cross-examined hundreds of nervous witnesses, including dozens who started out jittery and turned progressively jumpier as his hammering wore them down. Some wound up snarling; now and then one broke into tears, and—his fondest courtroom memory—the swindler Garrett Noble Watt had clutched his hand over his heart and flung himself off the witness chair and thudded face first onto the carpet.

Unfortunately for Garrett Noble Watt, he survived his fake heart attack and wound up paying the widow Gloria Lipcott $13.3 million in damages. Sam forced Watt to sell both his mansions and all his Lamborghinis, even the apricot one Watt adored. Two weeks later Watt died for real, maybe from a broken wallet. Sam hoped so.

Letitia Crump's was an unusual discomfort. Sam was only a few preliminary questions and halting answers into his cross examination when it sank in that Letitia's unease grew out of the fact she didn't comprehend what was going on in the court around her or what she was doing there.

She kept glancing to the prosecutor Harland Ellison for clues. Letitia's mute plea for help was so obvious that the jurors and Judge Moore all followed her glance and eyed Ellison too, waiting for some signal.

Ellison, a bald white man in a severe dark suit, stared without expression back at Ms. Crump from his own table to Sam's left. He knew better than to signal his witness with cues the jury would pick up on. If Ms. Crump wanted his help, it would have to be via telepathy.

Judge Moore, a solidly built black man, gazed with solemn neutrality down at all the players from his lofty perch on a high bench, implacable and unmoving as a stone idol. He prompted Letitia in a gentle rumble. "Ms. Crump?"

She glanced up at him. "Judge?"

"The Defendant's lawyer has asked you to read something aloud. Could you do that please?"

"I'm not sure, Your Honor. I'll try."

Sam reminded her, "Paragraph 2."

She stared at Sam.

Sam asked, "Do you see the words right after the number 2, near the top of the page?"

She nodded.

Sam said, "Please read those words."

She tapped the paper with her index finger. "Here?"

"Yes, there."

The three yellow pages rustled as she shuffled through them. She said, "It's hard. It's not printed."

Her answer puzzled Sam for a moment. Then he got her point. "You mean because it's in cursive?"

"Yes. I don't know the cursive."

"Did you write this letter yourself?"

"No."

"Did you dictate it?"

"What is 'dictate'?"

"Did you say the words and someone write them down?"

"Yes."

"Who wrote them down for you?"

"Auntie Nola."

Letitia spoke low, barely above a whisper. Older jurors were leaning forward to hear her.

Sam asked, "But that is your signature at the end?"

"Yes."

"Do you think you can give it a try and read the part after the number 2, even though it's in cursive?"

She shuffled the paper again and pursed her lips and read, "I have personal knowledge of the facts stated..." She stopped.

Sam helped her out. "Herein."

She looked at him. "What?"

"Is the next word 'herein'?"

She looked back down at the page and smiled. "Yes. Thank you. Herein."

Sam smiled back. "You're welcome, Ms. Crump. Do you?"

"Do I what?"

"Do you have personal knowledge of the events stated therein? In this letter you say you dictated and signed? For example, that you were in the bedroom in Andre's apartment when someone knocked on his apartment door?"

Ellison said, "Objection. Asked and answered."

Judge Moore said, "Objection sustained."

Sam plowed ahead. "And Andre got up from the bed and left his bedroom to answer the door?"

Ellison said, "Objection."

Judge Moore said, "Sustained."

Sam asked, "While still in bed, from the next room, you overheard the conversation described in your letter?"

She tapped the paper. "What's written here."

"You heard Andre shout, 'Hands up! Don't Shoot!'?"

"Yes."

Sam asked, "If his hands were up, don't you think Officer Latham would have seen that?"

Sam's question called for speculation from the witness, but for some reason Ellison didn't object.

Letitia Crump glanced at Sam's client, Officer Stan Latham, sitting in the chair to Sam's right. Stan met her gaze unblinking, ramrod erect and expressionless, like the retired Marine he was. Throughout the trial, he'd remained stoic, guarding his dignity like an embassy in a hostile country.

Letitia glanced down at the floor in front of her. "I don't know."

"You have any idea why Andre felt the need to say that?"

She shrugged, her expression reminding Sam of a child caught with a broken cereal bowl and no good explanation.

Judge Moore reminded her, "Ms. Crump, you must make a vocal answer."

She said, "What's that?"

Judge Moore said, "You must speak your answer out loud so that the Court Reporter can write it down."

Letitia looked at the Court Reporter, a thin gray-haired woman who smiled back at Letitia over her machine.

Letitia gave her a shy smile back. "Okay."

Silence filled the courtroom. Sam repeated his question. "Do you have any idea why Andre felt the need to say that?"

"Say what?" she asked.

"To tell Officer Latham his hands were up if Officer Latham could see his hands just by looking at him?"

"Maybe he was being friendly? Andre was always a friendly person."

Sam asked, "Then you heard a gunshot?"

She tapped the letter. "That's what it says."

"And you stayed in the bed? You didn't rush to see what had happened?"

"I was terrified."

"But you heard Andre call out?"

"Yes. His last words."

"Which were, 'I've had a good life. Thanks to you, Jazmun.'?"

"Yes."

Sam asked, "Your name is Letitia but he called you 'Jazmun'?"

"'Jazmun' is a kind of nickname."

"Which is why you used the name 'Jazmun' when you signed the letter as 'Jazmun Wilcox' instead of using your own name Letitia Crump?"

"Yes. That's why."

Sam nodded as if that were a perfectly reasonable explanation. He glanced peripherally at Ellison at his table to Sam's left, leaning forward, poised like a coiled spring, waiting to leap to his feet.

Yes, something was going on.

Sam asked, "And then you escaped down the fire escape to avoid the police?"

Letitia paused as if considering her answer. "I don't recall exactly. I guess I must have."

One consequence of Sam's faithfulness to Preston Wilcox's commandment was that Sam had to prepare, prepare, and prepare, to know everything there was to know about a case, to immerse himself in all its facts and facets and nuances. Only then could he proceed to lay out his questions and get the answers he already knew in a logical progression which sold his client's story to the jury.

Here and now, in a homicide case, with his client Officer Stan Latham's freedom on the line, should Sam ask a question to which Sam suspected but did not know the answer?

Feet shuffled behind Sam, as if uncertainty riled the spectators as much as Sam.

At the thought of his upcoming reckless plunge, Sam felt a small thrill, like the thrill he'd felt back in tenth grade, about to unhook Mallory Horowitz's bra for the first time. Who knew then what unalloyed joy might follow?

On the other hand, maybe Mallory was going to punch him out?

Sneak up on it. Leave yourself an escape route. Start with something innocuous.

Sam asked, "Letitia, how much do you weigh?"

Ellison shot to his feet. "Objection! Harassing the witness!

"Your Honor, the question is not a personal attack. It goes to the credibility of the witness's testimony."

Sam guessed Letitia went at least three hundred fifty pounds. She looked about five foot three.

Judge Moore glowered at Sam. But Sam was defending someone on trial for murder. In Judge Moore's court that meant wide latitude. He sighed. "Go ahead." He nodded at Letitia.

Despite the interruption, this time Letitia remembered the question. "I don't know exactly how much I weigh. It changes a lot."

"Do you recall what floor Andre's apartment was on?"

"No, I don't."

"How many times did you visit Andre in that apartment?"

"I don't recall."

"More than ten, would you say?"

She shrugged, then corrected her mistake and answered aloud. "That sounds right."

"If I suggest his apartment was on the third floor, would that sound wrong?"

She glanced at the stone-faced Ellison, then admitted, "I guess that could be right."

"Are you aware whether there is an elevator in Andre's building?"

"I don't remember."

"Do you remember ever taking an elevator to get up to his apartment on the third floor?"

"I don't remember that."

"If I provide you with proof there is no elevator in that building, would that surprise you?"

"No."

"Do you remember if you perhaps took the stairs?"

"Yes. That must be it. I took the stairs."

"What were these stairs like?"

"They were stairs. I don't remember."

"Well, were they straight?"

"Don't remember."

"Curved?"

"Don't remember."

"Were they wood or metal?"

"Don't remember."

"Was there a banister?"

From behind Sam's back a scream erupted. The scream soared to a strident wail which fractured the air, a siren rising and dropping in pitch. Letitia froze, her eyes wide. Judge Moore glared—not this trial's first interruption.

Sam snuck a glance backwards. His friend Gus Dropo was watching from the gallery, sitting next to a wide black man. Even sitting, Gus towered over everyone else.

Three seats to Gus's right, a fat young white woman with stringy brown hair stood with both her hands clamped on her cheeks, her nails white from pressure, her face pointed ceilingward. She saw Sam looking at her and cut herself off in mid-wail. Looking directly at Sam, she raised the middle fingers of both hands and began to chant, "Give racism the finger! Give racism the finger! Give racism the finger!"

The two women on either side of her joined her in flipping Sam off. "Give racism the finger!"

Six burly male and female sheriff's deputies rushed to the three women and began hustling them out. The three women resisted. Pushing the women was like pushing heavy bureaus across a buckling carpet, involving a lot of shifting and twisting movements. The trial stopped while the deputies spent several minutes maneuvering the women down the aisle and out through the door to the hallway. It took a few extra moments for noise of their chanting to fade as the deputies bundled them off somewhere.

A quiet moment. Then, as if nothing had happened, Letitia said, "I don't remember about the stairs."

Sam snuck another sideways glance at Ellison. The Prosecutor sat with lips pressed tight, his cheeks compressed, his eyes almost bulging out of his head.

Ellison's edginess proved to Sam he was on the right track. Get to the real point. Forget the goddammed stairs. Ask the ultimate question. The question to which he did not know the answer.

Now or never. "Ms. Crump, do you know a woman named Jazmun Wilcox?"

"You mean my nickname like I sign on the Affidavit?"

"I mean an actual person named Jazmun Wilcox. A separate individual from yourself. Do you know her?"

Ellison was on his feet again. "Your Honor, what is the relevance of this? There could be a thousand people named Jazmun Wilcox in America. So what?"

Sam stood too. "Your Honor, I am not asking about random Jazmun Wilcoxes, but only about one specific person, and whether Ms. Crump knows her. It's a simple question."

Judge Moore sat a moment, a puzzled expression on his face, then: "Objection overruled. Ms. Crump, you may answer."

"Yeah, I do know someone by that name," she said.

Ellison sat down with a thump. He grunted and folded his arms in apparent disgust. He made a show of glaring upwards at the high court ceiling, away from and far above everyone else.

Sam asked, "This Jazmun Wilcox you know, that is not just her nickname, is it? That's her real name?"

"Far as I know, that her real name," Letitia said.

"She was also a friend of Andre's?"

"I guess."

"Don't you know it for a fact?"

Long pause, then Letitia muttered, "Maybe." Then she shook her head. She muttered something more.

But Sam thought he heard her. He asked, "What was that?"

Letitia said, "Nothing."

"But you said something, didn't you? And I think I heard what you said."

"Then you know what I said," Letitia told him. She looked Sam straight in the eyes, her expression regretful.

Sam felt regret too. "Go ahead, please, in case they couldn't hear you, please say for the jury what you just said so very softly."

She sighed. "I said, I feel guilty."

Sam's tone was gentle. "And what do you feel guilty about, Letitia?"

She sighed. "Guilty about what I said before."

"Because it wasn't true?"

"No, it wasn't."

"You weren't with Andre that night?"

"No."

"You didn't sign that Affidavit?"

"No, it wasn't me."

"It was the real Jazmun Wilcox?"

"Far as I know."

"It was the real Jazmun Wilcox who was with Andre that night?"

"Far as I know." Round tears welled in her eyes.

"Letitia, you don't have any personal knowledge of what happened that night, do you?"

"No." Fat tears rolled down her cheeks. "And I do feel guilty for saying all that stuff I said."

"I believe you," Sam said. He turned and stared at Harland Ellison. So did everyone else, among those Judge Moore, who had replaced his usual neutral expression with another more ominous one.

2 Owen

Owen Al-Amriki sat in a booth at the Hedgehog Barrel Tavern, savoring the moment.

He stared at the ice-cold Chumpster beer bottle on the table in front of him. He lifted the bottle and tilted it to his mouth and chugged. The liquid chilled his throat and carried its delicious coolness all the way down the center of his body. He felt the cold hit his belly. The cold radiated from his core outward through his chest and back up to his head.

If you're going to go bad, might as well go all the way.

Owen gave the bottle an extra squeeze with his right hand. The condensation wetted and cooled his palm and fingers. He lifted the bottle close to his face and sniffed at its neck top and inhaled the once-familiar smell of hops. The fragrance took him back to his high school days with his buddies, when beer had been the very currency of excitement and adventure and therefore of life itself.

For this single moment he lived again in one of those beer commercials where the guys ganged up for harmless fun, like dunking one another under the icy waterfall or flirting with slender black-clad women in the pool hall— never wondering what women in cocktail dresses were doing in a pool hall—or bunching up at the big game, dancing around, pounding their chests, clucking like apes.

"All right!" he said aloud and startled himself. He looked around, but none of the few other customers gave any sign of hearing him, not even the little black-bearded guy in the very next booth staring at a blank yellow pad and chewing the top of his black BIC ballpoint pen.

The only woman in the place squatted in front of the bar, paying no attention to anyone around her, her ass drooping over both sides of the stool, radiating hostility in case any of the men dared approach her, which seemed unlikely.

The Chumpster was like a religious experience. No, it wasn't *like* a religious experience, it *was* a religious experience.

Because alcohol was *haram*—forbidden. Owen hadn't drunk a drop since he said the *Shahada* to convert to Islam more than a year ago.

So having a beer was a religious act, right? In defiance of Sharia? A bold statement, even if made in secret, miles from his Al-Andalus Mosque.

Owen looked around again. Still nobody paying any attention.

The beer was tasty, but what Owen savored was to do something haram for the first time in like forever.

But what if someone from the cell saw him? No, Tayoub and Mahir were devout and would never go into a tavern. In fact, any Muslim who saw Owen there shouldn't be there himself and could have no good explanation for his own presence.

Suppose they explained they were only there to search for Owen?

Owen took another belt. He shook his head, not because of the beer but because of his own childishness. The second belt was no big thing, just more beer. So what?

What about the murder? That was serious.

He was sitting in this bar drinking a beer to avoid doing what he'd been told to do. In Tayoub's cell, the penalty for disobedience was death. Unless Owen followed his orders, Tayoub would be coming for him.

Owen was letting Tayoub down. Owen was letting the *Al Quds* Cell down. He was letting Allah down. He should probably give up being the pious rebel Owen Al-Amriki and go back to being plain old Owen Deutscher.

If Owen didn't do the deed, someone else would. He couldn't just sit and drink beer while someone hacked Professor Cobb to pieces.

The notion of talking to the police or the feds chilled Owen even more than the beer. He'd have to explain his own crimes. His part in the childcare fraud scheme, for example. He'd be implicating himself.

Owen needed a plan. And in the meantime, he needed to stay out of Tayoub's presence. Owen could come up with some excuse for not having killed the man—for example, maybe he hadn't found Cobb yet—but if Owen slipped up, Tayoub would spot it. Tayoub was uncanny that way. He tolerated no deviation, and he was a deviation savant. He detected it from the slightest dilation of a pupil or twitch of an eyebrow. Owen had seen him do it.

Owen didn't want to wind up like Steve O'Toole, disappeared forever into the Arizona desert.

3 Sam Bugs Out

Two hours after Judge Moore halted the trial, Sam
wheeled his suitcase thumpety thump down the stairs from
Judge Moore's chambers to a landing three floors below and
rendezvoused with his friend and all-too-frequent client Gus
Dropo.

"For all the business I provide, you ought to pay me
frequent flier miles," Gus had said once.

"You ought to pay me actual cash money," Sam had
replied.

The air was dank, as if the building's ventilation system
couldn't be bothered with it. The sweet fragrance of
marijuana lingered. Two dirty ceiling fixtures cast only dim
light.

Chants from the mob outside reverberated in the
stairwell. "No! No! No! No! Killer cops have got to go!".
Sounded like thousands out there. It was like huddling inside
a bass drum.

Gus was a behemoth as well as a veteran of dozens of
physical conflicts, most of them over in a few crisp seconds,
and therefore highly qualified to help out as Sam's first-call
bodyguard.

Maybe as a concession to the size of the mob outside,
Gus had brought along a partner, a large black man with a
huge chest and an even huger belly that jutted like a round
dome of concrete under his big shirt. Sam nodded a
greeting.

"This is Rolf," Gus said, "A reliable friend."

"I'm a man of the law," Rolf announced, as if that were
an explanation not only for his presence but for his entire
life.

Sam and Rolf shook hands. Sam asked, "Well, fellows, what's the plan?"

"There's a lot of lynchers out there," Gus said, "Howling for your neck."

"I'm not the one who put an impostor witness on the stand," Sam said. "That was the prosecution's brilliant idea."

Gus said, "Why do you think they did that?"

"The real Jazmun Wilcox wouldn't tell the story they wanted," Sam said.

"The mob's going to hate you for smoking out the hoax and wrecking the case," Gus said.

"Life is hard," Sam said.

"How'd you catch on?" Rolf asked.

"It started when I talked to Letitia before the trial and first met her," Sam said. "Not to be cruel, but she didn't figure to be cast as the main character in the romance novel she was telling. The rest was logic and an intelligent guess."

"Pretty lucky guess," Gus said.

Sam said nothing. Not everything need be told.

"What happens to Letitia?" Rolf asked.

"In chambers just now, I asked the judge to go easy on her," Sam said. "I think he will. It's the lawyers who should go down."

The chants outside surged in pitch and volume and changed from killer cops to "Shyster lawyers got to go!"

Gus nodded towards the noise. "They just heard how you torpedoed their case."

Rolf asked, "So, once we get you past that mob, where to? Home?"

"Haven't got a home right now," Sam said. "The day I took this case, I sold my Minneapolis house. I figured it would be a good time to get the hell out."

"Or what's left of it," Rolf said. "Maybe Judge Moore should consider the same move."

"I suggested the same thing to him, but I doubt he will," Sam said.

"Where you been staying?" Gus asked.

"In a crap motel on Highway 35W," Sam said. "Under another name."

"So where are we taking you?" Rolf asked.

"We could drive out to my place," Gus said. Gus lived ninety miles away on the edge of a jack pine wilderness. "You can hole up there for a while."

"Even out there, the zealots will find him and show up," Rolf said. "What then?"

"I've got plenty of open space," Gus said. "We'll see them coming."

Sam said, "Thanks anyway, Gus, but I've got no immediate happy future anywhere in Minnesota. Get me to the airport and I'll fly to Phoenix."

"You got a reservation?" Gus asked.

Sam waved off the question. "No need. All I need is this suitcase."

"Why Phoenix?" Rolf asked.

"I've lawyered there before," Sam said. "It's just as screwed up as Minnesota."

4 Owen Meets A Friend

"Owen!" The man's voice came from behind.

Owen kept walking down the sidewalk. Owen had waited for darkness before stepping out onto the street through the Hedgehog Barrel's swinging doors.

The same man's voice said, "*As-salamu alaykum!*"

At the traditional Muslim greeting, Owen turned.

Frank LaGuardia stood on the sidewalk grinning at him. Frank was a fellow member at *Al-Andalus*. He was a big Italian guy with a crew cut and black beetle brows.

What were the odds? Owen recalled Frank mentioning once that he worked downtown. That might explain it.

Frank belonged to *Al-Andalus*, but not to Tayoub's *Al-Quds* cell. But maybe some other cell? Who knew? That was the point of cells. Nobody knew.

Owen felt his face flush and hoped Frank didn't notice under the dim light from the street lamps.

If Frank did notice, he gave no sign. His big grin didn't waver.

Owen muttered the required response: "*Wa alaykumu s-salam,*" and pointed with his right thumb at the Hedgehog Barrel's swinging door. "Had to use the bathroom in there."

"Too many beers?"

Owen felt his flush burn deeper. He forced out a brittle bark intended as a laugh. "Good one."

Frank swung his arm up and gave a gentle poke to Owen's shoulder with the thumb side of his fist. "Just kidding, you know."

"Sure."

An awkward pause. Owen wished he could fill it with something funny but came up empty. He just grinned a pointless grin.

Frank said, "Where's your *kufi*? Always admired that blue knitted one you wear."

Owen pulled his hat out of his pocket. "Didn't want to wear it in a bar, even walking to the bathroom. Would send the wrong signal for a Muslim to be in there."

Owen realized he was still wearing his long-sleeved white *kurta* shirt and loose-fitting pants rolled up above his ankles. In fact, he still sported his full beard. Might as well wear an I-am-Muslim sign.

Nobody in the Hedgehog Barrel had shown any discomfort with his presence. Maybe they didn't care, but maybe they were just being polite.

Frank nodded, maybe also to be polite. "Makes sense. Well, it was fun running into you. Just heading home from work."

"Yeah. I had some personal business to handle in the neighborhood. I'll be heading back home myself."

Frank said, "*Ma'aasalaama.*"

Owen answered, "*Ma'aasalaama.*"

Frank smiled—it seemed to Owen a little sadly—and touched Owen's shoulder gently with his fist one more time and turned and walked away.

Owen watched him. Frank was a good guy, but so what? Would Frank mention the incident to Tayoub, even if only innocently? Tayoub demanded total devotion. To him, nothing was innocent.

Time to hide.

Where?

5 *Aviva Soriano*

"It was this rapper," Aviva Soriano said. "And his so-called song, which wasn't a song at all, just a nasty ignorant man shouting nasty ignorant things about Jews. And the crowd was laughing and clapping and shouting their own nasty things along with him. Disgusting."

Four plush easy chairs were arranged in a square in the front room of an old house near downtown Phoenix. A glass-topped dark oak coffee table was centered between them. One chair was empty. Sam and his only law partner Jacob Laghdaf sat in two of them, opposite each other. Aviva Soriano sat in a third, sipping a cup of tea Laghdaf had brewed for her, along with one for himself. As usual, Sam was having nothing.

Laghdaf had scouted ahead of Sam's planned flight from Minnesota and rented the house from a retiring Phoenix lawyer. Sam's first morning in Phoenix, Sam already liked the place a lot. It was comfy and roomy and gave a feel of the prosperity a lot of clients preferred in their lawyers. Maybe Laghdaf and he should buy it outright and make it their permanent Arizona office.

Even in English, Ms. Soriano's speech hinted at a Mexican melody, as if she were speaking words to an old Mexican song while an accordion played the melody behind her. One of those button accordions. Or did they call that a concertina?

Sam could recognize a lot of languages by melody. Even speaking English, her melody was the Spanish of Mexico, even though at this moment she was only speaking and not singing and her speech bore only a trace of an accent.

Sam decided he would like to hear Ms. Soriano sing. Sometimes he could tell a singer by her speech—something in the control and modulations of the voice. Maybe Aviva Soriano could sing.

And into the almost-sung speech of Aviva Soriano she mixed a counter melody, a distinct second tune enriching the first. This second tune was also familiar to Sam, but in the moment he couldn't think why.

Like a Bach invention or fugue. But with Bach, a third melody might come in, then a fourth and even a fifth. You could never tell with Bach. And you could never tell with a woman either, although it had been a long time for Sam and a woman.

This entire jumble of thought in a single instant. He'd lost focus and his mind wandered. He needed a few days to recover from the intensity and stress of his Minneapolis trial. But here he was, already back at work. What else was there to do?

This morning, let Laghdaf do most of the work and ask the questions. Sam would listen. He needed the practice anyway.

As usual, Laghdaf was on the job. "What rap was that?" he asked, "Which frightened you so?"

Aviva straightened erect and clutched her big black purse in her lap. She glared at Laghdaf. "It didn't frighten me. It angered me." She took her phone out of her purse and fiddled with a moment, then placed it on the table. The phone's tinny little speaker played:

(A beat boxer making a rap beat.)

A man's voice, in a foreign accent: "This is my anti-Semitic song. You don't expect me to be anti-

Semitic all by myself, do you? And you all look beautifully anti-Semitic."

(Crowd noise, laughter and garbled shouts.)

The same man yells, "All together now! I can't sing alone!"

The crowd shouts back, "All together now!"

He, "I'm in love with a Jew!"

They shout back, "I'm in love with a Jew!"

He, "Again! All together now! I'm in love with a Jew!"

They, "I'm in love with a Jew!"

(Much laughter. Shouting and more laughing.)

He shouts, "The Jew with her money and her nose!"

Crowd: "The Jew with her money and her nose!"

He, "I'm in love with her money and her nose and all the countries she controls!"

They, "I'm in love with her money and her nose and all the countries she controls!"

Laghdaf picked the phone up from the glass tabletop and punched the screen with this finger. The recording stopped. He placed the phone back on the glass. "Please. We get the idea."

Sam also liked to listen to Laghdaf speak. Laghdaf's mother tongue was the Wolof language of Mauritania in Northwest Africa, where he'd been born a Muslim slave. He was no longer a slave. Laghdaf's liquid vowels seemed to dissolve even the most rigid and brittle consonants of English speech into its own flowing music, almost like singing, even though Sam knew from disappointing experience Laghdaf couldn't carry a tune in a donkey cart.

Two years ago, Sam had taken Laghdaf on as a partner. It had been a long time for Sam and a partner.

Aviva said, "I just wanted to show you what I heard. And it gets much worse."

"We can listen to the much worse part later," Laghdaf said. "Where did you make this recording?"

"At SWASU," she said. She paused. "SWASU is our nickname for South West Arizona State University."

"Of course," Laghdaf said. He nodded to reassure her he knew that. "And the occasion?"

"A conference," she said. "They advertised it as a learning opportunity about Israel and Indigenous Peoples, but it turned out to be about nothing but Jews and how rich and evil they are and how they secretly run the world."

Laghdaf asked, "Who sponsored this conference?"

"Everyone," she said. "Almost every department. The History Department. The Gender Studies Department. Comparative Literature. Latinx Studies. The School of Dentistry. And Pharmacy."

"Pharmacy?", Laghdaf asked.

Although he'd planned to say nothing, Sam couldn't help himself. He muttered, "Dentistry?"

For the first time, Aviva looked directly into Sam's eyes. He saw the depth of feeling there. "Dentistry," she repeated. "They advertised they were going to talk about

Israel and indigenous peoples and what was behind the
fighting there. But it wasn't like that. It was just all about
the awful Jews. That the Jews have all the money and they
use it to control all the governments in the world."

She pulled a folded yellow sheet from her big black
purse. She unfolded in into a poster and placed it face up on
the glass. The poster blared **ISRAEL AND INDIGENOUS
PEOPLES** in big block letters, and in smaller letters listed
dozens of SWASU departments as sponsors, including not
only the usual suspects but departments like the Schools of
Pharmacy and Dentistry.

Laghdaf let the poster lay. Laghdaf asked, "Why were
you at this conference?"

"I was there to help organize things. Get things done. I'm
good at that. They're not."

"You work at SWASU?" Laghdaf said.

"For the Latinx Studies Department," she said. She
pronounced it "Latin-ex." Sam guessed the idea of the name
was to include everyone of every gender who spoke a
language descended from Latin, and not just males or
females. He wasn't sure how many other genders there
could be, though the catalog burgeoned.

Did Romanians count as Latinx? Their language came from
Latin too, but they were east Europeans, the whitest of the
white, at least according to the people who kept close track
of such things.

Laghdaf said to Ms. Soriano, "Please continue."

She said, "They got a lot of federal money too. Two
hundred thousand dollars. And they paid this rapper ten
thousand dollars."

"How do you know how much they paid him?"

"I told you, I get things done. I fill out the forms. I file
the requisitions."

"You saw the check?"

"I wrote the check. I handed it to him. That was before I heard him. His name is Tayoub Abawi. He calls himself a 'recording artist', but he's no artist. Just another gutter hater."

She spat out the phrase "gutter hater."

Sam was not surprised by the audio she'd played. Jew hatred was nothing new to him. Just the same, the rage bubbled far down beneath the surface, the way it always did, a dormant volcano that had erupted only a few times in his life, into scenes he preferred not to brood over. One more reason to keep his trap shut.

Laghdaf asked, "Do you know which part of the government gave SWASU this two hundred thousand dollars?"

"They got their grant from the U.S. Department of Education."

Laghdaf asked, "Does your boss know you made this recording?"

"I have two bosses," she said. "Professors Gomez and Escobar. "I don't think so. I certainly haven't told either of them"

Laghdaf leaned back in his chair and folded his hands on his lap, signaling the most important question. "What would you like to do about it?"

"I don't know. That's why I came here. For you to tell me. You're the lawyers."

Laghdaf asked, "How'd you find out about us?"

"I know you two sued SWASU last year and beat them in court. They all hate you. Especially this woman Sterns-Stuyvesant." She shuddered.

Laghdaf shot a quick glance at Sam, then asked Aviva, "You know Dean Sterns-Stuyvesant?"

Professor Sterns-Stuyvesant was the Bias Committee Dean and Diversity Honcha who had lorded it over their client Amos Owens. Sam had relished ripping Sterns-Stuyvesant a new one when he cross-examined her at trial.

Aviva said, "Only a little bit. She's no longer just a dean. She's President of the entire university."

"Fascinating," Laghdaf said. "She cost them millions of dollars." He smiled his broad smile at Sam. "Then she fails upwards."

Sam nodded. In government jobs, failing upwards was the norm, especially for university administrators. The more you toed the line, the more you proved you belonged with the elite, the higher you soared. No matter the institutional cost.

Taxpayers pay those bills anyway. A mutual protection society. Otherwise, they'd have to admit their tribe could do wrong, which they couldn't, being on the right side of history.

Laghdaf asked her again, "What would you like to do about this?"

"SWASU will fire you for using the wrong pronoun," she said. "Then they bring this hater on campus and pay him government money. Doesn't that break some law somewhere?"

Sam was liking this potential client. She just told them what happened. She didn't try to explain the law. Sam and Laghdaf hated it when clients lectured them on the law.

Laghdaf asked, "Have you had any problems at work personally?"

"Like what?"

"Demotions? Pay cuts? Harassment? Negative performance reviews?"

She shook her head. "To my professor bosses I'm just another Mexican. Even the Latinx Studies people. They can't tell us apart. They don't know."

"They don't know what?"

She smiled at Sam. "I'm a Jew myself."

Sam asked, "They don't know you're a Jewish Mexican?"

"I don't keep it secret. They just never ask. It never occurs to them."

She looked first at Sam, then at Laghdaf. "Will you represent me?"

Sam glanced at Laghdaf. With just a flicker in his eyes, Laghdaf signaled agreement, and Sam finally said what he'd been thinking all along. "It will be our pleasure."

6 *The Mujahid*

"Is this boy Owen you sent to kill Professor Cobb trustworthy?" the Mujahid asked his lieutenant Mahir Darwish.

"We will see, Abu Jihad," Mahir said. "We can consider his mission an initiation. If he succeeds, he is truly one of us and we have recruited a valuable new *jihadi*. If he fails, we can deal with him. We have others who will not fail."

Although Mahir usually reported to the Mujahid over the Internet, every week or two he reported in person. This Tuesday morning they sat sharing tea in the kitchen of the Mujahid's safe house near Phoenix.

Unlike most of the Mujahid's Arizona operatives, who'd been mere thugs like that Mexican Jabali or total idiots like that American Ali, Darwish was an honored guest. Darwish spoke fluent Modern Standard Arabic as well as the Mujahid's own dialect of Darija. Mahir possessed brilliant technical skills. Most important, he was Tribe.

The Mujahid doled out crumbs of trust only to Tribe, and the more distant the relationship the smaller the crumbs. His teachers had drilled into him their fundamental doctrine: "I against my brother; I and my brother against my cousin; I and my brother and my cousin against the world."

For the moment at least, it was Mahir Darwish and Abu Jihad against the world, although that intimate relationship could sever in an instant. The Mujahid suspected from brutal experience it eventually would.

"I tell you again," the Mujahid said. "I have grave doubts about this Owen Al-Amriki. He seems weak to me. And a weak horse can trip."

"Any horse can trip, Abu Jihad," Mahir said.

The Mujahid eyed Mahir. Was the quote of the familiar Arab proverb intended as disrespectful? No hint of such an intent appeared on Mahir's face.

Mahir had so much to learn. The Mujahid asked, "Do you have anything else to report?"

Mahir went on to report on some of their various ventures. They had added a new training compound to the dozen rural compounds spread from northern Mexico into the United States. Their network continued to accumulate an ever-greater treasury and to develop ever more profitable business contacts with the narcotics cartels, as well as with the human traffickers and weapons smugglers whose business intertwined with those cartels.

All progressed in a satisfactory manner. "Anything else?"

"You told me to keep my eye out for this Jew lawyer Lapidos who defeated SWASU in court," Mahir said. "He's back in Phoenix. And there's this female clerk who works there. She visited Lapidos and his African *abd* Laghdaf this morning."

The Mujahid said "Tell me more about that."

"Is this important, Abu Jihad?"

"Perhaps. Do you know why this woman visited the Jew lawyer?"

"There's nothing specific on her work computer," Darwish said. "I know only that she searched the Internet by name for the lawyer's phone number and called his office. Later I tracked her phone physically to the office he is now using in Phoenix. If her phone went there, so did she."

"You don't know what they talked about?"

"No. But I'll be installing the necessary tools as soon as possible," Darwish said. "Then we'll know everything passing between them."

"Good."

They sipped their tea. The Mujahid came up with an idea. He said, "Perhaps you should visit Sam Lapidos yourself."

"Why so, Abu Jihad?"

"We could hire him. For our Anti Islamophobia League."

Mahir wore a puzzled look. "To do what?"

"This Sam Lapidos is a very famous lawyer. He could represent us in some matter or another."

"But why should he?"

"Why shouldn't he?"

"I don't understand."

The Mujahid didn't mind taking the time to instruct a bright young mind. "American lawyers generally take on all comers, correct?"

Mahir smiled. "They are not known for their fastidiousness, Abu Jihad."

"And our Anti Islamophobia League is a reputable and respectable organization, isn't it? Members of Congress, the big media, the State Department, they all consult us."

"True."

"And we can afford a fat retainer, right?"

"A retainer?"

"A regular monthly fee we pay him regardless whether he actually does any work. Lawyers like monthly retainers."

Mahir smiled again. "If to wager were not haram, I would wager they do."

"Now, if this particular lawyer represents us, we get his services, which are useful. I understand he's good at it."

"But isn't he a Jew?"

"Better yet. He's famous. He has defended Hollywood perverts and gotten them off. They made a movie out of one of his cases. He is a loudmouthed and effective apologist for the Zionist Entity in writing and on television. He even taught for a while at a law school. Once he takes our money it becomes a conflict of interest for him to go against our interests. He's off the table. You see?"

"I see. But what if he refuses?"

"If he refuses, we learn something about him, and when we find out why, we will know more about what he is up to here in Arizona, whatever that may be."

"Whatever that may be." Mahir gave a slow nod. "How much should I offer, Abu Jihad?"

"Ten thousand dollars per month should get his attention."

Mahir pursed his lips and blew out a soft breath. "It surely should."

"You have to understand, Mahir, these prominent lawyers operate on a different scale." The Mujahid didn't add that ten thousand a month was also small scale for AIL and for himself personally.

Mahir promised to carry out his assignment. The Mujahid dismissed him. They hugged and Mahir left.

The Mujahid bussed the plateware to the sink. Living alone and womanless as he must for security reasons, the Mujahid had surprised himself by coming to enjoy mindless kitchen chores. Washing the plateware from their tea service as well as his morning's breakfast dishes gave him time to think.

He congratulated himself: his idea that the Anti Islamophobia League should hire Lapidos was brilliant.

The founding of AIL had itself been brilliant. Bigotry was bad and AIL stood against bigotry, which made AIL an easy sell. The American media had come to treat AIL as their go-to source for understanding Islam. AIL had helped convince many of the highest U.S. authorities to bend from their previous unwavering allegiance to the Jews. On university campuses, a Muslim could do no wrong.

And the Jews? The whole situation was absurd. Here was this vast *Ummah* of more than a billion Muslims, constantly fending off threats from this tiny conspiracy of cowardly Jews, hardly worthy of contempt. Apes. Imitations of real men.

How did they do it?

Gold. Jews had amassed control through their legendary prowess with money. That was the only answer.

But how did Lapidos fit in?

7 *Mahir Darwish*

After his report to Abu Jihad, Mahir sped home to his little house near the Interstate. He found Maria just starting out with her work cleaning his kitchen. She protested in her broken English, but he sent her home and told her to come back another time.

Abu Jihad's doubts about Owen had rattled Mahir. As soon as he chased Maria out, he sat down at his desk and logged into his laptop. He opened his GPS tracker application and checked the tracking device he had installed on Owen's automobile. Owen's car was stationary, only a few blocks from the SWASU campus, presumably parked there. This was a good sign. Maybe Owen was carrying out his mission this very moment.

Mahir relaxed back in his chair, feeling relief, but also irritation with himself. He couldn't take a chance on losing Abu Jihad's confidence. If Owen failed, it should be on Tayoub. Mahir should have clarified to Abu Jihad that Owen was Tayoub's choice. Mahir had relied on Tayoub's pledge that Owen was ready, and in reliance on Tayoub, Mahir had repeated Tayoub's avowal to Abu Jihad.

Mahir admitted to himself that some of his frustration flowed over against Abu Jihad as well. Of course, the man had much experience and knowledge, but sometimes the man seemed too cautious to lead a *jihad*. He was almost timid, often too slow to take action.

Take the Cobb execution. This khaffir professor had mocked the Prophet with his cartoons. How could he be allowed to live? What example would that set?

Mahir had seen an American gangster movie. The younger more modern gangsters chafed under the yoke of the older

Italian immigrant gangsters they called "Mustache Petes." The older gangsters deserved respect, but for their Mafia to prosper, aggressive modern leaders had to replace them.

Abu Jihad certainly possessed knowledge, but some of it was suspect. For example, he had given Mahir a piece of advice: before you come to America, read Danielle Steel novels.

By their limited nature, women sometimes had deeper understanding of domestic issues, which were after all their proper realm. This Steel woman made penetrating insights into America's Khaffir culture. Reading her books had been a good way to improve his English while at the same developing a better understanding of America.

Nonetheless, her books also operated according to Khaffir assumptions. It was harmful to the soul to internalize her infidel point of view. Mahir had stopped after the first two.

And Abu Jihad was also behind the times. Imagine, a man of his stature and importance doing women's work, cleaning his own house, even scrubbing his own toilets.

He had insisted Mahir follow his example, but of course, Mahir was not going to perform these menial and disgusting tasks. For Mahir, having a woman around presented no security risk. Mahir was hi tech. He wrote nothing on paper. He left nothing important lying around. Everything was properly encrypted and secure on his laptop.

And the Mujahid had insisted Mahir keep watch on the Jew lawyer's so-called "partner." This command Mahir had followed, even though the man Laghdaf was an *abd*. Mahir's family had enslaved these people for centuries. In fact, Mahir's cousins back home were continuing to do so.

Despite all the surveillance, Mahir had never observed Laghdaf doing anything to suggest he was anything more than what he appeared, Lapidos's mere helper, hardly worth notice.

The Jew Lapidos was another matter. From an independent tribe with a long history of obstructing the advance of the Ummah.

When Mahir was fifteen and big and strong for his age, his father took him along for a fight with another independent tribe.

Men from this other tribe had insulted and beaten a cousin in an argument about a missing goat. They had broken his arm. Mahir didn't recall having met or even having seen this cousin. In fact, just two weeks before, Father had been eager to attack this same cousin's family over a dispute with Father's brother about some palm trees.

It didn't matter. That argument was past. This argument was present. The man beaten was a cousin, descended from the same great ancestor as Mahir and Father.

As Father walked with Mahir to the gathering place for the fighters, Father reminded him, "If we let our family member be abused, who will stand with us when we are abused? We will lose not only our family honor, but hope of future help from others in our family. We will need that help to defend ourselves when the time comes."

This was maybe the fiftieth time Father had delivered this particular lecture. But Mahir loved and admired Father and didn't mind when Father repeated himself. Old men did that a lot.

What mattered was the prospect of exciting action, and this time Mahir would be part of the action himself, as one of the men, and not just a boy hearing about it afterward. Mahir's step was light and he felt a prickling in his arms, as if they were independent beings eager to set to work.

The gathering place was a patch of open desert. Dozens of men milled around. Father stood in front of the men and made an exciting speech reminding everyone of their obligations. The fifteen-year-old Mahir was proud to see Father as a leader of men. Maybe someday Mahir could be a leader of men too.

Two more cousins drove up in a pickup truck. The truck bed was filled with clubs, axes, sickles, and brass knuckles. The driver and his partner got out and went to the back of the truck and began passing out the weapons. The fifteen-year-old lined up with the others, but he worried they'd reject him as a mere boy.

The driver was a grey-bearded old man with a livid three-inch scar on his left cheek. He inspected the fifteen-year-old up and down and glowered for an instant, but then he flashed a stump-toothed grin and handed over an especially thick knotted stick and growled, "Time to learn."

Words of respect which thrilled.

Three more pickup trucks arrived. Everybody climbed onto the beds of the trucks and bounced along for half an hour until they reached a village. For the boy wedged in the pack, the ride was another exhilarating phase in the new experience. He enjoyed even the stink of all these unwashed men crammed together.

At the target village, the village men were unprepared. Since they were not the particular men who had beaten the cousin, they had no idea the attack was coming.

But they were members of the same clan as the ones who had beaten Mahir's cousin, so they shared responsibility.

The invaders spilled off the truck beds and launched into the village. The melee left several men unconscious on the ground. The young Mujahid himself suffered a thunk to the back of his neck. It was sore for an entire week. As the bruise turned from black to purple to green, he showed it off to all his friends and rivals as proof of his manhood. Even some of the seventeen-year-old boys were jealous.

Father's group was winning when a dusty blue four-door Mercedes pulled up and the driver leapt out and opened the back door. A fragile old man got out and started waving his thin arms and ordering everyone to stop the fight.

Other fighters echoed the call, including Father. The two bunches of men separated. The old man waved his arm in the air and tottered into a house. A few men from each side followed him in, Father included.

For the next two hours the men left outside milled around or sat on the ground and glared at one another across the neutral space between them.

Finally, the old man and Father and a few cousins and the village leaders all came out together and declared that they had reached a deal.

Father's clan received five goats, and, more important, maintained honor and respect for their family.

Everybody separated and Mahir rode the truck back home and got to be part of the men's celebration which followed.

Of course, this was all before the University, where Mahir matured intellectually and learned more about the Jews.

Mahir learned much about the Jews from his close study of *The Protocols of the Elders of Zion*. In 1865, two Germans named LaSalle and Faust had chanced to overhear a speech given by a Rabbi named Reichorn at a clandestine meeting in the Prague Jewish cemetery. It turned out representatives from each of the twelve Jewish tribes met every hundred years to plan and review progress towards Jewish world domination.

Mahir knew from the Protocols that the Jews' claim to a religion was a fraud. Their real goal was to infect every society with the idea of freedom, so called "liberalism," so that authority would give up its power to the licentiousness and greed of unchecked mobs.

Mahir's teachers explained that likewise fake were the Jews' fraudulent claims to any historical connection to Palestine. There had never been any Jewish Temple in the city they called Jerusalem.

And to Mahir it followed that any Christian claim that the prophet Jesus had been a Jew living in Jerusalem and visiting this imaginary Temple must also be a lie.

The Protocols proved that even thousands of years ago, at the time of Pericles in ancient Greece and Augustus in ancient Rome, the Jews had worked to subvert the moral order of any thriving culture.

The Jews had organized the seventeenth century execution of Charles II of England. The Jews had prepared the French Revolution of the 1790s. In 1897, the Jews reissued the Protocols at Theodore Herzl's first Zionist Congress in Basle, Switzerland. Herzl had also predicted and planned the destruction of the Turkish Caliphate, which in turn freed up the Zionists to seize Muslim land and set up their Zionist Entity on the land.

One had to know his enemy to defeat him. Mahir had studied his enemy and knew him well. Every Jew bore watching, and any noteworthy Jew bore particular watching.

Sam Lapidos was a noteworthy Jew.

8 Is This A Case?

After Laghdaf went over their lawyer-client agreement with Aviva and she signed it, Laghdaf escorted her out the front door. Sam stayed seated in the front room, thinking over the possibilities. Laghdaf turned and said, "You caught me by surprise."

"How so?"

"When I told you I'd made this appointment, you complained we already have too many clients, and you just arrived in Phoenix, and you wanted a day or two to relax."

"You didn't mention she was from SWASU," Sam said.

"Something is rotten at that University," Laghdaf said. "And I wanted us both to hear her story. But she admits she's suffered no personal harassment or discrimination."

"So far," Sam said.

"She has no money," Laghdaf pointed out.

"If she blows the whistle on her bosses, they're sure to retaliate."

"This is true," Laghdaf said. Functionaries always retaliated. Suing for their retaliation was a rich source of work and income. Since Ms. Soriano's story threatened SWASU's access to millions of federal dollars, this upcoming retaliation would be worse than usual.

Laghdaf said, "And I suspect you're interested in her."

"Yes. I'm interested in her situation."

"Though she has no money."

"That's why God created contingency fees," Sam said.

"You're interested in her situation," Laghdaf repeated. He smiled his frequent semi-mysterious smile. Laghdaf found many things amusing for reasons known only to Laghdaf. After all, he came from a culture very different from Sam's.

"You admit she may not have a big case?"

"She will," Sam said.

"I agree," Laghdaf said, "By the way, how are Lily and Sarai doing back in Minnesota?"

"Sarai won't answer my phone calls," Sam said.

"Too busy?"

"She insists I text," Sam said. "And I refuse."

"Your granddaughter is of a new generation," Laghdaf said.

"And her mother's busy," Sam said. "Lily is holed up in her house working on a novel."

"Really. What about?"

"She won't say. She just tells me she wants to be the next Danielle Steel. Which I guess means writing about furniture and women's clothing and shoes. Lily knows a lot about couture and coffee tables."

"Oh, Ms. Steel writes about more than consumer goods."

"Really? I've never read any of the woman's novels."

"I've read many," Laghdaf said.

"You have? Why?"

"Before I immigrated to America, I asked some friends for suggestions on things to read to get an understanding of American life and culture. Many friends recommended Danielle Steel novels. So I read several."

"In English?"

"No, in Arabic."

"They've translated Danielle Steel books into Arabic?"

"She's sold 800 million copies. What did you expect?"

"Did the novels help you?" Sam asked. "Understand American culture, I mean?"

Laghdaf nodded. "Oh yes. Very much so."

"And what you found here when you got to the U.S. was what you expected from reading her books?"

Laghdaf nodded. "Exactly."

Sam said, "It's been a long time since I read a novel. All I read is law, with some occasional history thrown in."

"Perhaps you should broaden your interests," Laghdaf said. He checked his watch. "Get you in touch with the human side of things. Excuse me."

Laghdaf went to his office in the back and came back out carrying a briefcase. "Off to court," he said, and left through the front door.

Laghdaf's final throwaway comment irritated. What involved Sam with the human side of things more than the law? People came to Sam with their most personal struggles and Sam helped them. Laghdaf had taken off without giving Sam a fair chance to answer. That was a cheat.

9 *Aviva's Computer Takes Sides*

After signing the lawyer papers, Aviva rushed through the awful traffic to get back to her office. She arrived an hour late anyway. She didn't want anyone who mattered to see her, so instead of parking in her normal spot in the lot behind the Latinx Studies building, she picked a side street two blocks away and made her way through the crowds of students.

She'd skipped breakfast and now she'd missed lunch, but she ignored the Student Union and its cafeteria and hurried into the Latinx Studies building through the back door.

As far as she could tell, neither Gomez nor Escobar had spotted her. She scooted down the back flight of stairs and took a left and then into the Chicana Studies Suite at the end of the hall. The Suite contained just two windowless offices, one for each professor, and a cubicle for Aviva just inside the Suite door.

Neither Professor Gomez nor Professor Escobar had made it into work before Aviva left for the lawyers, which was good, and the professors' offices were still dark even after lunchtime, which was even better.

Neither of Aviva's bosses came around much anyway. Aviva had no idea where or how they spent their time. Aviva was a stickler for her own duties, and their routine absenteeism irritated, if only because it obstructed Aviva's workflow while she waited for them to show up and sign things, often days after their due dates. But just this moment their truant work habits were a convenient relief.

Aviva opened the big lower right drawer and dropped in her purse. She sat down on her swivel chair and was about to click on her desktop before she saw from her monitor the computer was already running.

Which was odd. She was sure she'd powered it down before leaving. Or at least put it in "sleep" mode. De-activating a computer was the recommended security precaution at SWASU, and Aviva always followed security rules. There was too much confidential student information on these computers to leave them open to every random passerby, though she'd noticed neither Gomez nor Escobar bothered to follow the policy.

Files scrolled by on the monitor, opening and closing too fast to read all the way through: meeting agendas; emails; announcements; expense spreadsheets for events like the fake Israel conference; a private letter she'd written to her sister in Tel Aviv, and so on.

One loud whirr and a loud startling click and a blank gray screen.

It had turned itself off. Had it turned itself on?

Should she call her lawyers?

She'd never had her own personal American lawyer before. What kind of things did lawyers want to know?

They'd said to call if anything intimidating or even odd happened.

But one hour after hiring them? The same day? Would they think she was crazy?

The whole thing was crazy. She had barely summoned the courage to see the lawyers in the first place. Though they both seemed nice. But she couldn't just let things ride. That awful rapper. The awful so-called "song." The awful crowd.

Her mother and father had told her about some of what happened back in Saloniki where she'd been born, and then she'd seen and heard a little of it herself as a girl in Fez. The Jew hatred.

She'd think it over before calling the lawyers.

She didn't want them to think she was crazy, calling them right away, one hour after they met.

Tomorrow would be okay.

10 Sam In The Evening

After Laghdaf took off for court, Sam went back to his
own office and sat at his desk. For the next two hours, he
diddled with some research for a web magazine article on
Israeli elections, trying to explain Israeli politics to the
uninitiated. Then, frustrated in the effort to unsnarl the
tangle of bellicose factions and abrasive personalities, and
reminding himself he had just escaped a vicious Minnesota
trial and should be outside enjoying such a beautiful
February day, he gathered up his stuff. He locked up the
office behind him and took off.

Phoenix on a February afternoon was a sunny 65 degrees.
Fresh from Minnesota's winter hell, Sam made a point of
letting the sun and breeze play on his face as he meandered
the six blocks from the edge of downtown to the Vauxhall
Arms Hotel. From time to time he stopped to window shop
or to watch the restaurant customers eating, drinking and
talking—mostly talking about themselves, he supposed.

Halfway there, he seated himself at a sidewalk café to
sip a bottle of water and watch the cars, marveling at how
clean and rust-free they all seemed, even the nineteen-
nineties models. No snow, therefore no road salt, therefore
no rust. Amazing. He promised himself never to buy a used
car in this part of America—a shiny rust-free paint job on the
outside could sucker him into buying a lemon.

Once back at his hotel, Sam rode the elevator up to his
room and set his laptop case on the floor by his bed. He took
off his suit coat and hung it in the closet. Careful to
maintain the creases in his pants, he hung them in the
closet. He untied his tie in the order reverse to the one in
which he'd tied it. He hung that up as well. He removed his

dress shirt and put it into the bag for the hotel laundry. As always, he checked the "light starch" box on the laundry instruction sheet.

Sam put on his track suit and his headphones and went down to the hotel gym and lifted dumbbells for a half hour and rode the elliptical machine for another half hour, listening through his entire workout to an audio book called *Between Cross and Crescent,* which told a story of Jews in Christian and Muslim countries for the thousand years separating the Arab prophet Mohammad from the Amsterdam philosopher Benedict Spinoza.

Sam didn't waste time, and workout time was like any other. He could study while he exercised. Efficient.

Sam rode the elevator back up to his room and hung his workout clothes in the closet and showered. He put on black jeans and a blue-checked button-down shirt and a sports jacket and went back downstairs and ate the Vauxhall Bistro salad, which for Sam was a meal all by itself. This took another hour.

It was now 7:30 PM, which was 8:30 in Minnesota. He punched the speed dial for his ten-year-old granddaughter Sarai. The call rang through to her voicemail: "Hi, this is Sarai; I'd love to talk, but I can't right now. Please leave a message!"

He said, "Hi, it's Grandpa—just checking in. Call when you can, Sweetheart," and hung up. He punched the same speed dial again. This time he hung up right after her message—he just wanted to hear her voice again.

Sarai would see from her caller ID that he'd called the second time. Later when they did talk, she'd pester him to text instead, which he refused to do, not just because he was a relic—although he was—but because he needed to hear her sweet voice. A few tiny black letters on a white screen

46

was a dismal substitute. Like ice milk when you expected ice cream, he'd told her, but of course, she'd never heard of ice milk, nor of black-and-white TV, nor for that matter, of record players, phones with dialers, or Walter Mondale.

Not even eight PM. Sam performed his ablutions and put on the silk travel pajamas Bea had given him right before she fell into her final sickness fifteen years before. He said his prayers. He pulled the covers open and lay down in bed and pulled the covers up to his chest.

He put on his headphones again and chose Bach's *Well Tempered Clavier* on his MP3 player. He took a paperback from the night table and picked up where he had left off in John D. MacDonald's final novel, *The Lonely Silver Rain*. Travis McGee was an adventurer who'd lived past his time, contending with new intrigues more complicated and better organized than he could fight his way through alone. There'd be no fair fight; to survive this time, Travis had to finagle.

The Bach piece was a long series of short preludes and fugues. When Fugue 22 in B Flat Minor came on, Sam laid down his book to concentrate on the music.

The little piece was his favorite Bach. Bach started with a few simple notes and then introduced variations until he was interweaving five distinct strands of melody.

The player had to delineate all five tunes so that the listener could trace each one and at the same time recognize each tune's kinship with every other. Sam tried to follow as it all unrolled in real time. This was a challenge for a non-musician like Sam, but he felt he owed it to Bach, who'd gone to all that trouble, as well as to himself, given his continual need to reinforce the self-discipline of listening.

Somehow the Bach led Sam back to the two melodies he'd already detected in Aviva Soriano's voice and to wondering what other tunes he might hear from her.

Nuts. He'd failed once more to focus on Bach's little three-minute piece all the way through.

Sometime later, his phone beeped, but by then he'd drifted too far into the relief of blessed sleep to wake up and answer. Tomorrow would be soon enough.

11 Owen Goes To School

Wednesday morning, Owen was standing in line for breakfast at a coffeehouse called *One Swallow Does Not Make An Arizona Summer*. It was a few blocks off campus from SWASU. SWASU was located on the far southwestern outskirts of the Phoenix metro area, which sprawled for dozens of miles in every direction.

After his mutinous beer, Owen had driven to SWASU to warn Professor Cobb of his upcoming murder. Professor Cobb didn't seem grateful; in fact, he had chased Owen out of his office. After a few harsh words, he snarled, "Don't bother me."

Owen had slept in the back seat of his car, where he'd parked it on a street near the campus. Owen hoped any cops he might have to deal with would only be the SWASU variety instead of the real thing. He supposed SWASU police would be more relaxed about a young guy sleeping in his car than real police. As it happened, nobody bothered him, and he slept a full eight hours.

Owen used a classroom building restroom to wash up the best he could. No one else was there at 5 AM. On his phone, he checked the Internet for this year's fashionable beards. He bought a disposable razor from a vending machine and trimmed his full Islamic beard to a pure goatee with no mustache.

Thinking he was still young enough to pull it off, he visited the campus bookstore and outfitted himself to look like a student: flared wide-leg blue jeans; a "No Justice No Peace" tee shirt in white letters on black; white running shoes with the SWASU Swashbuckler crossed-cutlass logo in blue; blue SWASU socks with white stripes and the same logo in white, and to top himself off, a brand-new blue and white cap with the same logo.

Swashbuckler as a team name? They'd probably wanted a nickname starting with the letters "SWAS." The only other SWAS word Owen could think of was "swastika." But "SWASU Swastikas" didn't sound like a winner. And if they used a logo to match the nickname, that would create obvious problems.

Was he making a joke? Joking seemed another thing Owen hadn't dared to do for the past year, even if only to himself.

Owen checked the young people in line in front of him and then behind him and the others sitting at their little wood tables, studying alone or chattering in bunches. Nobody else dressed like him. Mostly they wore regular tee shirts under big checkered shirts and jeans and sneakers. Not a single person wore a SWASU cap.

He paid for his vegetarian egg dish and some wheat toast and a tall coffee and placed his tray on the single remaining empty table in back.

The free newspaper rack stood by the door. He walked over and picked up the one on top and returned to his table to read while he ate. It turned out to be the college paper, inevitably also called the *Swashbuckler*. Its frontpage headline blared in big black letters:

"Injustice Anywhere is a Threat to Justice Everywhere."

Below in smaller print was the famous quotation:

"Injustice anywhere is a threat to justice everywhere. We are caught in an inescapable network of mutuality,

tied in a single garment of destiny. Whatever affects one directly, affects all indirectly."
Martin Luther King, *Letter From A Birmingham Jail.*

The injustice the *Swashbuckler* editors were covering was a failed prosecution. The "anywhere" in question was Minneapolis, Minnesota.

According to the *Swashbuckler*, a notorious Neo-Nazi lawyer named Sam Lapidos had pulled one of his infamous tricks to derail the trial of a racist cop who had murdered an innocent unarmed black man. The judge had declared a mistrial, and now no one could guarantee the racist cop would ever be convicted.

Lapidos had even gotten the prosecutor in trouble as well. This was the great fighter for justice Harland Ellison. He worked out of the Minnesota Attorney General's office.

The article was vague about the trick Sam Lapidos had played, but it sounded racist. The article also kept mum about what the prosecutor had done to get himself into trouble.

The *Swashbuckler* quoted Mahir Darwish from the Arizona branch of the Anti Islamophobia League: "Islamophobia, white supremacy and Zionism are all threads in the same interwoven fabric of oppression. Sam Lapidos has been a notorious defender of Israel and its genocidal crimes against Muslims. It is no surprise that he also represents killer cops and obstructs racial justice here in the U.S."

Owen knew Mahir Darwish only a little. He was a member at Al-Andalus Mosque, but far above Owen's station— powerful and important. Even Tayoub deferred to him, which had surprised Owen the first time he saw it happen, because Darwish didn't even look like a Muslim was supposed to look, which was also the way Owen had tried to look.

Darwish didn't wear a beard or *kufi* cap or other Muslim clothing. He went clean shaven and usually wore khaki slacks and white sneakers and a pinstripe oxford shirt. He presented as a "regular" American, whatever that was. He looked like an investment banker dressed for a casual weekend at his yacht club.

Nevertheless, the routinely domineering Tayoub made a display of elaborate deference to Mahir Darwish, almost to the point of servility.

Darwish taught a lot of classes on Islam at Al-Andalus, including a regular Tuesday night class on basic Islam. Darwish always spoke in a voice of authority, definitive and certain. No one ever dared ask Darwish a challenging question. If someone asked a foolish question, Darwish lifted his head and stared off into space while Tayoub jumped in to squelch the offender.

To Owen, there was something very convincing and comforting about Darwish's certainty. Owen had grown up in a Reform Jewish synagogue where there seemed no religious certainty at all, and the only certainty was the commitment to the ever-evolving politics of Social Justice.

In the Swashbuckler interview, Darwish explained, "Yet again the Zionist Lapidos has displayed his raging hatred towards people of color."

In the Tuesday night sessions Owen had heard Darwish complain that so many black Americans were *khufar*— infidels—because so many were Christian. He seemed to blame American-born Muslims like Owen for their failure to convert more African Americans. "Get yourselves into the prisons," he demanded, glaring about the room. "That's where black men are. And the Khaffir authorities have stuck them in prison because they have proven they are willing to fight Khaffir law. They are warriors. Those are the converts we need!"

In the interview, Darwish went on, "The interwoven web of oppression extends not only to Muslims and people of color, but also to women and our feminist and LGBTQ allies."

Owen had heard Darwish drum into his students the fundamental principle that Islam required the separation and subordination of women. No women had ever spoken at any of these Tuesday nights or any other event during Owen's experience. Women weren't even allowed in the room; they were kept out of sight.

As far as Owen could tell, women listened from a small basement space through a speaker. When Owen got up the nerve to ask how women could ask any questions, Tayoub explained that women could submit their questions in writing. Owen never saw this happen.

Darwish's mention of LGBTQ "allies" caught Owen off guard. No one on any Tuesday night ever questioned Darwish's weekly pronouncements that Islam demanded the summary execution of homosexuals.

In the interview, Darwish said, "The U.S. Constitution should not protect racist cops."

When Tayoub mentioned to Darwish that there was a new young mosque member—Owen—who was considering law school, Darwish pulled no punches. "The study of U.S. law requires supporting the U.S. Constitution, which contains much that is inconsistent with Islam," Mahir declared. "No Muslim can affirm support for the U.S. Constitution." Everybody in the room looked at Owen as if they were waiting for him to wilt in shame.

Owen wondered if he might have been the victim of a bait-and-switch. The Islam he'd converted to in college was a progressive Social Justice Islam, concerned with the rights of victims of racism, Islamophobia, homophobia, and sexism.

In the Islam to which Owen had converted, words like *jihad* meant only internal struggle to become a better person. People who claimed jihad meant violence and war were at best just misinformed, or, even more likely, were themselves racists and Islamophobes.

But in the Islam Mahir Darwish taught, and then in the cell into which Tayoub recruited Owen, everything the Islamophobes said seemed to be turning out true, especially the part about jihad.

After the Darwish interview, the *Swashbuckler* article went on to quote the SWASU President, Petra Sterns-Stuyvesant: "Arizona does not need this man Lapidos. He carries the virus of racism and division wherever he goes."

Why did the President of a University in Arizona care about some Minnesota lawyer setting up shop in Arizona?

In the very next paragraph, the *Swashbuckler* spelled it out: "Sam Lapidos and his partner Jacob Laghdaf were the attorneys who successfully sued SWASU for the process by which SWASU expelled the Islamophobic basketball player Amos Owens."

Interesting.

The article then doxed Lapidos, listing the address and contact information for his Arizona law office as well as Lapidos's personal phone number and email address.

Owen stood. He tore the article page out of the newspaper and folded it and stuffed it into his jeans back pocket. He bussed his tray and walked out onto the sidewalk.

When he stepped through the coffeehouse door, a crowd swamped him. Hundreds of young people were all streaming in the same direction. Some wore tee shirts and hats with the Swashbuckler crossed-cutlass logo. They were chattering about an upcoming big basketball game.

Owen recalled all those movies where the hero escapes his pursuers by hiding in a parade.

Was anyone following Owen? If not already, soon. He stepped into the stream and strolled along for a few blocks, trying to hide himself in the middle, the babble of the kids a soothing elevator music for his nerves.

When the crowd passed Owen's parked Tercel, he stopped and let the kids pass on. He got in his car and drove away.

12 Sam in the Morning

Sam awakened still lying on his back. Something under him was poking his right shoulder blade. He felt around. He'd fallen asleep with his headphones on. They'd slid off his head and his ears onto the bed and under his back. He hoped he wouldn't wind up with an all-day back spasm.

He opened his eyes. No light filtered through the window shade. Still night outside. The hotel clock read 6:20 AM. Sunrise should be soon.

He sat halfway up and grabbed the headphones and laid them on the end table next to the clock. He dug through the blankets and sheets found that his MP3 player was disconnected from his headphones. He laid the player on the table next to the headphones.

He swiveled his feet onto the carpet and stood. He recited the blessing customary on awakening, thanking God for returning his soul from wherever it went while he slept. He walked on bare feet onto the cold bathroom tile and stood and relieved himself and came back and lay down on his bed and pulled up his covers again. Cozy.

The window shades turned from dark to yellow. Sam waited an extra ten minutes to make sure sunrise had come. He got up again and walked over and opened the bureau drawer where he kept his prayer gear. He laid all of it on the top of the fake wood desk—the tallis bag with its prayer shawl inside, the smaller black bag containing his tefillin— one black box for his arm, one for his head—a small prayer book, a hand towel, and a special portable basin and accompanying two-handed cup for hand washing.

He carried the cup into the bathroom sink and filled it from the tap. He brought the cup out of the bathroom and positioned himself and poured the water over each hand three times and let the water fall into the basin. He picked up a towel and said the Hebrew blessing for hand washing and dried his hands on the towel.

He faced Jerusalem and draped his prayer shawl over his shoulders and back and put on his tefillin, at each point along the way saying the appropriate blessings and prayers. He said the eighteen morning blessings and few more for good measure. He reversed his original process to remove his tefillin and tallit and packed up everything and put it all back in the same bureau drawer.

Now he could start his day.

Although Sam had once savored every moment of his morning prayers, the sad truth was that since Bea passed, he hadn't felt like doing any of this. But he'd been praying every morning for decades and he'd long ago vowed he wouldn't miss a morning.

And so far he hadn't, except for those few desperate U.S. Army days in the Iraqi desert decades ago, when life-and-death priorities had demanded his complete attention, which the rabbis had assured him was the right choice. You were supposed to live by the commandments, not die by them. *Pikuakh Nefesh*—saving a life.

Sam always said all his morning prayers alone. He'd long ago stopped joining *minyans* of ten or more to pray with other Jews. Maybe he didn't want to infect others with his bad attitude—or maybe he was afraid others would infect him with their good attitude. Same difference.

Once he finished, Sam wasn't even sure he remembered doing every part of the process. It was like commuting a well-traveled route and arriving home and not remembering any of the familiar landmarks you'd passed.

Maybe it had all become mechanical, but a mechanical process was better than none. Doing the right thing was always better than not doing it, even if your intention and attention weren't what they ought to be.

After all, you found yourself operating just as mechanically in your profession. You listened to clients with half a mind, nodding along, sometimes asking them to repeat facts you missed the first time through.

In court, more than once, after opposing counsel made some argument, you stood up with no idea what you were about to say, then watched yourself from outside deliver the exact argument needed to win some point. Where did that come from?

You often wrote briefs and other documents by copying older ones and just plugging in new names and dates and a few changes to details.

You're a law machine, a robot which has programmed itself to come up with the output it needs whenever it needs.

But the results are generally good, so why pick on yourself?

And why should the way you pray be any different from the way you do your life's work?

Sam shaved while he showered. He dried himself off. He went to the closet. He chose one of the custom-tailored suits he'd brought to Phoenix, the gray pinstripe.

He put on a blue Luigi Borrelli dress shirt. It was single cuff. Sam shied away from cuff links. Jurors appreciated successful-looking lawyers. A successful lawyer reflected well on the client. But jurors were suspicious of showoffs who flashed gold and diamonds in their faces.

To complete today's ensemble, Sam chose a yellow Salvatore Ferragamo Gancini Print Silk Tie figured with a black diamond pattern. To show he was a serious man, he knotted it full Windsor.

He picked his Berluti dress shoes off the floor of the closet and removed the cedar shoe horses and sat in the desk chair and used his long walnut shoehorn to pry first the right and then the left over sole and heel. He checked the shine on the toe box for blemishes and found none—a military grade shine, just the way they'd taught him at Fort Benning one brutal summer decades ago.

On the way out, he reviewed himself one last time in the full-length mirror by the door. Perfect—ready to sue the world.

Sam skipped breakfast. He had no court appearances today. He'd be able to churn out his research and writing chores in a couple of hours, so he took his time and enjoyed his walk to the office.

He passed a bakery, A moment of madness took him inside. He surveyed through the glass case and picked a single one-inch-round 70% cacao chocolate truffle for five dollars. The woman passed it over the counter to him in a brown ruffled paper cup.

Sam sat at one of the two little white Formica tables in the bakery and nibbled slivers off the truffle for a few minutes, until about a third of it remained, then in his second wild impulse of the morning tossed down the whole thing. Delicious.

Feeling a little lighter on his feet from the sugar, or maybe giddy from the trace of caffeine in the chocolate, Sam meandered down the street.

His phone rang just as he arrived at his building.

13 A Call From Ms. Soriano

Sam pulled his phone out of his inside jacket pocket. He couldn't read the screen in the Phoenix sunlight. In Minnesota, he hadn't faced that problem for months. He stepped over to a shady spot by the front of the building. This wasn't an obvious spam call. He clicked it to answer and said, "Law Office."

"Mr. Lapidos?" A hesitant voice, but with the intermingling melodies he already recognized.

He said, "Ms. Soriano?"

"Yes. I'm sorry to trouble you."

"No trouble. Did something happen?"

"Well, I don't know. It's very strange."

"What's strange, Ms. Soriano?"

"My work computer turned itself on and then off again."

"How do you know this?"

"I watched it happen. Right in front of me. Yesterday, right after I got back. I'm sure I turned it completely off when I left to see you. But it was already on. Then it went off again all by itself."

He could hear the wobble in her voice. She'd seemed a strong woman, but this might be a scary business for her. Time for his patented Sam Lapidos Voice of Calm. "Well, things happen with computers."

"I've never seen it before. In years. Have you?"

"Well, no, I haven't."

"I didn't want to bother you with this," she said.

"It's no bother."

"But you said I should call if anything happened."

"You're right to call," Sam said.

"What should I do?"

"For now, go on at work like nothing happened."

"And then?"

"Tell you what. I've got an ex-son-in-law who's a whiz with computers. I'll ask him about it and see what he says. Maybe it's all perfectly normal."

"Thank you, Mr. Lapidos."

"It's my job, Ms. Soriano."

A pause. "Well, thank you anyway. And I'm sorry to trouble you. I promise I'm not one of those stupid women who panics over every little thing."

"I already know that."

"I realize it's probably nothing."

"You're probably right. But I'll check and we'll talk again soon."

She clicked off. He put his phone back in his pocket and unlocked his front door and went in.

14 The Grilling of Aviva Soriano

Aviva had stepped outside and across the street to make her call to Sam. She put her phone back in her purse and walked back to her building and down the stairs to her office.

Odd—the office front door was unlocked. And when Aviva stepped through it, she saw the light on in Professor Escobar's office. Oliva rarely came in before 11 AM.

Aviva's monitor was still dark.

Aviva sat down and turned on her monitor and computer. Even before everything finished booting up, Professor Gomez was standing by Aviva's cubicle. Professor Gomez said, "Good morning, Aviva."

Aviva looked up at her. Aviva said, "Good morning, Elia."

"Do you have a few minutes? There's something we need to talk about."

"Of course." Aviva stood and followed Elia Gomez into Oliva Escobar's office, where Oliva waited behind her desk. She was tapping a pencil in her palm. Elia seated herself in the guest chair on the right and Aviva took the remaining one. Elia had been the one who hired Aviva. Aviva rarely spoke with Oliva.

Aviva smoothed her skirt down over her knees and waited.

Oliva wore very large black frame glasses, Aviva suspected to cover her slightly protruding dark brows and eye sockets. Oliva leaned her wide form back in her chair and said, "Well."

Aviva suppressed the impulse to say "Well" back and waited, sitting straight, her hands folded on her lap.

"Something has come to our attention," Oliva continued.

"Yes?" Aviva asked.

"It's not something I'm eager to discuss, but I feel I must."

Aviva said nothing.

Oliva said, "Were you using your work computer for personal purposes?"

"I don't know what you mean," Aviva said.

"What I mean is that we have reason to believe you were using Department equipment for some kind of personal business."

"What reason is that?"

Oliva said, "We think you were writing some kind of non-departmental documents on it."

"Well, we all from time to time make a personal call on our work phones or glance at a website or two," Aviva said. "As long as we get our work done, there's no rule against that, is there?"

"No, there isn't. But it depends what the personal business is."

Did Oliva already know about Aviva seeing the lawyers? How would she know that? "What is it you think I'm doing?"

"Well, you're writing things."

"Writing things is part of my job."

"Well, something in Hebrew. Which is not part of your job."

"Hebrew?" What was the woman talking about? And why so hostile?

"Of course, we can't read it, at least not yet. But we recognize the alphabet."

"I assure you I have never written anything in Hebrew on my work computer."

"Really?" Oliva leaned forward. She seemed barely able to suppress her triumph.

Aviva answered, "Really."

Oliva picked a couple of white pages up from her desk and handed them towards Aviva. "And this? How do you explain this?"

Aviva stood and took the document and sat again and looked at it. A hardcopy of her email to her sister Etti in Tel Aviv. She glanced up at Oliva. "Yes?"

"Whatever else you do, it's not a good idea to lie to us." Oliva raised her eyebrows high enough for Aviva to see them hovering like black caterpillars over her black frame glasses. "That is Hebrew, isn't it?"

"No," Aviva said, "It's not."

"Who do you think you're fooling?"

Elia cut in. "Aviva, what are you talking about? They do look like Hebrew letters."

Aviva said to Elia. "They are."

"Which is it?" Oliva demanded.

"Both. It's Ladino."

Oliva asked, "Ladino? What's that?"

"Of course," Elia said, "Now I get it. It's an older form of Spanish. It's just written in the Hebrew alphabet."

"Right," Aviva said, a bit surprised that Elia knew that. Looking for an ally, she smiled at Elia. Elia smiled back.

Oliva asked, "What are you talking about? Why would anyone do that?"

Elia and Aviva both started to answer. Aviva stopped and nodded to Elia. Let the professor handle it.

Elia said, "Spain expelled all its Jews in 1492. The exiled Jews dispersed all around the world, but they kept their Spanish language. What do they call it, Aviva?"

"Ladino," Aviv said.

"Yes, of course," Elia said. "They wrote Ladino in Hebrew letters. It's a lot like the Castilian Spanish people speak in Mexico, but old-fashioned."

Aviva nodded. A nice summary of her early family history. She told Oliva, "You see, what I told you was true. The document is not in Hebrew. It's in Ladino."

"So you're Jewish?" Oliva asked.

Aviva nodded.

"But when we hired you, you said you were Mexican," Oliva said.

Aviva nodded again. "I am."

Oliva frowned.

Aviva said, "I grew up in Mexico. I learned English there. I was married there. I had my son there."

"But this is the Department of Chicana Studies." Oliva said. "We chose you over other candidates, some of whom are authentically oppressed. In this institution, we are engaged in affirmative action. The purpose of affirmative action is to benefit the oppressed, not the privileged."

"How am I privileged?" Aviva asked, genuinely curious. "Because I'm Jewish?"

"The point is, you deceived us," Oliva said. "You led us to believe one thing when another was true."

"I don't agree to that," Aviva said. Mr. Lapidos would be impressed when she told them about this encounter, which she would do as soon as she could. She was keeping her cool. "I am in fact a Mexican American. I am also Jewish. Why not?"

Why not indeed? A long pause. Oliva looked like she was trying to think of some other point of attack. But why the attack?

Oliva demanded, "So what was it about?"

"I beg your pardon?"

"What were you writing about in Ladino?"

"It's a private matter," Aviva said. Enough of this nonsense.

"I really think we have a right to know," Oliva said. She glanced at Elia as if looking for an ally. "After all, you wrote it on a Department computer."

"I'd rather not say."

"We'd rather you did." Aviva also glanced at Elia, who shrugged back a semi-apologetic "might as well go ahead" signal.

Whatever. "It's a letter to my sister," Aviva said.

"About what?"

"A family recipe."

"Really? A recipe?"

"From our mother. My sister lost it."

"A recipe for what?"

"Chicken soup."

"Is that meant to be a joke?" Oliva stared at Aviva through her big glasses in what Oliva must have intended as a steely gaze. "Okay," she said finally. "Then if that's all it is, you should have no problem reading it to us."

"Are you serious?"

"Yes, please."

What an idiot. Aviva smiled sweetly at each of her bosses in turn. She picked the papers up off the desk and read aloud in Ladino, "Start by heating some olive oil in a large oven over medium heat. Add onion and sauté until you soften the onions, which usually takes about five minutes. Season with salt and pepper. Then you add the chicken broth and bring to a boil."

Aviva paused. "You want the whole thing?" Though Aviva was leaving out vital details about spices. Why share a private family recipe with these two?

"Please," Oliva said.

"Are you following the Ladino?"

"Of course," Oliva said. Something defensive in her manner confirmed a ripening suspicion.

Aviva shrugged and read the rest of the recipe aloud, ending with a triumphant flourish: "And then you season to taste." Again, she smiled as pleasant a smile as she could muster at Oliva.

"I see," Oliva said.

But Aviva didn't think Oliva saw. Aviva recalled she'd never actually heard Oliva speak any Spanish beyond a few hackneyed catch phrases. And Professor Elia's Spanish was good enough for a Mexican-American, but not as natural and effortless as the Spanish of someone like Aviva, who'd actually grown up in Mexico.

Oliva said, "I'm wondering. How is it you still have this recipe and your sister doesn't?"

Another stab at smoking out a lie? If so, truly feeble. Aviva answered, "When she left Morocco for Israel, she lost touch with a lot of family traditions."

Oliva stared. "Your sister lives in Israel?"

15 Sam's Laptop Too?

When something troubled Sam, he liked to pace his office floor. He also paced when he was trying to sort out the facts of a complicated case or trying to think up a convincing argument or when he was just bored with sitting.

He was pacing now, for all these reasons and more.

You could never tell with a new client. More than one promising new client who spun a convincing account of abuse had turned out a fruitcake. And tales in which computers turned themselves on and off while files flashed by bordered on fruitcake.

On the other hand, the rapper audio she brought had been all too real. And she seemed, well, what? Sane? Reliable? A woman of substance, not given to panic?

Sam lifted his laptop bag off the carpet and laid it on the desk and unzipped it. When he touched the black metal case of his laptop, the heat stung his fingers.

Had it been on? In the bag?

He sat down and touched his fingertips to his lips and stared at the computer.

Good news and bad news.

Good news: okay, so maybe Aviva Soriano wasn't a fruitcake.

Bad news: was someone messing with Sam's computer too?

This was no ordinary laptop. He'd paid his ex-son-in-law Hack to set it up for him. Although Hack insisted his nickname came from a physical resemblance to a squat old-time baseball slugger named Hack Wilson, Sam discounted Hack's claim. People called Nathanael Wilder "Hack" because of his computer skills, which were legendary. And

Sam had paid him good coin to set up a laptop as secure and impenetrable as possible.

The precautions were necessary. Sam often went up against public authorities and private tech giants with unlimited budgets and limited morality. They had ready access to their own high-powered and highly paid computer talent, as well as to judges with slow minds and slippery consciences, who gave pseudo-constitutional cover to all kinds of assaults on citizens' rights.

Sam took his phone out of his jacket pocket and cradled it in his left hand and with a single flick of his right index finger speed-dialed Hack.

16 Hack Wilder, Ace Songwriter

Hack was sitting in a booth at the Hedgehog Barrel taking occasional sips of Chumpster beer from its trademark brown bottle, hoping his favorite beverage would inspire a good song.

His trusty yellow pad lay in front of him on the table. His black BIC ballpoint lay sideways across the pad. So far, he'd used the BIC to scribble across the top of the page only a single word:

Song

That was two hours and three Chumpsters ago.

Songwriting was always painstaking, but this time it was slower than usual. He didn't even have a hook or a catchphrase for a title or chorus. Nothing.

This morning Mattie had dispatched him to the Barrel, scolding, "Since we joined up with Dudley, you've written just two songs, and they're songs for men to sing. What about me? I'm the singer in this marriage."

All true. His most recent songs were songs for a man to sing, which meant him, which was a joke, because he couldn't sing a lick, although he could play a lick or two on his keyboard.

But Mattie could sing for real. Her singing was the main reason people paid to hear Dudley and Mattie and Friends. Hack's keyboard was there strictly for atmosphere and to fill in the empty spaces in the songs.

Hack could croak words in rhythm, and Dudley let him croak out one of his songs nearly every gig, though usually towards the end of the night when the crowd had thinned down to a few drunks and loyal fans with nowhere else to go, who tolerated even Hack's vocals.

Now Hack had to come up with a real song for the real singer Mattie. Another novelty number like his two most recent wouldn't cut it. Mattie hated both *It Ain't Gamblin' When You Know You're Gonna Lose* and *One Emotion Behind*.

Hack's notion was to write about Mattie being pregnant. She'd announced her pregnancy only recently. But it couldn't be pop pap like *Papa Don't Preach* or *You're Having My Baby*. Hack had to do better than that. It was a matter of self-respect.

If Hack had a songwriting strength, it was being self-deprecating and maybe even goofy. A serious song required a serious state of mind, and Mattie's pregnancy had knocked the goofy out of him. He was just too damned giddy over the whole amazing thing—a new person coming.

Was that a title? *A New Person Coming?*

His phone rang the unique ring tone he'd loaded into it—a riff from one of his own tunes. No matter how large the crowd or how noisy the room, he could always identify his own phone's ring. He picked the phone off the table and checked the caller ID: Sam Lapidos.

Excellent—another excuse to shirk. Even after the three Chumpsters, he could only visit the head so many times, and unlike a soft lead pencil, the BIC ballpoint required no sharpening.

Hack answered the phone with a question. "Sam, what's happening with my lawsuit against ZNN?"

"You should ask Laghdaf. He's taking the lead on that."

"I will."

"But the last I heard there's nothing new. It's still oozing its sluggish way through the bowels of the U.S. legal system."

"I don't think so," Hack said. "I don't think it's even reached the stomach. Probably still blocking the esophagus."

"Or stuck in the throat," Sam said.

Enough of that. Hack asked, "How's Minnesota?"

"I'm not in Minnesota. I'm in Arizona. Like you."

"What are the odds? It's like we travel in tandem. Here for the warm weather?"

"Minnesota's a little hot for me just now."

"In February?" But Hack had read what his ex-father-in-law had been up to and why he'd bugged out of Minnesota.

"What about you?" Sam asked.

"We're getting ready for a perpetually promised mini-tour with Dudley and Mattie and Friends."

"What's that?"

"The band we're in. What's up?"

"I've got a computer problem," Sam said.

"The only reason you ever call me."

"I have a new client, and she's having weird experiences with her work computer. She thinks she's being hacked."

Hack asked, "Is this her employer's computer?"

"Yes."

"Then I think the word is 'monitored', not 'hacked'." If it's theirs, they can do what they want with it."

"Maybe," Sam said. "But what about my own laptop, the one you set up for me after I paid you for a hackproof one?"

"What about it?"

"What does it mean when turns itself on and then off again while it's still inside its case?"

"It means it's not hackproof, which you should remember I never guaranteed. I just did the best I could at the time. You remember me saying that?"

Sam skipped past Hack's excuse. "You got time to take a look?"

Hack glanced down at the blank yellow pad with the solitary word "Song" staring up at him. "Where are you now?"

17 A Generous Offer

After Hack hung up, Sam sat staring at the laptop on his desk. He touched his finger to it. It had cooled to room temperature. Was it safe to turn on?

The doorbell rang. Too soon for it to be Hack. A delivery? Sam took his suit jacket off its hanger in his small office closet and put it on. He checked the mirror on the front of the door and adjusted his tie and went to the door.

He opened the door to the porch and saw a fit dark-haired man in business-casual khakis and button-collared oxford shirt. The man was smiling. He said in a faint accent, "Mr. Lapidos?"

"Yes."

"I am in need of counsel. Do you have a few moments?"

"I'm expecting someone soon," Sam said.

The man said, "This won't take long."

Sam stepped back. No harm in listening.

The man smiled his way in and looked around.

Sam gestured the man towards an easy chair in the front living room. "Please take a seat anywhere."

"Thank you."

Sam said, "Would you like something to drink?"

"No, thank you." The man chose one of the plush easy chairs. Sam took the chair directly across from the man. While Sam did that, he patted the outside of his coat pocket to turn on his phone's "record" app.

Sam had perfected his sneak recording maneuver over years of practice. It was legal; in both Minnesota and Arizona, only one person needed to consent to recording a conversation, and Sam always consented to himself. Of course, Sam didn't record his clients.

The man gave no sign he noticed the move.

Sam settled back and crossed his legs. "How can I help you?"

"My name is Mahir Darwish. I work with an organization called "AIL"—the Anti-Islamophobia League. Have you heard of it?"

"I'm familiar with it."

"We need legal help."

Sam said, "I'm afraid I can't help you, Mr. Darwish."

"Are you sure? You haven't given me the opportunity to explain the situation."

"It doesn't matter," Sam said. "My partner and I are very busy now, and we're not in a position to take on new clients. But I can refer you to some other attorneys."

"Your current workload will not be an obstacle. Ours is not an immediate need. And even if you happen to do no work any particular month, we are willing to pay you a substantial monthly fee."

"It doesn't matter."

Darwish said, "My orgnization AIL has authorized me to offer you as much as ten thousand dollars per month."

Sam shrugged.

The man said, "I already spoke with Mr. Laghdaf, and he seemed very satisfied with such an arrangement."

Darwish was lying. Neither Sam nor Laghdaf would agree to represent anyone without checking with the other. And Laghdaf was even more cautious than Sam. Maybe paranoid. Laghdaf's life had given him stunning reasons for that.

"Perhaps if I explained," Darwish said.

"Perhaps, but I doubt it."

"I understand you take cases involving discrimination."

"I do," Sam said.

"And our current situation finds us in partnership with Southwest Arizona State University, working to fight Islamophobia."

"I see."

"You do that kind of work, I believe," Darwish said. "You sued SWASU for its horribly unfair treatment of that young African-American student, did you not?"

"Yes."

"And that case has completed, hasn't it?"

Sam said nothing.

"And if I understand your attorney rules, there would now be no conflict of interest in representing SWASU, am I correct?"

It was easy to see where Darwish was headed. Conflict of interest rules prevented lawyers from representing parties with adverse interests. For example, it was standard practice for environmental activist organizations to hire the most noted environmental lawyers in any state, not only to buy them off, but to create conflicts of interest ahead of time. A lawyer already representing the activists couldn't defend some corporation they sued. And a lawyer getting a fat monthly retainer was less likely to want to.

AIL was trying to hire Sam to protect SWASU?

It didn't matter. Sam wasn't going to work for AIL, not because they were Muslim—after all, Laghdaf was Muslim—but because they'd inspired SWASU to shaft his previous client Amos Owens. And there was a good chance they had something to do with the Jew-hatred festival Ms. Soriano wanted to expose.

AIL must know all this too. So what was this guy doing here? Fishing for information?

No matter. Darwish would come up empty. All Sam said was, "We're very busy now, and we're not really taking on new clients. But I can refer you to other lawyers in town who may be able to help you."

"Is there something we should know about?"

"Who?"

"AIL?"

This Darwish guy didn't work very hard to hide the ball. "I don't know what you mean. But it doesn't matter, I can't represent AIL."

"At this time?"

"I think I've said all I need to say. Do you have a business card or something like that?"

Darwish blinked. "Why?"

Sam smiled and lied. "I can show this to some attorney friends of mine and see who might be interested."

"I do have a card." Darwish reached into his pocket and handed Sam a business card.

The card listed Mahir Darwish as an officer in the "Anti Islamophobia League" and gave an email address and a phone number. No mailing address, but Sam supposed that was now common practice. The world was fading from hardware to software in front of his eyes, like the Cheshire Cat in the light of the moon.

Darwish said, "Do you think I came here under false pretenses?"

"No pretense at all," Sam said. "Now, it's been interesting, but as I said, I have a meeting in just a few minutes." He stood.

Darwish stood too. "Thank you for your time," Darwish said. "I'm sorry we didn't get further in our conversation. Perhaps some other time."

"Perhaps," Sam said. He escorted Darwish to the door. They shook hands and Darwish walked off into the Arizona sunlight.

Sam closed the door and took his phone out of his pocket and played back a little of the recording. The app had worked fine. He put his phone back in his coat pocket and returned to his office and hung up his jacket in his closet again.

He sat behind his desk. His laptop was cool to the touch. He took a chance and turned it on. It seemed to boot up as normal. He wrote and sent an email to AIL at the email address on Darwish's card, outlining his entire conversation with Darwish and identifying five other attorneys who might be interested in representing AIL.

The point was to make a written record, just in case Darwish later lied about what they'd discussed. Sam had no clue what lie Darwish might come up with, but why take chances?

18 Suspension of Disbelief

Sam's phone rang again. His jacket was still hanging in the closet. Sam stood and struggled a bit to get the phone out of his jacket pocket but managed on the sixth ring. The caller ID said Aviva Soriano. Sam answered.

"They suspended me," she said. "Without pay."

"That was quick. Did they find out you're going to blow the whistle?"

"They never said anything about that."

"Did they find out you hired lawyers?"

"They didn't mention that either."

"Okay. What reason did they give?"

"Israel."

He paused, his mind racing through possibilities and making connections. "I see," he said.

"You do? Because I don't."

He said, "Let's get together in person. I'll explain."

"As of now, I've got nothing but time. I can come right down to your office."

Sam looked around. His computer had acted odd. What if the office were bugged? Hack should check that too. What then? He said, "Come to the lobby of the Vauxhall Arms Hotel downtown."

"Okay. Why there?"

"It's where I'm staying. They have conference rooms there. I can get us one."

"Are you afraid your office is bugged?"

Very good—she was making her own connections. And quick too. Which would only help. "I can't rule it out."

Sam's doorbell rang again.

"Hang on a moment, please," Sam said. "Someone at the door."

"Of course," she said.

Sam went out and opened the front door.

It was Hack. Sam told him, "I'm on the phone, but come on in." Sam signaled Hack with a single upraised finger of his right hand and led him to his office and pointed to his laptop.

Sam returned to the front room and told Ms. Soriano, "Okay. That was my computer expert ex-son-in-law. He's here to check things out. He'll take a look at your work computer as soon as he can."

"If he can," she said. "I've just been suspended, remember? I don't know if I can get him in, or even get myself in anymore."

Sam said, "Hack has ways. Meanwhile bring any document you have with you to the hotel."

"Is there good parking nearby?"

"Use the hotel's Valet Parking."

"How much is that? I just lost my paycheck."

"Laghdaf and I validate. We're full service."

She laughed. It was the first time he'd heard her do that. "Thank you."

"Great. See you soon."

"See you soon."

The conversation hung a moment.

Sam said, "Goodbye for now."

Ms. Soriano said, "Goodbye for now" and hung up.

19 Hack Inspects Sam's Office

It had taken Hack only twenty minutes to drive from the Hedgehog Barrel to the address Sam had given him. Hack navigated by phone, since his Audi Fox had no GPS, or for that matter, any other electronic feature dreamed up in the generations since 1973.

Hack didn't care what they wouldn't think of next.

His route took Hack to a residential neighborhood about a mile from downtown Phoenix. Sam's office turned out to be an elderly but well-maintained white cottage with an attached carport instead of a garage. The carport was empty. Hack parked on the street in front and walked around to the other side and lifted his small equipment bag off the floor in front of the passenger seat. He hoisted its strap over his shoulder and carried it up the narrow concrete path towards the front porch.

A palo verde tree about twenty feet high grew to the right of the path, casting no meaningful shade. Two stakes held it upright with wires. Two sprinklers cast thin spray onto the two sides of the tiny front lawn of genuine green grass, which seemed an extravagance in the Arizona desert.

Hack liked palo verde because it was thorough in its greenness. It was green all the way, in every detail, not only in the yellowish green of its sliver leaves, but also in the darker greens of its branches and trunk.

Sam and Laghdaf's bungalow had a little front porch shaded by an overhanging roof. Hack stepped up onto the porch. On each side of the door stood two wide crimson flowerpots as high as Hack's waist, each sprouting lush yellow hibiscus.

Hack rang the doorbell. Ten seconds later, Sam opened the door. He was holding a cell phone to his left ear. He said to Hack, "I'm on the phone, but come on in," and signaled Hack with a single upraised finger of his right hand and led him through an expensively furnished front room to an alcove office. A dark natural wood desk and a plush chair took up most of the place. Bookshelves filled with law books covered the wall behind the desk. Sam pointed to his laptop sitting on the desk and took himself and his phone back to the front room, abandoning Hack to the work.

Hack laid his bag on the desk next to Sam's laptop. For the moment, he ignored the computer. Instead, he started with a physical sweep of the office. He looked under the desk. He looked inside all the drawers and checked them for false bottoms or backs. He clambered on top of Sam's desk and poked into the smoke detector on the ceiling above.

He wheeled the swivel chair over and stood on it to get at the air vents. He wheeled it again and unscrewed the globe off an old-fashioned ceiling light fixture and inspected inside and screwed the globe back on.

Nothing so far.

One at a time, he lifted and put back each of the three framed abstract art pieces off the wall. Nothing worth seeing behind them. Nothing worth seeing in front either.

He eyed the dozens of law books on the shelves behind the desk and sighed. Cameras and microphones were easily hidden in books. He spent the next half hour yanking each book off the shelf and opening it. Still nothing.

Hack looked for any unexplained wires, but found none.

While Hack was snooping around the room, he was also listening for the hums, clicks and buzzes motion tracking cameras might make. He heard none of that.

Hack called his voice mail on his cell and moved around, phone pressed up to his left ear, listening for clicks or other sounds of interference with the call. He walked his phone back to the front room, where he found Sam locked upright like a wiry yard troll in a business suit, stuck in one of his deep trances, staring off into the void.

Hack had seen Sam do this many times. It was a way Sam had to think through any serious problem. Sometimes he even snapped out of his trance with a solution.

Hack sidestepped the Sam sculpture and repeated in the front room the same thorough search he'd conducted in the office.

Nothing here either.

Hack hung up his phone. He pulled down the shades and turned out all the lights and prowled in the darkness through all the rooms of the house, hunting for little glowing red or white lights from cameras or other devices. No such lights.

From the kitchen, Hack heard Sam shout from the front room, "What the Hell?"

Sam must have snapped out of his trance. Hack shouted back, "I had to turn out the lights. I'm done now, go ahead and turn them back on."

Sam grumbled something Hack couldn't make out. Hack heard a thud and what sounded like a few choice words.

No luck so far, in the kitchen or any other room in the house. Time to go electronic.

Hack returned to the alcove office and turned the lights back on and opened his equipment bag and took out his RF meter, a black device about six inches long and a couple of inches thick. A bunch of buttons were mounted on the front along with a small screen.

Hack flicked it on. Of course, Sam's office was awash with the normal electronic emissions of the contemporary world. Hack recognized typical frequencies of local wireless internet modems, routers, cell phones, Bluetooth devices, microwave ovens and all the others.

Hack was particularly interested in signals from 8 MHz to 10 MHz, a range of frequencies common to electronic surveillance. He did find one signal near 8.5 MHz which he didn't recognize and whose source he couldn't pinpoint.

Sam came in. "You almost done with my computer?"

"Haven't even gotten to it yet. I've been sweeping the place for bugs."

"Find anything?"

"I found you have terrible taste in art."

"Those pieces came with the place. They belong to the landlord. I've been meaning to tell him to take them away."

"Don't wait. Meanwhile, I found this." Hack held out the RF Meter so that Sam could see the little screen.

Sam shrugged. "Means nothing to me."

Hack asked, "Have you had any unusual visitors?"

"Of course. It's a law office. Every visitor is unusual."

"Okay then, anyone unexpected?"

Sam said, "We had a new client we expected, and then someone unexpected did come by. He left right before you got here."

"Did any of them drop anything or leave anything behind?"

"Yes, actually. Our new client left her sunglasses behind."

"You got them?"

Sam walked over to the closet and reached into the inside suitcoat pocket. He pulled out a pair of black sunglasses and handed them to Hack.

Hack inspected the sunglasses. His RF meter ignored them. He handed them back. "These are okay. And the unexpected visitor?"

"A young man who said he was from the Anti Islamophobia League and they wanted to hire me on a fat retainer."

"How fat?"

"Ten thousand a month guaranteed, even if I do no work that month."

"That's not fat. It's morbidly obese. Did you take it?"

"Of course not. Conflict of interest."

Hack shook his head in wonder. These lawyers. "Did your potential new client leave anything behind?"

"Just his business card," Sam said. He went back to his desk and opened a drawer and retrieved a manila folder. He lifted the folder and showed Hack the white card stapled to the inside.

Hack took the folder and fingered the card up off the manila. "That's not it."

"Not what?"

"I'm getting a signal I haven't identified yet. But I don't think it's coming from in here." Hack walked out to the front porch. Sam followed.

Hack bent over and looked into the flowerpot on the right. He poked his hand in among the tangled hibiscus stems and blossoms and found nothing.

He looked in the flowerpot on the left and poked his fingertips around again until he felt the cold touch of metal.

Hack put thumb and forefinger together and grasped and pulled up a flat silvery disk about a quarter the size of his thumbnail. He showed the tiny item to Sam. "Here it is. Audio microphone and radio transmitter. You're bugged."

Sam said, "I watered those plants yesterday. It wasn't there then."

"You sure?"

"Not a hundred percent sure. But I don't just sprinkle the water from on high. I stick the spout in deep to make sure the water will soak into the soil and down to the roots. I should have noticed it."

Hack asked, "So what do you want me to do with this?"

Sam took the bug in his hand. Such a small item for such a big intrusion. Who was it this time?

Criminals masquerading as law enforcement? If so, local or federal? The private legal profession crawled with crooks, liars and deceivers, but the government was worse.

But rage was a useless emotion. He put it away, back where it could do him or clients the least harm. He said, "Put it back. Maybe I can use this to my advantage."

"How?"

"No idea yet."

Sam's phone was ringing again. While Hack put the bug back, Sam went back inside and looked at his phone's screen. Laghdaf. Sam answered.

Laghdaf asked, "Have you tried to check your voice mail?"

"No."

"Well, don't bother. It's full."

"Okay," Sam said. "Why?"

"You're doxed," Laghdaf said.

"Who this time?"

"I'll explain when I see you. I just got a call and there's somebody we need to talk to in person as soon as possible."

"You're kidding," Sam said. "Didn't you just get us to take on Aviva Soriano as a client?"

"This is different."

"By the way, I was right about the retaliation. Her bosses already suspended her."

"For talking to us?"

"Not clear. I just got into town and already a lot of things are popping."

"Get used to it," Laghdaf said. "This man who called me wants to tell us about an imminent terrorist murder."

"And Ms. Soriano? I said I'd meet with her today."

"You decide," Laghdaf said.

"Murder comes first," Sam said. "I'll call her."

Right after they hung up, Sam called Aviva Soriano. He explained that something urgent had come up.

"I understand," she said.

"In the meantime, there is something you can do," he said. "I'll have Hack call you. You can set things up with him to check out your work computer together."

"I can't imagine how," she said. "I'm suspended. They took my keys. I can't even get into my office anymore. What can he do?"

"He'll think of something."

20 Hack Inspects Sam's Computer

Hack leaned back in Sam's luxurious swivel chair and lifted his feet and gave himself a couple of twirls. Sam knew how to live. Sam was staying at that fancy Vauxhall Arms Hotel while Hack and Mattie made do in their bachelor band mate Dudley's tiny back bedroom.

Dudley was a good guy and a generous host, but no one called his old Arizona home swank. And unlike Sam's hotel, there was no room service or laundry or changing the bedsheets. Mattie and Hack took care of all their own domestic stuff. In fact, she'd wound up cooking for Dudley too, which was part of the reason Dudley charged them no rent.

Hack heard a door slam. He went to the front room. No one there. He opened the front door. Sam was sprinting away down the street, hard shoes clacking on the concrete, suit coattails flying behind.

Of course, no explanation for the sudden takeoff. Sam was always in a hurry; for Sam, the "overbooked lawyer" cliché was an understatement.

Which was no excuse for the fact that Sam had followed exactly none of Hack's written list of warnings and instructions about protecting his laptop.

It was riddled with worms, keystroke loggers, rootkits, trojans and viruses. The viruses included system viruses as well as file and macro infectors. The malware in Sam's laptop was singing and dancing in a festival that rivaled that old time Woodstock in its joyful and muddy abandon.

Sam must have opened every attachment he ever received in an email. Worse, he'd ignored all the notices to upgrade the protective software Hack had installed. Each upgrade contained updated definitions and controls to fight the latest threats, but like Sam, Sam's laptop was stuck in the past.

Hack spent the next two hours cleansing the laptop while mentally composing and rehearsing a fierce scolding.

Hack decided to encrypt the entire laptop. Sam would just have to learn the steps to go through and memorize all the necessary passwords.

In trial, Sam was a smart guy. He remembered what was on Page 163 of some witness deposition or in the unreadable small print on page 27 of some contract. He ought to be able to remember a few passwords and a few necessary written steps to protect himself and his clients.

Hack set up and initiated the encryption process. Encrypting the entire hard drive was going to take a few hours. He went to the kitchen and brewed a pot of coffee and poured himself a cup. He carried the cup back to Sam's office. He scanned the bookshelf. He took out Brian Dirck's book *Lincoln the Lawyer* and went into the front room and took a seat in one of the plush chairs. He set his cup on the wood trivet on the coffee table. He curled up to read.

He could upgrade Sam's laptop, but could he upgrade Sam?

21 Owen and Sam and Laghdaf

"I feel like I've coming out of a cave and my eyes are blinking from the light, like I've been living in this gloomy oppressive space for a year and I was trapped underground like a mole in a constricted burrow with the walls clenching me ever tighter and the massive dirt ceiling pressing down. And now I've come out and my eyes can't stand the light and I want to close them again against the pain, but I can't. I don't dare close them. I have to stand erect in the light and tell the truth. But how? Maybe you can tell me. That's why I called."

All this in a rush, one uninterrupted expulsion of breath and voice, then Owen Deutscher stopped, chin trembling. He waved his upraised open hands in little circles in the air, as if he didn't know where to put them.

He looked to be in his early-to-mid-twenties. He wore jeans and a tee shirt and a black fleece watch cap pulled down tight. His dark eyes bulged from adrenalin. He wore no beard, but the faint trace of unshaven mustache quivered over his lip.

Sam and Laghdaf were sitting with him in a Vauxhall Arms conference room. Sam sat in a swivel chair at the end of the glass-covered conference table, Laghdaf to his right and Owen to his left. Sam had laid a bottle of water and a blank yellow pad in front of him. Laghdaf had put nothing in front of him but a cup of tea, steam rising from it.

Owen wrapped both hands around his tall paper coffee cup and stared into it, as if he hoped a quick fix for his troubles would float up to him out of the blackness.

Despite the leftist doxing and the hate mongering Laghdaf had told him about, Sam felt safe at the hotel. He'd registered there in his original name, the one on his birth certificate. Enemies were generally slow to make the leap to connect the Vauxhall Arms guest "Shmuel Lapidoth" with the lawyer better known as Sam Lapidos.

One big plus: unlike the Minneapolis courthouse, no threatening mob surrounded the hotel. At least not yet.

Sam and Laghdaf had bought their firm's new phone account under the name "Lapidos and Laghdaf," with several phone numbers. As usual, the doxers had overlooked Laghdaf, whose phone and voice mail stayed available. After getting the "voicemail full" message at Sam's number, Owen had called Laghdaf and arranged the appointment.

So the kid had at least some minimal resourcefulness.

Sam glanced at Laghdaf, who signaled with barely perceptible nod that Sam should take the lead this time.

Sam told Owen, "On the phone, you told Mr. Laghdaf you know something about a terrorist plot, but you wouldn't say what. And we still don't know what you're talking about."

Owen said, "I'm a Muslim, at least I think I am, or maybe I was. I don't know." He stopped again.

Sam said nothing. Sometimes you just had to wait and eventually they talked, even if only to fill the uncomfortable silence.

This silence stretched half a minute before Owen gave in and said, "I'm worried about being prosecuted myself."

Sam said, "Anything you tell your lawyers is privileged. We can't tell anyone else without your permission. But we have to know."

Owen sighed. "Even if it's a crime?"

"Like what?"

"Like fraud?"

"When you spoke with Mr. Laghdaf on the phone, you weren't talking about fraud, you were talking about a terrorist murder. That's what got our attention and got us rushing to talk with you here."

"Okay, so there's this group I'm involved with. And they want me to do something," Owen said, "But I don't want to, and I'm scared."

"Scared of what?" Sam asked.

"Scared they'll kill me."

"Why would they do that?"

"I've disobeyed an order."

"What was the order?" Sam asked.

Owen said, "I already said. To kill someone."

"Who wants you to kill someone?"

"Tayoub Abawi."

Laghdaf sighed a barely audible sigh. Owen gave no sign he noticed.

Sam asked, "Could you spell that please?"

Owen did, and for the first time Sam wrote something on his yellow pad. Sam asked, "Who is Tayoub Abawi?"

"He's the leader of my cell."

"Whom does he want you to kill?" A little correct grammar couldn't hurt.

"A professor at SWASU."

Sam often wondered whether his job was more like dentistry than law. Getting information could feel like strapping his client to a chair and extracting one impacted fact at a time. "And what is this professor's name?"

"Hans Cobb. He's an Emeritus Professor at SWASU. He only teaches one course. He calls it American Literature on the Border."

Sam wrote down the name "Hans Cobb" next to the name "Tayoub Abawi" and drew an arrow from Abawi to Cobb. Sam asked, "And why does Tayoub Abawi want you to kill Professor Cobb?"

"Tayoub found out—from a student on the Bias Response Team, I think—that Professor Cobb was talking about book banning and freedom of speech in his class and he showed cartoons of the Prophet Mohammed, *alayhis salam.*

At the Arabic expression, Sam raised a single eyebrow at Laghdaf, who spoke for the first time: "Peace be upon him."

Owen asked Laghdaf, "You're a Muslim?"

Laghdaf tilted his head in a barely perceptible nod. His dark lidded eyes expressed no emotion, but there was some in there.

Sam asked Owen, "When is this killing supposed to take place?"

"I was supposed to do it yesterday. I was supposed to go to his office and make sure I had the right guy and then kill him."

"And did you?"

"No. Of course not. I mean, I went there, but I warned him instead."

"What did he say when you warned him?"

"He told me not to bother him."

Laghdaf commented, "Professor Cobb is a renowned scholar of international literature."

"Really?" Owen said. "He sure didn't look like a scholar. He dressed like an old-time desert prospector. He was wearing blue jeans stuck into high brown boots and a big loose yellow shirt and a black vest. He said he'd be goddammed if he was going to let some"—Owen glanced at Laghdaf—"person scare him out of doing his job or expressing his opinion. Then he told me not to bother him."

Sam took over again. "Do you think he's still in danger?"

"Absolutely. That's why I'm here."

"Why not just call the police?"

"I want to, but I want a lawyer to help me with that."

"Because of your fraud?"

"Yeah. And a few other things."

"Let's summarize and see where we are," Sam said. With his right index finger he ticked the points off on his left palm. "You *(tick)* joined some Islamist terrorist cell and *(tick)* they ordered you to kill a college professor and *(tick)* instead you warned him and *(tick)* now you want our help contacting the authorities?"

"That's most of it."

"What else?"

Owen ticked back. *(Tick)* "I'm on the run and *(Tick)* I don't want to wind up dead like Steve O'Toole."

22 Steve O'Toole

Laghdaf spoke up again. "A man named Steve O'Toole is dead?"

"Yes."

"What happened to him?" Laghdaf asked.

"I don't know for sure. I only know he's dead."

Laghdaf said, "You believe this Tayoub Abawi killed him?"

"Yes. Or had him killed."

Laghdaf asked, "On what do you base your belief?

"I heard Tayoub say it."

"What were his exact words?" Laghdaf asked.

Owen said, "I asked Tayoub why Steve hadn't shown up at this meeting we were having and Tayoub told me, 'Steve is dead. He disappointed Allah and me. Don't you disappoint Allah and me.'"

"Those exact words?" Sam asked.

"Yeah. It's something hard to forget."

Sam asked, "Did you ever see Steve O'Toole's body?"

"No."

"Besides what Tayoub told you, do you have any reason to believe O'Toole is dead?"

"He was always there at the office every day and then suddenly he wasn't there anymore, and he doesn't answer his personal phone, and someone emptied out his desk at work, and I went to his apartment and knocked and no one answered. Yeah, and no one will tell me where he is."

Sam asked, "And how did you get involved with this Tayoub Abawi in the first place?"

Over the next several hours, late into the evening, in halting and confused and not-very-chronological order,

Sam's and Laghdaf's questions hauling Owen upriver against the current a few yards at a time, Owen got out his story.

As far as Sam understood, Owen's story went something like this:

Owen's parents were Jewish and he had grown up in a Reform Jewish Synagogue in Connecticut.

The temple rabbi—Owen called his synagogue a "temple"—was a woman named Cam Holtzmann. She was a motherly woman who became his mentor and teacher. She encouraged him to work in social justice causes, which he did, even as a teenager, for example, when he joined protests against transphobia.

Owen's Bar Mitzvah speech covered the Torah portion *Shoftim*—"Judges"—a section of the Bible which contained the famous commandment to pursue justice. Rabbi Holtzmann explained that justice meant social justice.

Owen grew up seething with disappointment that so many Americans object to social justice. They were the white supremacists who profit from injustice, along with their easily manipulated allies and pawns, like the American religious right and other crazies who foster racism and homophobia and transphobia because of their greed and ignorance and bigotry and fear. So Owen believed.

When Owen went to college in Boston, Owen continued his activism for each new social justice cause as it arrived. He earned extra spending money by participating in a Bias Response Team, which patrolled the campus hunting for hate speech and reporting it to the Administration. Through the Team, Owen met and become close friends with a Pakistani man named Hamza Khan, who explained to Owen that despite all the lies and slanders, Islam was a progressive religion which opposed racism, supported women's rights, and abhorred violence.

To Owen's natural open mindedness, Owen's progressive upbringing in the Temple added a sympathy for Muslims, whom he was taught to see as victims of Islamophobia. Even worse than their current victimhood were the shameful historic crimes of Western civilization, which Owen studied at the university in the social justice courses required for his majors, which were accounting and music.

Under Hamza Khan's kind guidance, Owen had eventually converted to Islam, which required only his repeating out loud what Hamza called the *Shahada*, the confession of faith: "There is no god but God. Muhammad is the messenger of God."

After his conversion, Owen spent a dream-like few months with Hamza in communal spiritual efforts, studying, praying and chanting. Hamza was a genuinely brilliant and kindly man and the best friend Owen had ever known. Hamza taught Owen many beautiful spiritual practices, some of them from Islam's mystical Sufi tradition.

With the proverbial butterflies fluttering against his insides, Owen summoned up the nerve to tell his parents about his conversion to Islam. They seemed surprised, but they professed only pleasure that Owen had found a path on his spiritual journey which was "comfortable for you," as his father put it.

His parents' reaction shouldn't have surprised Owen as much as it did; they were both kind people who rarely spoke ill of anyone, especially those they saw as victims.

Owen's friend Hamza Khan graduated in winter and went back to Pakistan. In his final few months of college, Owen felt lost without him. Owen saw an advertisement on a Muslim website: the Al-Andalus mosque in Phoenix needed someone to handle their accounting. The pay was meager, but Owen was an unmarried new graduate with no serious financial obligations and no marketable experience. The promise of immersing himself in an authentic Islamic experience intrigued him. He applied, and after a twenty-minute online interview he got the job.

In a painful scene which left both crying, Owen broke up with his girlfriend. She was not going to convert along with him, and he needed to seek his own spiritual path. Tears in his eyes, he got in his car and set out for Arizona.

23 The Al-Andalus Mosque

When Owen arrived in Phoenix, an Al-Andalus Mosque member named Steve O'Toole found Owen a cheap efficiency in a nondescript apartment building near the mosque. Every morning Owen walked two blocks to work at the mosque, which was a new two-story octagonal building faced with red bricks, occupying a small dirt lot. Owen generally entered through a side door and walked up the narrow stairs to his small office on the second floor.

The financial accounts were a mess and Owen spent his first two months untangling them, often laboring deep into the evening. Owen liked numbers and the work was pleasant for him, especially after a lifetime trapped in classrooms and libraries.

The Al-Andalus leadership rewarded Owen's efforts with lavish praise. The praise was especially enthusiastic from a leader named Tayoub Abawi, who seemed to function as the organizer for many Al-Andalus activities and kept tabs on Owen's development as a Muslim.

Tayoub became Owen's mentor and Steve O'Toole became Owen's closest Phoenix friend. Steve was Tayoub's direct assistant and worked from another small office connected to Owen's by an open doorway. Steve was a thickset barrel-chested man about thirty who cut his hair close to his scalp and sported a bushy brown beard.

Steve had grown up on a small ranch in northern Arizona. Steve had come to Islam after a long period of study and reflection. He seemed able to recite every tenet of every religion, even nuances of beliefs of indigenous peoples from faraway continents. Steve explained that Islam incorporated all the best beliefs and practices of all the religions in the world. To be a good Muslim required one also to be a good Jew and a good Christian, and indeed the best according to every religion. These other pre-Islamic religions had been corrupted. The perfect man Mohammed had delivered the final perfect revelation.

Steve could be volatile: he could switch in an instant from harsh doctrinaire condemnation aimed in general at those who rejected Islam to a disarming kindness aimed at individual human beings.

Once, in the middle of delivering a harsh diatribe against heretics, Steve interrupted himself and sprinted down the stairs and across the street to help an old man. Steve had seen the man slip off a sidewalk curb through the window. Steve called an ambulance and stayed on scene until he was sure the medics were treating the man's injuries correctly. He saw the ambulance off as if it were a yacht bearing royalty.

Al-Andalus was a hermetically sealed environment. Owen worked and prayed and studied only there. At some point, Owen wondered if it was a good thing to lock himself away from the rest of the world. But he decided he didn't mind. His new safe bounded space was a comfort after all the bustle and confusion of his earlier life, especially in wide-open Boston.

Owen spent all his time with other Al-Andalus Muslims. Once, Owen saw an announcement for what looked like a thought-provoking class at another local mosque. He showed Steve the notice on his computer screen. Looking over Owen's shoulder, Steve said, "Dude, you don't need to go over there to learn. It'll be less confusing for you if you stick with the classes we run right here. Ours are all from one consistent point of view."

Education at Al-Andalus was intense. There was a class almost every night. Under Tayoub's guidance, Owen started studying Arabic and began trying to read the Quran in the original. He found websites full of explanations detailing ever more abstruse and arcane doctrines in what Owen began to understand was true Islam.

As he progressed, Owen came to realize that his Pakistani friend Hamza Khan had misunderstood many things. Owen sometimes wondered whether he should pass on to Hamza some of what he was finding out, but Hamza seemed occupied with his new job and marriage in distant Pakistan and was no longer truly available to Owen.

It was not Hamza's Islam but Tayoub's and Steve's Islam which Owen studied in the mosque classes and reinforced in the Internet articles they directed him to read.

Despite their strict interpretations, Tayoub and Steve always remained gentle when they corrected Owen in some of the misconceptions Owen had started out with. And Steve was always right next door to answer in his firm but friendly way any of Owen's doubts.

At first the absence of women at prayer or in the classes caught Owen off guard, but he soon began to enjoy this all-male world.

Owen now realized how repressed he'd often felt growing up in his female-centric Reform Temple in Connecticut, although at the time he accepted it without question. He certainly had never summoned up the nerve to complain.

For example, Rabbi Cam Holtzmann seemed to favor girls to head any youth committees and social justice efforts. Girls were the ones chosen to sing at services. Robbie Stein had sung a few solos, but Owen wasn't sure that counted, since Robbie made a big deal about saying he was gay. No matter. Owen sang better than any of them. He'd even sung solos in front of his high school and college choirs.

Rabbi Holtzmann disliked any behavior she felt smacked of masculinity, toxic or otherwise. Even rambunctiousness seemed to irritate her. She hated what she called "arena sports" like football. Looking back, Owen realized that she expected Jewish boys to act just like Jewish girls—although of course not to be as good at it.

Owen admitted to himself that in Al-Andalus classes and in the mandatory five-times-a-day group prayers, the absence of distracting female bodies and voices did seem to help him focus on Allah and not lose himself in destructive thoughts and desires.

Some Islamic strictures did seem unnecessary and even extreme. One morning, Owen had stopped outside the Al-Andalus to pet a stray black dog that followed him into the front yard. The dog was obviously desperate for affection. Steve must have seen Owen through the window, because upstairs in the office, he said, "Dude, don't you know you're supposed to kill black dogs?"

"What do you mean?"

"There's a lot of *ahadith*. You shouldn't even let a dog touch you, and if it's a black dog you have to kill it."

By this time, Owen had learned not to argue. All Owen would get back in return was disapproval from his only local friends. Pretty soon, Steve would find a way to raise the topic in front of Tayoub, and Tayoub and Steve would double team Owen until he caved. Instead, Owen said, "I didn't know that"—a phrase he found himself using more and more often.

When Owen looked it up on the Internet, he found the Muslim attitude towards dogs was more nuanced than

Steve's. But knowledgeable as he was, nuance wasn't part of Steve's toolkit.

The same strictness applied to Owen's shaving his face—it made men look like women, as did wearing a bracelet; shorts that didn't cover his knees—even in the blazing Phoenix summer; and an infinite list of all-encompassing and ever-tightening restrictions on Owen's food, dress, habits and ultimately his most private thoughts.

The toughest break from the past was to give up music. Owen loved music. He especially loved to sing, and he knew he sang well.

Many moonlit nights, Owen had sung Muslim verses along with his friend Hamza Khan from the roof of Hamza's Boston apartment building. Owen loved to listen to Hamza playing his Pakistani *rubab*. It was like a guitar, but tuned differently, and with a lot more strings. Hamza's finger flew over the frets, and the exotic sounds thrilled Owen in modes different from western music.

But music turned out to be haram.

On this subject, Steve allowed no doubt. He stood erect in front of Owen's desk and lifted his clenched right fist in the air and declaimed, "Dude, music leads you to Hell."

Steve brought his big fist to his thick chest and recited, "The noble Quran says, 'And of mankind is he who purchases idle talk like music and singing to mislead men from the Path of Allah without knowledge. For such there will be a humiliating torment in Hell'."

Steve added, "Or almost those exact words. You get the idea. The point is that idle talk sends you to Hell."

Owen had to ask, "How is listening to music or singing any kind of idle talk? I mean, even if it's to praise Allah?"

"There's a lot of *ahadith* that prove it," Steve said. *Ahadith* were recorded sayings of Mohammed. "Music is idle talk. Music distracts you from Allah's path."

At Al-Andalus, to way to settle any question was to appeal to the authority of the Quran or Ahadith or other ancient Islamic source. The the more ancient the source, the more authoritative. Reasoning from facts outside that authority was pointless, off the subject, out of place, didn't matter.

And even though Owen did his best not to notice, he became more and more aware that if he ran across two or more sayings in the Quran or Ahadith or other authorities which seemed inconsistent with one another, his Al-Andalus teachers always chose the strictest possible interpretation.

So Owen didn't argue about music either. Owen read the Ahadith Steve pointed out to him, and after a heart-breaking two weeks of inner struggle against yet another of his endless supply of personal weaknesses, Owen cancelled his Spotify account and erased his Pandora apps and links. In a vigorous gesture of penance, he took a hammer to all his CD's, even his Home Free and his Mozart. He bagged the shards and threw the bag into the dumpster behind his apartment building. That would teach himself.

Owen was dedicating himself to the greater jihad, *al-jihad al-akbar*, the inner struggle for personal self-improvement against the self's base desires.

The other jihad was the lesser jihad, *al-jihad al-asghar*, that is, military struggle, which ignorant *Khufar* called "holy war."

When Owen had been a lot younger, the French satirical magazine *Charlie Hebdo* had blasphemed against the Prophet Mohammed by publishing cartoons showing his image. Enraged Muslims responded by killing the offenders.

The violence had appalled Owen. Before Owen converted, he asked Hamza about it. Hamza expressed the same disgust.

But when a new cartoon killing happened in the Netherlands, Steve asked, "What are our brothers supposed to do? We can't let the *Khufar* blaspheme against our Prophet." And he pointed to passages in the Quran and the ahadith which supported him.

Violence was a terrible thing, but violence could be an understandable response to provocation. And even if the blasphemers had some abstract free speech rights to say what they said, they didn't have to actually exercise their so-called "rights," did they? They didn't have to say everything they thought. By choosing to indulge their wickedness, hadn't they just brought the violence on themselves? Had Hamza Khan had been wrong about *Jihad*, too?

Owen started to read the news in a different way. As he pored through the Internet news sources recommended by Steve and Tayoub, he began to understand how the American and other western media distorted events. All over the world Muslims were struggling against violent regimes which oppressed and repressed Muslims with massacre and torture.

How could Muslims defend themselves from violence other than through violence? And a lot of so-called "free" speech was merely hate speech inciting violence against Islam. Why punish the bad actions, but ignore the language which inspired them?

As Owen traveled his spiritual path, there did come one moment he almost rebelled. He had accumulated a few vacation days, and he mentioned to Steve he planned to take a long weekend and travel back to Connecticut for his younger brother's Bar Mitzvah.

Steve's big jutting beard seemed to harden to concrete. "That's not right, Dude. That's another religion."

"I'm not going to participate," Owen said. "I'm just going to watch. But he's a lot younger than me and I haven't paid enough attention to him. He and I are still part of the same family. My parents supported me when I converted to Islam, and it will reflect well on Muslims if I support family members in their religion as well."

"Are you going to congratulate him?"

"I hadn't thought about it. I suppose I might, if it comes up."

"Don't."

"Why not?

Steve reached into his desk and pulled out a book of ahadith. He leafed through it and found the page he wanted and read aloud:

> "Congratulating the *khufar* on the rituals that belong only to them is haram by consensus, as is congratulating them on their festivals and fasts by saying 'A happy festival to you' or 'May you enjoy your festival,' and so on. If the one who says this has been saved from *khufar*, it is still forbidden. It is like congratulating someone for prostrating to the cross, or even worse than that. It is haram for a Muslim to accept invitations on such occasions, because this is worse than congratulating them as it implies taking part in their celebrations."

At this moment in telling Sam and Laghdaf his story, Owen stopped and fell silent. He stared down at his now empty coffee cup. Tears started in his eyes. He said, "Excuse me," and stood and walked out of the room.

After a moment of silence, Sam asked Laghdaf, "Do you think he went to the Bar Mitzvah?"

"Of course not," Laghdaf said. "Although I can't help wondering what a world-famous Muslim like Muhammed Ali was doing at his own grandson's Bar Mitzvah."

"Supporting his grandson?"

"As he should," Laghdaf said.

Sam had a great tolerance for meandering witness stories, but Owen was burning through it fast. "We need to hurry him along. He still hasn't explained how they convinced him to kill this professor."

"Patience," Laghdaf said, not the first time in their partnership. "He is not explaining just to us, he is explaining to himself. But I need a break too." He stood. Sam did the same.

Twenty minutes later, the three gathered again in the same conference room, sitting in the same places. Sam had stopped by the hotel coffee shop for another cup of coffee for Owen, herbal tea for Laghdaf, and a bottle of water for himself.

Sam leapt ahead. "You were about to tell us how you decided to kill Professor Cobb?"

Owen said, "I didn't really decide. It was just presented to me as a fact."

"Who presented it? Steve?"

"No, Tayoub. Steve was already dead."

"Why?"

"I never found out."

"Did you have a guess?"

"I guess he did something he wasn't supposed to do or didn't do something he was supposed to. But I don't know any specifics. Or maybe it was something he knew he wasn't supposed to know."

"What did he know?"

Owen sighed. "I'm not sure. But for example, there was this Arizona state official who came sniffing around about our childcare accounting. There's a state subsidy for childcare. We were claiming way more children than we had in our childcare. We were moving kids around from room to room ahead of the inspector, changing their shirts and hats. It was like a movie farce. That way we got way more money."

"Fraud," Sam said.

"Yes, fraud."

"How much?"

"Maybe five to six million dollars."

"Where'd the money go?" Sam asked, although he could guess.

"I don't know," Owen said. "Tayoub said education, but I never saw specifically. They just drained it into some other accounts, and after that I don't know where."

"You never tried to learn?"

Owen shook his head. "Wasn't my business."

Owen looked first at Sam, then at Laghdaf. Owen said, "None of this makes me look too good, does it? But it was all a gradual progression, one small step at a time. You agree to one little thing, like not to wear shorts above your knees even if it's 115 degrees, and then you're giving up music, and then the next thing you're stealing."

"And after stealing?" Sam asked.

"I won't say it was like a nightmare, because I remember it all, and I don't remember all the details of my nightmares," Owens said. "All I can tell you is that I found myself in some kind of mental state and I was walking around SWASU and I asked people how to get to Cobb's office and they told me and I was standing there in his office doorway looking at him and I couldn't do it. So I warned him and took off and now I'm here with you."

A brief pause, then Owen said, "You tell me. Am I that easy to manipulate? Am I a total sucker. A loser?"

"Son, I won't tell you not to be so hard on yourself," Sam said. "Because you should be hard on yourself. It's true the people you're dealing with are experts, but that's no excuse."

"They possess great knowledge and long experience with human psychology," Laghdaf said. "You're not the first."

Owen appealed to Laghdaf. "But it is true, isn't it? How Westerners have oppressed and victimized Muslims throughout history?

"Don't infantilize us," Laghdaf said. The normally unflappable Laghdaf surprised Sam by snapping out his words. "We are not children. Muslims are human beings. We are capable of great wrongs, just like all the other human beings. History is full of terrible crimes by all sorts of people. As full human beings, we've committed our share. If you're going to talk about history, you need to learn it, and I mean really learn the fullness of it, not some distorted version that reduces Muslims or Africans or anyone else to a mass of weak, helpless, passive victims. As one historian wrote, that image originates in the mind of the oppressor."

That was a long speech for Laghdaf. He leaned back and flickered an almost apologetic glance at Sam.

Sam said, "I'm no way a Marxist, but Marx said one thing that fits my experience with life and people. Marx said, 'Being determines consciousness'."

Owen said, "What does that mean?"

"You are what you do," Sam said. "If someone can get you to do things, the more things you do, the more you believe these must be the right things. After all, you're doing them, aren't you? And your ideas follow your actions, not the other way around, the way most believe."

"Do you think that's true?"

"At least sometimes. You're here in this fix, aren't you?"

"Yes," Owen said, "I'm here in this fix."

Sam glanced at Laghdaf, whose face had flattened to a mask. Sam guessed Laghdaf was still seething under his controlled exterior.

Sam also kept his seething to himself. Sam was no way surprised to learn from the little asides Owen had dropped here and there that Owen had spent his childhood in a Jewish synagogue and yet knew next to nothing about Jewish history or the Jewish religion, and what little he did know was usually untrue.

It's not true that in the Jewish religion there is no afterlife.

It's not true that there's a vengeful Old Testament God, or that the Hebrew scriptures demand revenge for wrongs, as in "an eye for an eye and a tooth for a tooth"; this was never meant literally, but as a financial measure of damage, just as in contemporary American law.

It's not true that in the Jewish religion it is the wife's duty satisfy her husband sexually at his demand—in fact, any such duty is on the husband, and the wife has no corresponding obligation.

It's not true the Hebrew phrase *Eretz Israel* means "Greater Israel," signifying some master plan for Israel to take over the entire Middle East. The phrase just means "land of Israel," the indigenous Jewish home country.

And so on. But what did Sam expect? After all, at Owen's Bar Mitzvah, everyone had no doubt lavished Owen with praise after he chanted Hebrew phrases with no comprehension of the words he was parroting.

Most grating to Sam was Owen's incessant incantation of the phrase "social justice." Sam pursued justice one human being at a time. That was enough of a grueling effort without taking on the entire world according to yet another Utopian master plan.

Social justice was what the communists and socialists and fascists and religious fanatics were always trying to impose. They imposed more individual injustice on more individual human beings than their most hostile opponents had imagined, including famines, catastrophic wars, and genocides.

Fine. Owen wants to make the world a better place. Who doesn't? But what Owen needs is a kick in his narcissistic butt, along with some humility and some doses of real-life experience, which he is getting willy-nilly right now, good and hard.

Though Owen might be running out of chances for new experiences of any kind.

Sam said none of this. Sam's job was to give Owen legal advice, not religious instruction. And time was precious. All Sam said was, "You keep hiding out—don't tell us where. We'll contact some authorities we trust and you call Laghdaf."

"How long?"

"It's too late tonight," Laghdaf said, "Early tomorrow morning at the latest."

Sam said, "Meantime, you lay low for just the next few hours."

Laghdaf asked Owen, "Do you have a gun?"

Owen stiffened. His eyes widened. "A gun? No, of course not. Why would I want a gun?"

"To protect yourself," Laghdaf said.

"I could never shoot anyone," Owen said. "That would reduce me to their level."

Laghdaf snapped his words out again. "You plan to allow your enemies to reduce you to the level of meat?"

Sam flashed Laghdaf a cautionary glance. Laghdaf pressed his lips together and leaned back in his chair. He folded his hands in his lap.

Sam asked, "If you have no gun, how were you planning to kill Professor Cobb?"

Owen said, "Tayoub gave me a knife."

Sam asked, "Where is it now?"

"I threw it away. It made me sick to look at it."

Brilliant. First toss the evidence, then see a lawyer.

Owen went on, "I couldn't kill Professor Cobb, and he insulted the Prophet. How could I kill another Muslim?"

"Muslim or not," Laghdaf said. "If what you say is true, Tayoub and his gang are murderers. You are allowed to defend yourself against murderers. In fact, it's a duty."

"I've already decided I'm not going to kill anyone. That's why I'm in the trouble I'm in."

Sam said, "That's part of why."

24 Professor Hans Cobb

Professor Hans Cobb was a dinosaur. This was just one reason so many other professors couldn't stand him—and not only the professors, but the teaching assistants, the social justice warrior students, and especially the administrators, including the SWASU President Petra Sterns-Stuyvesant, she maybe most of all.

The SWASU people who could stand Hans Cobb were the typists and clerks and maintenance people and cleaning ladies and many of Cobb's students. They loved him, in part because he had remained one of them even as he racked up one extraordinary intellectual accomplishment after another.

His accomplishments may have caused his colleagues to hate him, but they were also the reason SWASU couldn't dump him, even at his advanced age. Cobb was SWASU's only professor of legitimate academic distinction.

Cobb was a scholar of international renown. He taught at SWASU only because he loved the nearby Sonoran desert where he had been born and where his parents had raised him in their isolated shack far from any town. Family members drew their water from their own private well, which made them relatively wealthy by neighborhood standards, although they gladly shared the precious liquid with anyone who asked.

Hans—or Harry as everyone called him—grew up hiking the desert, ranging on foot farther and farther from home. After school and chores, like clearing out brush from the water pump, he toughened himself climbing hills that felt like mountains to his short young legs and yanking cholla cactus spines from his calves with a pair of needle nose pliers he learned to carry at all times.

The desert was a paradise of spectacular vegetation: not only the nasty jumping cholla, but barrel cacti like spherical watermelons sprouting porcupine quills; ironwood trees twenty or more feet high; thorny-branched mesquite trees near any open water; short cylindrical hedgehog cacti with their red cup-shaped summer flowers; and the grandest of all, the branching saguaro cacti shooting like green majestic candelabras fifty feet in the air.

Not to mention the prickly pear, whose tasty fruit his friends among the local Gila River people taught Harry to collect and to turn into a delicious marmalade.

Of course, in case he had to scare off coyotes, Harry always carried his father's 1922 Colt Army Special revolver with the 4-inch barrel, chambered in .38 Special, finished in fine brushed blue.

Young Harry planned to become a botanist until, at the age of twelve, he read Homer's *Odyssey*. This mere book thrilled him even more than the many real-life wonders he'd encountered in his short life. Dark desert nights he lay in bed listening to the whistle of the passing Southern Pacific locomotive, wondering where it was going and whether he'd ever get to go there himself. He craved his own odyssey, his own impossible journey through terrifying danger to faithful love.

The habits of hard work and independence his parents pounded into Harry paid off. Harry rode those disciplines to a full scholarship to Harvard, then to Oxford and to the Sorbonne. He came back to America thoroughly read in the world's literature, all the way back to Homer and even the Sumerian Gilgamesh. He was fluent in Homeric and Attic Greek, all forms of French, Old Slavonic, Russian and a formal Castilian Spanish he fused with the rough and sometimes obscene Mexican he'd picked up from his amigos of his home desert.

After getting his Ph.D. Harry coasted through his two-year break in the U.S. Army as a quartermaster's clerk. The Army regarded Harry's twenty-six years of formal education as excellent preparation to do the work of a low-level clerk, and this time the Army got it right. Harry had great clerical skills.

His fellow soldiers liked him too, though to some it seemed odd the way he was always hiding himself away to study and write. During his relaxing two-year hitch, Harry found time to write three books on world literature. The books made him famous in the academic world, which in that remote epoch still prized genuine scholarship and insight into the written heritage of humanity.

By the time the Army discharged PFC Hans Cobb, great universities all over the world were offering him professorships and chairs endowed especially for him.

Young Harry shocked everyone by signing on to teach at SWASU, the Siberia of academia, three cruddy Quonsets in the Sonoran Desert, barely worthy to credit as a university, or for that matter, a high school.

Professor Hans Cobb immediately became SWASU's pride and joy as well as the grounds for SWASU's endless exorbitant funding requests to the Arizona State Legislature. Soon modern buildings and parking lots sprang up all over what once was rough desert.

SWASU was the house that Hans built.

Harry liked to write in the evenings after most had left. This Wednesday evening, Harry was sitting in his office writing an article on his trusty Smith Corona 220 electric typewriter, a device he cherished as the acme of modern writing technology, in part because it gave him the power to type in red ink. That had been an exciting new feature when he bought one of the first ones sold in 1972.

Harry chuckled to himself as he compared the vengeful female furies of the ancient Greek play *The Eumenides*—remorseless and unforgiving harridans and harpies—to the crew of likewise vengeful contemporary feminists who launched hysterical personal attacks against Harry whenever he published his ruminations on stories and poems written by dead European males or dead Chinese males or dead Hindu males.

Harry heard a knock at his open office door and glanced up. A young guy garbed and bearded like a Muslim terrorist from a low-budget action movie stood in his doorway.

Just the day before a young guy garbed and bushy bearded like a Muslim had knocked on Harry's office door and brandished a knife. The young guy stared at Harry. Harry stared back from his office chair. In a shaky voice, the youngster warned Harry that someone might come to kill him and he should hide out right away.

Harry told the youngster not to bother him and the youngster disappeared.

Here was a different young guy garbed and bushy bearded like a Muslim knocking on his office door. Although well past eighty, Harry was sharp enough to make the connection.

The young guy asked, "You are Professor Hans Cobb?"

Harry swiveled his chair to face the man. "Yes."

"In your classroom you showed cartoons depicting the Prophet Mohammed, *alayhis salam*?"

In a casual gesture, Harry lay his right arm across his torso and snuck his hand under his big yellow shirt to his

116

below-the-waistband holster. He tickled the handle of his father's Colt. "I did that."

"Did you realize that when you committed this atrocity you were blaspheming?"

"Don't bother me," Harry said. The past few years he'd taken to packing his pistol on his left side, convenient for a cross body draw, which he could execute even sitting down, something at his age he found himself doing more than he wanted to.

The man cocked his head as if puzzled. "Do you mean you don't want me to bother you, or that you are not bothered by the fact you blasphemed?"

"Both," Harry said.

The man reached his right hand across his body to his left side and drew a dagger from under his belt. He took one step forward.

Harry executed his own cross-body draw and doubled-tapped the idiot, shooting him once center mass and once more in the same spot.

25 Laghdaf Calls The Cops

After Owen left the hotel to hide out for a few hours, Laghdaf stepped outside and walked about a mile to one of his favorite local parks. It was another Phoenix February night, too cold for Laghdaf's taste. Even Phoenix days were not sufficiently "Africa hot," as the joke went. He found a bench and sat and took a special encrypted burner phone out of his pocket.

He dialed a friend at a private number, also encrypted. The friend worked in a little-known state law enforcement agency which followed terrorism, as well as the human and narcotics and weapons trafficking that plagued the state's Mexican border.

This was a friend Laghdaf trusted. Laghdaf did not trust Feds.

The friend answered. "Yes?"

"We need to meet," Laghdaf said.

"About what?"

"I have a client who wants to turn himself in first thing tomorrow morning. He has information about a planned terrorism-motivated murder."

"Who is your client?"

"A young man named Owen Deutscher," Laghdaf said.

"Who's supposed to be murdered?"

"A Professor Hans Cobb. At SWASU."

"Cobb. Did you say Cobb?"

"Yes."

"Your client is too late," the friend said.

"What do you mean?"

"Someone tried to kill Cobb, but Cobb shot him dead."

"I see."

"Do you? Because I don't."

Laghdaf asked, "Whom did Cobb shoot?"

"A man named Tayoub Abawi."

"I see."

"Does that name mean something to you?"

"Possibly," Laghdaf said. "Or at least it may or may not mean something to Mr. Deutscher. He may or may not have information about an organization. This Abawi character may or may not have something to do with the organization. We are interested in arranging an immunity deal."

"And where may or may not Mr. Deutscher be located right now?"

"I don't know," Laghdaf said truthfully. "But I believe he should be available tomorrow morning."

"Then bring him in at 8 AM tomorrow. You know where."

"Yes," Laghdaf said.

The phone clicked off.

26 Two To Kill

"Now there are two we need to kill," The Mujahid told Mahir.

Explaining away the failure to kill Cobb was a time to be submissive. Mahir said, "Of course, Abu Jihad. I assume you mean both Cobb and Owen."

"That is exactly who I mean," the Mujahid said. He was standing on the other side of his kitchen table. He leaned across the table and poured tea into Mahir's cup and put the teapot on a big green trivet. He sat down. Sunlight streamed through the windows. Steam rose from the cups.

Mahir waited.

Abu Jihad said, "And I am disappointed but not surprised that this Owen Deutscher of yours failed."

"Yes, Abu Jihad."

"As I predicted."

As Mahir had predicted to himself that Abu Jihad would say exactly that. But all Mahir responded was, "Yes, Abu Jihad."

"And now Tayoub is dead as well," the Mujahid added. He shook his head in apparent disgust. "A valuable man."

Mahir said, "I don't think Tayoub anticipated Cobb would be carrying a gun."

"Did anyone check ahead of time to see?" Abu Jihad asked. "This is America, after all."

"That is an excellent observation, Abu Jihad."

Abu Jihad narrowed his eyes, as if suspecting insubordination. Mahir was careful to keep his composed submissive expression on his face.

Abu Jihad asked, "So what is your next step?"

Mahir said, "Finding Owen is easy. I have a GPS tracker on his car. I know everywhere he goes. Finding Cobb will be harder. It seems he has taken refuge in the desert."

"You yourself are a man of the desert, are you not?"

"Of course."

"Then take care of it. We cannot afford to look weak and foolish, which is exactly how we look right now, not only to the public but also to our many business partners, everywhere between here and Venezuela. It can be a matter of life or death to maintain their respect."

"Yes, Abu Jihad."

27 Car Life

After meeting with the lawyers, Owen had driven towards the SWASU campus and parked for the night on a nearby street.

Owen tried lying across the back seat, but the car wasn't wide enough. No matter how he twisted, he couldn't find a comfortable place for his head. He folded and wadded his big shirt under his head as a pillow, but that didn't work either.

He moved to the front passenger seat and wiggled around for a comfortable position to sleep. He pulled on the lever to recline the front seat as far back as it would go, and that felt okay, but then he wondered what if someone saw him like that from the sidewalk? What if it attracted attention?

Owen was miserably aware of his failure. He was a failure as a jihadi, a failure as a Muslim, a failure as a human being. He'd blown his mission. He'd let Tayoub down. He'd let his cell down. He'd let Allah down. And now he was an informer.

What now? What way out?

Run away? To where?

Or leave Islam altogether? But the penalty for leaving Islam is death.

Owen grabbed his phone out of the console. The phone lit its own screen in the darkness. He confirmed the rule on the Internet site Steve had shown him once:

> "A man joined Islam and then went back to Judaism. The Prophet's companion Mu'adh bin Jabal saw the man sitting with another companion, Abu Musa. Mu'adh asked, "What is wrong with this man?" Abu

Musa answered, "This man joined Islam and then went back to Judaism." Mu'adh said, "I will not sit down unless you kill him according to the ruling of Allah and His Apostle."

Sahih al-Bukhari,9:89:271

The penalty for leaving Islam is death.

Owen had asked Steve, "Even if it's to convert to another Religion of the Book, like Christianity or the Jewish religion?"

"Yes," Steve said.

"What if someone was born a Christian or a Jew and just went back?"

"Same rule," Steve had said, and directed Owen to the passage Owen was looking at now.

The penalty for leaving Islam is death.

No exceptions?

None.

Was there any appeal within Islam? There must be. Of course. Allah was merciful.

Allah, sure, but what about Tayoub?

Maybe someone in authority could talk to Tayoub.

Mahir Darwish? Tayoub deferred to Mahir. But how could Owen convince Mahir?

Maybe there was a path. How about that rabbi, what was his name? Bostick, that was it. Rabbi Bostick. Owen had seen him once, helping lead an event to which Tayoub had brought Owen. Christians and Jews and a few Muslims gathered in an Indian restaurant. It was billed as "interfaith" but the speeches focused less on religion than on politics, especially on defeating Islamophobic candidates.

Mahir had introduced Owen to Rabbi Bostick. The rabbi seemed friendly and open minded. When Mahir bantered with the rabbi about Owen's conversion from Judaism to Islam, Rabbi Bostick took it in good humor and just smiled.

So, Rabbi Bostick was friends with Mahir. Mahir was Tayoub's superior. Maybe Rabbi Bostick would intercede with Mahir on Owen's behalf, and then Mahir would talk to Tayoub, and then Tayoub would go easy on Owen.

How to find Rabbi Bostick? He had an organization—what was it? The Foundation for Multifaith Peace and Goodwill, or something like that.

Owen looked up the foundation on his phone and called the number on its website.

After five rings, a man answered. "Foundation for Multifaith Peace and Understanding." A resonant baritone.

Owen said, "May I speak with Rabbi Bostick, please?"

"Speaking."

"This is Owen al-Amriki. We met once."

"I'm sorry, I don't recall."

"Well, I used to be Owen Deutscher. Mahir Darwish introduced us last month at the Interfaith Conference Against Islamophobia. I was born Jewish but I converted to Islam."

"Oh yes, I remember you. How are things going for you?"

"Not too well, I'm afraid." Owen said.

"I'm sorry to hear that," Bostick said. "Is there a way I can help?"

"That's the reason I'm calling. I have a favor to ask."

"Well, please go ahead and tell me your favor and I'll see if I can help."

Owen said, "I wanted to ask you to talk to Mahir Darwish about something for me."

"Me? Why? Is there some reason you can't talk to him yourself?"

"It's complicated."

"I've got a few minutes," Bostick said.

"Well, there's this man Tayoub Abawi. Do you know him?"

"Not well, but I've met him. He introduced himself at that same conference. Seemed like a friendly fellow."

Before answering, Owen paused. How to explain? Finally, "Tayoub Abawi wants me to do something and I don't want to do it."

"And that's the problem you want me to speak with Mahir about?"

"Yes."

"I see. What does he want you to do?"

"He wants me to kill someone."

A long emptiness at the other end of the call. Then, "To be honest, Owen, I find that very hard to believe."

"I know. It's hard for me to believe too."

"And why does Tayoub supposedly want you to kill this person?"

"The person is a blasphemer. It's Professor Cobb at SWASU. The one who showed cartoons of Mohammed in his class."

More pausing. Then Bostick said, "If this is true, why not contact the police?"

"I've arranged for that."

"So how do I fit in?"

"You're friends with Mahir Darwish, right? He's Tayoub's boss, I think. See, I was hoping you could talk to Mahir and he could talk to Tayoub and help straighten out the situation."

"Uh-huh."

Another long pause. Owen held his breath.

Bostick spoke. "You know, if what you say is true, and to be perfectly frank, I have a hard time believing it, this seems like either a police matter or a matter between you and Mahir. I'd be very reluctant to interfere in another faith leader's congregation anyway. As a pastor myself, I don't like to intrude into another pastor's flock."

Strange. Owen had never heard a rabbi call himself a "pastor" before.

Bostick spoke again. "Owen, I wonder if you might benefit from psychological counseling or other help. Are you sure you understood what Tayoub was asking you to do?"

"I'm very sure."

"And you're claiming Tayoub asked this of you as a religious obligation?"

"He didn't ask. He commanded. And he commanded it in the name of Islam."

"Again, hard to believe. I mean, I know there are some few who have hijacked Islam, but I don't put Tayoub Abawi in that category, and especially not my friend Mahir."

"I could quote you some Koran passages that Tayoub used to justify this," Owen began, "But"—

Bostick cut him off. "But as many have pointed out, we have some pretty bloodthirsty-sounding passages in our own Jewish scriptures. But we've moved beyond that."

"Tayoub hasn't."

"And Mahir?"

"I don't know for sure," Owen said. But in fact, as he thought about it, he did know.

"What did the police say?"

"I don't know yet. I mean, I haven't personally talked to them, but I've talked to my lawyer Mr. Lapidos, and he's going to call them. Or already has."

"Your lawyer is Sam Lapidos?"

Owen heard disdain in Bostick's voice. "Yes. Why not?"

"Well, there are concerns about Mr. Lapidos, about his questionable stances on hate speech and social justice and, to be honest, whether he's altogether trustworthy. He's taken the wrong side on several issues."

Owen said nothing.

"Beyond that," Bostick continued, "I firmly refuse to believe you or this professor are in any serious danger, and you're in touch with the police anyway, so I guess that's covered. And I do recommend some counselling for you. Can you promise me you'll call someone? I can give you some names and numbers right now."

"No need."

"Please, let me."

"I'll think about it. But I don't want any names or numbers right now."

"Then that's all we think I can do for you?" Bostick said.

"Yes," Owen sighed. "That's all."

A click. Owen's phone screen read, "Call Ended."

Owen leaned his head back against the seat rest. He stared for a few minutes through the windshield into the darkness. Then he closed his eyes.

A noisy rapping on Owen's passenger side front window jarred Owen awake. Through the window, Owen saw a knuckled fist. The knuckles disappeared and a bearded young man peered in. He wore a dark kufi. He had a dark face. His smile revealed bright teeth that seemed to glow in the darkness. He said, "Excuse me. Sir?"

Owen heard his heart knocking inside his chest. "Yes?"

"Does your automobile happen to possess a working cigarette lighter?" The smiling Muslim man waved an unlit cigarette in his fingers.

Owen glanced at the dashboard clock. 9:32. He had slept about an hour.

It seemed Islamophobic to say "no" to the smiling Muslim man. Owen said, "No lighter, but I have some matches." Owen turned on the ceiling light and fumbled open the lid of the center console and dug through the junk until he found a small pack of matches. He lifted them out, then realizing there was no other way, he pressed the button rolling down the passenger window and with trembling right hand offered the matches.

The smiling Muslim man took them in his hands tore out a match and struck it and lifted its flame to light his cigarette. He took a deep breath. His smile broadened. He offered the pack of matches to Owen but Owen had already rolled the window back down.

Owen told him through the closed window, "You keep them. I don't smoke."

"Thanks," said the still smiling Muslim man, and disappeared into the darkness.

Owen sat frozen, waiting to see if the man's departure had been some kind of trick. Ten minutes passed. Nothing happened.

Had Owen become a bigot? Was he going to jump out of his skin every time he saw a Muslim?

Only a year ago, back in Boston, Owen been an enthusiastic convert. Seeing other Muslims in a university class or on the street delighted him, and simply on the basis of shared Islam, he'd struck up friendly conversations with total strangers.

Owen leaned back in his car seat again. A stream of students came and went on the sidewalk. At one point, three giggling girls in hijabs passed by. Was he going to cringe in dread every time he saw some harmless innocent girl?

The lawyers should have called the FBI by now. Or had they said they'd do it tomorrow? Now that Owen recalled, they never said "FBI." They'd just said, "some authorities we know," or something like that.

Which authorities? And then what? Witness protection? A new name and identity for Owen? Would he have to disappear forever? Never talk to his family again?"

And what about Professor Cobb? Had Owen acted in time? Could the authorities protect Professor Cobb? Would they?

Maybe Owen should take action.

28 Hack Hard At Work

"Another Islamophobic murder, this time in Phoenix!"

ZNN talking head Lauren Goodwell glared in devout indignation from the screen behind the bar. Hack could always measure her indignation by the frown wrinkles creasing her forehead. This was a three-wrinkle indignation, surpassed only by the four-wrinkle rage she mustered every time the world's most famous white supremacist crackpot demagogue criminal committed one of his verbal atrocities against any of the thousands of ever-changing but inviolable principles she prized beyond reason.

Hack was sipping a Chumpster beer from his seat on a barstool in the Hedgehog Barrel. He'd never sat at the bar before, only in booths or at tables. But Hack had made no progress on his song in any of the booths or tables. Maybe if he gave this barstool a proper chance, he might get somewhere.

He stared at the blank yellow pad in front of him. He had finally come up with a possible title: *Stranger in the House*.

Not a bad start, because true: Hack knew from experience with his daughter Sarai that having a baby was the same as inviting a total stranger to move in for decades.

But Hack also knew from experience in song-writing that there weren't a lot of good rhymes for "house." "Mouse" and "spouse" made no sense. "Louse" for a new human being was not a word Mattie would want, although sometimes all too accurate.

How about "home"? *Stranger in the Home* was almost as good. And he could rhyme with some good words like "roam," "dome", and "loam." Some of them might even make sense if Hack could figure out how to put them in the right order.

The word "home" had definite advantages. He could rhyme "home" not only with words ending with "m", but also with words ending in "n." Words ending in 'n', like "unknown" and "stone", didn't technically rhyme with "m" words like "home," but everyone did it, even Nobel Prize winners:

How does it feel
To be on your own,
With no direction home,
Like a complete unknown,
Like a rolling stone?

In a booth, Hack could see ZNN, but he didn't have to hear it. Now all the spite Lauren spouted came through loud and clear from the wall TV hung over and behind the bar, only about six feet away from Hack's tender ears.

But why did management tune the TV to ZNN? Everyone Hack knew hated ZNN. Maybe ZNN was paying Hedgehog for the exposure, the way ZNN paid airports and hotel lobbies to torment hapless travelers. But how did ZNN even know the Hedgehog existed? It was just one obscure bar out of thousands spread out all across the Southwest.

And why would management ever agree to this? Maybe it was the Hedgehog's plan to drive out lingerers, the way McDonald's set out only plastic furniture too hard and cramped for customers to sit in for more than a few minutes. To McDonalds, faster customer turnover meant more money.

Hack looked around. Except for that one couple necking in a corner booth, the Hedgehog was empty. Maybe management hadn't thought it through. The Hedgehog Barrel didn't have the McDonalds customer base; no customers lined up outside, or even inside. What worked for McDonalds wasn't working here.

Hack wrote on his pad:

A stranger in the home
From which I'll never roam

The worst lines Hack had ever written? Not even close. It took only an instant to recall lines even worse, song lyrics so atrocious Hack allowed no one else ever to become aware of their existence.

On the TV, Lauren's fury raged more intense. She could barely sputter out her contempt: "An innocent young man came to visit a professor this evening. And merely because of the way the young man dressed, dressed as a Muslim, this college professor, a professor named Hans Cobb, shot him dead. This was in America, or at least in Arizona, which may not even be part of America anymore, or at least an America I want to recognize as my own."

Hack tore off the top yellow sheet and crumpled it and took a big swig from his Chumpster bottle. The brown liquid foamed over the top and dribbled down the sides and wetted his hand. Felt good. He glanced around to see if anyone was watching. No one was, but he decided not to lick it off his hand anyway. Civilization imposes limits.

Licking off his cheeks was another matter. That didn't count. Hack appreciated that Chumpster didn't come on tap.

The camera panned back to show that Lauren was sitting behind one of these low TV anchor desks. Lauren lifted a square green silk cloth from the desk in front of her. She folded it into a triangle and draped it over her head. She pinned it under her chin. She crossed the corners of the scarf over her neck, the left side to the right and the right side to the left. She draped the tails over her shoulders. She reached behind her to pin the tails of her scarf behind her.

A hijab. She stood and announced in triumph, "Today, in solidarity with our brother Tayoub Abawi and all other victims of Islamophobia, we all dress Muslim."

The camera panned back. A Lauren clone stood on each side of her behind the low desk, each wearing a green hijab. Lauren said, "They can't shoot us all, can they?"

There must be more to the story. With ZNN, it wasn't "trust but verify." Hack didn't trust ZNN far enough ever to reach a need to verify. ZNN had slandered Hack himself the winter before, labeling him an Islamophobe who had murdered his friend Amir Mohammed. Despite Hack's proving himself innocent, ZNN never retracted. Hack had hired Laghdaf to sue. The lawsuit was taking forever.

Lauren said, "Our guest is Mahir Darwish, chair of the Arizona chapter of the Anti Islamophobia League. Mr. Darwish, are you and other Arizona Muslims feeling despondent about this murder?"

The screen showed a fit dark-haired man in business-casual khakis and collared oxford shirt. He said, "Yes, Lauren, many are indeed despondent about the fact that this Professor Cobb has yet to be arrested and charged. And we are working to make sure that happens and that he faces justice."

"What are your next steps?"

"You and other supporters of justice can help a lot, Lauren. Speak out. Help us put pressure on the authorities to take action."

"As of now, Cobb just goes about with his life as if nothing happened? As if he didn't shoot another human being to death? What excuses are the police giving for refusing to arrest him?"

Darwish answered, "This Cobb man claims self-defense. And of course, the only surviving witness is Cobb himself. He left no one alive to contradict his story, a story quite unbelievable to those of us who knew and loved this young man Tayoub."

"Of course," Lauren said, "And we at ZNN find Cobb's account just as unbelievable. Thank you, Mr. Darwish. Now let's hear from another recognized voice of social justice, Rabbi Aaron Bostick, who is an AIL supporter living in the Phoenix area."

The screen showed a bearded man in his sixties sitting at a desk. A bookshelf full of Hebrew-looking books was visible behind him.

"Rabbi, how are members of your congregation reacting to this terrible event?"

"Well, Lauren, I'm currently between congregations, but I can tell you that my own heart is broken. I knew this young man Tayoub Abawi only a little, through my good friend Mahir Darwish, a man with whom I have often prayed for peace. Tayoub often joined us. We sup together. We seek peace together. And although I never personally heard him perform, I understand he was a rap artist who made it his mission to speak out against injustice. I ask only that my friends in the Muslim community do not become despondent. The arc of history bends towards justice. We just need to grab that arc from time with our own hands and bend it more strongly."

"Of course," Lauren said.

"If I may add, this Professor Cobb's story makes little sense," Bostick said. "And even if some of it is true, or even if he were just a small town gun nut who in his madness believed it to be true, why did he have to shoot to kill? He could have just shot Tayoub in the legs or shot the knife out of his hands."

Hack took Bostick's suggestions as his cue to hustle his ass off the barstool. Maybe that last booth in the corner. Hack hadn't tried it out yet because he didn't want to be the sole occupant of a booth built for six. But the Hedgehog was almost empty anyway, so it wouldn't hurt them any, and Hack couldn't take any more ZNN.

It was almost impossible to shoot and hit any rapidly moving creature in the legs. And when you missed—you were 99% certain to miss—there was no telling where the bullet would go or who you would maim or kill.

Every shooter took credit or blame for every round he fired. That's why law enforcement trained officers to shoot in the torso, center mass, reducing the chance of missing and hitting an innocent bystander.

And shoot the knife out of Tayoub's hand? Something out of an old cowboy movie, where Hopalong Cassidy never missed. Even if Cobb could have made this impossible shot, a knife would never stop a bullet, and then where would the bullet go? Half a mile onward, to hit some random young woman strolling across campus with her friends?

Hack finished off his Chumpster and set the bottle down on the bar. He grabbed up his pad and pen and headed toward that big empty corner booth, where he hoped salvation, or at least inspiration, lay waiting.

29 Owen In Action

Midnight, and Owen wasn't sleeping anyway. He got out of his car and closed the door as quietly as he could. He walked to the sidewalk and looked both ways up and down the well-lit street. Only a few young people here and there.

He walked the three blocks to Professor Cobb's building, trying to keep alert to any danger. No one looked suspicious.

From the parking lot behind Cobb's building, it was clear Cobb's office window was dark.

No surprise.

Also, no problem. Tayoub had given Owen Cobb's home address. Owen turned around and went back to his car.

Cobb lived only a few miles away. Owen followed his phone's GPS directions down several side roads, at first down a well-paved four-lane, then a two-lane, and finally an unlit potholed street. Occasional houses were set back deep in the roadside darkness.

Owen slowed down to ten miles per hour on the bumpy road. Slowing turned out to be a wise decision, because the street dead ended at a formidable five-foot-high barricade of phosphorescent orange pipes, each at least three inches in circumference. Ramming it would have been tough on his grill and his engine.

A four-foot-square white sign hung across the barrier. Someone had hand-painted in large black letters:

DON'T BOTHER ME

Owen pulled off onto the gravel on the left side of the narrow road. He turned off his engine and got out of his car.

He checked his phone GPS. He switched the transportation mode from driving to walking. Looked like only about a mile. The GPS projected a twenty minute walk.

Owen used his phone's flashlight app to light his way over the rough ground and through the desert vegetation. Owen buttoned his long-sleeved big shirt up to the top. He should have worn a coat, but he hadn't even brought one west to Phoenix.

The nighttime desert cold bit harder as night grew deeper. About a half hour into his trek, he almost collided with a strange cactus. It was only a few feet high. Chains of pear-shaped fruit draped from it in all directions. When Owen leaned closer to examine one of the fruit, his shirt sleeve brushed a long spine on a branch. The spine detached and almost seemed to jump onto Owen's shirt sleeve. He flicked at it with the fingers of his free hand several times until he knocked it off.

As we stepped around it something stabbed his thigh. He saw a rip in his jeans just above his knee. Another even longer spine had stuck him and scraped his thigh. He tugged on it but the pain was excruciating, as if a small fishhook had embedded itself in his flesh.

For the moment, Owen let the spine stay in his thigh and limped on. He'd look for a better lit place to remove it.

Another half hour later, Owen shuffled over a hill and saw a dark house lit from three directions by tower spotlights hung on towers.

The house surprised Owen. It looked modern and well-kept, unlike the shack Owen expected to find in this barren place.

Owen must have approached from the back, because the first portion of the house he saw was its patio. The patio was about twenty feet wide and twelve feet deep. Three rectangular pillars supported a roof, underneath which sat a couple of glass-topped tables, each with three wicker chairs pulled up beneath it. It was like something out of a glossy magazine about gracious desert living.

"Don't turn around." The voice was gravelly, the same growl that had ordered Owen not to bother him a day and a half before. Cobb.

"I won't," Owen said, "But I'm not here to hurt you."

"Oh, it's the Muslim kid," Cobb said. "I wondered if you'd show up again. But you've changed clothes. You can turn around after all."

Owen did. Cobb wore drab dark clothes and a backpack and high black boots. If he carried a gun, it was invisible to Owen. He inspected Owen up and down. "What's that on your leg?"

"A thorn, I guess," Owen said.

"Don't move," Cobb said.

Cobb stepped forward. Owen stood still as told. Cobb took a pick out of his rear pocket. It was the kind of wide toothed comb people use to comb out their Afros. With a little stiffness, Cobb knelt and used the pick to pull the thorn out in a single quick but smooth motion.

The pain stung Owen, but he steeled himself and made no sound.

"Come with me," Cobb said, and walked away into the darkness. Owen followed.

They traveled about twenty minutes over the rough ground. Cobb stopped. He turned and pointed to a waist-high boulder. "Sit."

Owen sat. The stone felt cold under him. He wrapped his shirt and arms around himself.

Cobb took off his pack and laid it on another wide flat boulder. He unzipped a pocket in the pack and reached in and pulled out a small tube. He handed the tube to Owen. "Spread that on your scratch."

Owen unscrewed the tube cap and squeezed some goo out of the tube onto his palm. He rubbed the goo through the tear in his jeans onto his wound, which had turned into a four-inch-long welt.

Owen handed the tube back to Cobb and Cobb sealed it up and put it back in his pack. He sat on the boulder next to his pack and inspected Owen.

Neither spoke for a few moments. Finally, Cobb asked, "You thirsty?"

Owen nodded. Cobb reached into his pack and took out a bottle of water and handed it to Owen. Owen accepted it and unscrewed the cap and drank.

Cobb asked, "What on earth are you doing out here?"

"I was worried about you."

"You expecting more hit men to come after me?"

"More?" Owen asked.

"More." Cobb inspected Owen's face. "You don't know what happened?"

"What happened?"

"A man came to my office this evening. He dressed the way you dressed yesterday, though I see you've changed your style. He tried to knife me."

"What did you do?"

"I shot him dead. You expecting more like him?"

Owen began to shake. Was he going to faint? He inhaled and exhaled a deep breath.

Cobb said, "You didn't know about this, did you?"

Owen shook his head. He didn't want to know, but he had to ask. "Do you know who it was?"

"I didn't at the time, but it turned out to be a man named Tayoub Abawi. You know him, right?"

Owen flashed on Tayoub's face—the two faces, really, the patient one who had tutored Owen and the adamant one who had terrified him.

Cobb repeated, "You know him, right?"

"I did." Owen drank a few more swallows of water.

"Son, I know my way around this desert, and I have friends here myself, some of them at least as dangerous as your friends."

Owen said, "They're not my friends," and with a shock realized it was true. They were not his friends. He repeated, "Not my friends."

"That's a start, I suppose. What's your name?"

"Owen Deutscher." Owen took yet another slug of water. Delicious, even in the cold.

"Well, Owen Deutscher, in this desert, nobody bothers me. I appreciate your concern, but I'm in little danger. You on the other hand I'm not so sure about. Why don't you stick around and I see if I can make sure nothing very fatal happens to you?"

"I have to get back to town," Owen said. "I promised my lawyers I'd go see the authorities with them tomorrow."

"Lawyers? Authorities? You counting on those people to protect you?"

"I hadn't thought that far ahead," Owen said, and realized this was another thing he said that was true. He hadn't. He was just improvising, and badly. Then, "One thing at a time."

The old man studied Owen some more. Then, "You seem to have good intentions."

Owen sighed. "I try."

"Have you ever been convicted of a felony?"

Owen considered becoming indignant, but it wasn't worth the trouble. "Of course not."

"Would you like me to sell you a gun?"

"A gun?"

"I'll sell you a fine new revolver. Reliable. Idiot-proof, almost. Revolvers almost never fail."

"I don't have that kind of money."

"One dollar. That's my price. Take it or leave it."

"I don't know how to shoot a gun," Owen said.

"I'll give you free lessons right now. I can teach you about gun safety and how to work the thing. Couldn't be simpler."

"I don't think so."

"Why not?" The old man's eyes seemed to glow in the dark.

"That's just not who I am."

Cobb took another water bottle out of his pack and handed it to Owen. Owen realized his first bottle was already empty and that Cobb had noticed right away. Owen looked around for a place to discard the empty. Finding none, he handed it to Cobb.

Cobb grinned and stowed the empty in his pack. Then, "You know ancient Greek stories?"

"A little."

"You know who Narcissus was, don't you?"

"The name sounds familiar."

"Narcissus was a young guy who saw his reflection in a pond. He fell so in love with his own beauty he leaned over to get a closer look. He fell in and drowned. It's a tough story with an instructive ending. Very Greek."

"Now that you tell it, I recognize the story," Owen said.

Another pause.

A more powerful shivering seized Owen. It was a deep winter chill, the kind he thought he'd left behind in the North East. It was the kind of chill to the bone it could take hours to warm up from. He crossed his arms and rubbed his upper arms. "I didn't know Arizona could be this cold. I'd better get back."

"Promise you'll hide out someplace safe?"

"Sure," Owen said. "I'm not stupid." He stood up from the boulder and he looked around. Little needles stung the backs of his thighs.

Cobb stood. "Do you know the way back to your car?"

"I'm not sure," Owen said.

"Follow me," Cobb said. Like a magician, from behind his own boulder he produced a rifle. The rifle had a pistol grip and bristled with attachments. The thing looked one of those assault rifles Rabbi Holtzmann had warned against.

Cobb set out into the darkness and Owen followed.

Twenty minutes later, the two stood on the desert side of the orange barricade. "There's your car," Cobb said. "Whatever you do, don't come back here. Find yourself someplace safe to hide."

"That's my plan," Owen said. He sprinted to the car and stopped and fumbled in his pocket for his keys.

As Owen unlocked the driver door, Cobb called out something. Owen turned and yelled back, "What was that?"

Cobb cupped his hands in front of his mouth and shouted, "Don't fall in!"

30 Dudley and Mattie And Friends

"Where's my song?" Mattie asked.

Hack glanced up from his seat in the booth. His wife was trying to peek over his shoulder at his yellow pad. Luckily, her small baby bump distanced her enough to frustrate her evil design.

Hack ripped the top sheet off the yellow pad. He considered stuffing it in his mouth but settled for standing up and cramming it into his jeans pocket. He sat again and said, "The song is in progress."

"No way. I saw. You've only two lines."

"That's not true. Anyway, if I did, they'd be really good lines. Poignant and piquant. Practically poetic."

"Like what?" She asked.

"What do you mean?

"What are they?

"What are what?'

"The lines," she said with exaggerated patience, like she thought she was talking to a six-year-old, which she probably did think, and occasionally told him out loud. "The really good lines. The poignant and piquant lyrics you just packed down your pants."

"Please don't press. Poetry pokes along."

"Like pregnancy. You don't see me dawdling."

"That's not fair," he pointed out. "You've got an inexorable biological process pushing you. All I've got is my will power, which is weakened by love."

She settled herself into the seat opposite him in the booth. She made a point of sitting sideways with her legs poking out into the aisle, as if her pregnancy kept her from getting her body behind the table, which in fact it didn't yet do.

She darted her left hand across and snatched the blank yellow pad and examined it. She said, "You know, I could detect what you've written from the impressions underneath on this pad. I saw how they do it on TV. All I need is a pencil."

"You'd do that, too, wouldn't you?"

"Tell me what you've got so far and maybe I won't."

"All I've got is a possible title."

She propped her elbow on the table and cupped her chin in her right hand. He'd seen his wife do this thousands of times. The weight of her chin in her hand raised the muscles in her trim right arm like small ridges on a three-dimensional map. She looked as strong as a teenage boy. Her long brown hair framed her lightly freckled face. Her strong nose endowed her face with more character than any conventional Hollywood prettiness. But it suited her. Her dark brown eyes probed him with their permanent provocation, the irresistible challenge which kept him knocking himself out to please her.

She said, "Fine. For now, I'll settle for the title."

"That much I can say. *Stranger in the House*."

"Actually, that's not terrible," she said. "Although I don't know how you'll rhyme anything with the word 'house'. But it sort of makes sense. Babies are strangers."

"It's what I've got so far," he said. "And that's all you're going to get out of me for now." But even as he said it, he was wondering if *Babies Are Strangers* might be a better title. But why give her the satisfaction?

She said, "You know, there already is a country song called *Stranger In The House*, by Elvis Costello."

"Really? Is it about a baby?"

"No," she said. "It's about a guy in a romance gone bad and he thinks it's his fault."

"Sounds like a standard country song."

"No, it's an original idea. The stranger is himself. It's got good words to it." She smiled and his love for her again flamed incandescent, as if some vagrant breeze had blown over the natural gas pilot light. She reached her left hand across the able and squeezed his forearm and said, "Let's see what you can do, Soldier."

He laid his hand across hers on top of his arm and squeezed back.

An electric guitar twanged from the stage. He glanced over. Dudley was bent over his amp. Without straightening up, he grinned and waved at Hack.

Of course. Mattie had ridden here with Dudley.

The clang of wheels on a hardwood floor. It was Marty, rolling his drum kit to the stage on his metal cart. The bass player Bob followed right behind, carrying his electric bass in one hand and rolling his bass amp alongside him.

"It's 8:30. Time for me to set up too," Hack said.

"Yes, you should," she said. "I'll just sit here and keep waiting for our little stranger. It's what I do best right now."

Hack had brought his gear into the club when he first arrived to write. He stood up and got out of the booth and walked to the edge of the stage. He hoisted himself onto it. He went over to his keyboard stand and unfolded it and stood it up.

Marty said, "Hey, brother, how are you doing on that song?"

Hack bluffed. "What song?"

"Don't talk that static," Bob said. "We're hip to your jive."

"And we know just what cooks," Marty said.

"Can you dig it?" Bob asked.

Marty and Bob were identical twins. Hack glanced back and forth between the two men and saw four identical pale blue eyes peering at him from two nearly identical faces wearing two identical bland expressions. Their hobby was ragging on him. He said, "I take it Mattie's been talking with you two."

"Mattie's been spreading the word," Bob said.

Marty said, "She's tripping, man. She wants her song and she wants it now."

"We'd offer to help," Bob began,

"But we both know that when it comes to songwriting, you're the man," Marty finished.

"We know it's a bummer, and we don't want to get in your face," Bob said.

Marty added, "Just chill, baby, it'll come to you."

"Keep on trucking and go with the flow," Bob said.

Hack was trying to recall his seventies slang, but the seventies were before his time, and before Marty and Bob's time, by the way. Maybe this was their flakey way of giving him moral support.

With these two, who knew?

"Hack the man!" Marty told Hack again, and the two brothers low-fived each other.

Hack tried to think of a snappy comeback, but all he came up with was, *"Et tu, Marty and Bob?"*

Hack spent the entire gig that night trying to think up something better, but he never did.

31 Owen

Unable to think of anywhere else to spend the night, Owen drove from Cobb's back to SWASU. He'd sleep in his car again. He should be tough to find parked on a dark street in his nondescript Toyota Tercel. Morning was only a few hours away. Then he'd call the lawyers and they'd take him to the authorities and then maybe all this would be over.

It took the Tercel's engine a few minutes to warm the heater and passenger compartment. Owen drove with his left hand on the steering wheel and waved the stiff bare fingers of his right in front of the center heating vent. After some sensation came back to his right hand he steered with his right and held his left in front of the left side vent.

He drove around the dark streets near campus, scanning for a parking spot. On the right was a single space big enough for two cars. He drove straight in and stopped.

He got out the car and walked around and got into the passenger seat and pulled the lever beside the seat. He leaned back and closed his eyes.

With the engine off, the car turned too cold to sleep. He should have asked Cobb for a spare coat or blanket. That old man probably had all kinds of gear. But Owen hadn't thought of it at the time.

Should Owen keep the engine running for heat? Was that safe? What about carbon monoxide poisoning? And just how safe was this old car's exhaust system?

Owen checked his phone for the temperature. Forty degrees—above freezing anyway.

Two silent men walked by in the darkness. Owen couldn't see their faces. They disappeared.

He shifted around in his seat. He began to shake from the cold. He couldn't stay like this for an entire night. Maybe he should get out and move around. Maybe sneak into a building for warmth and find a cozy spot where he could sleep.

He got out of the car and started jogging towards campus. It took only a few minutes to arrive at the parking lot for Cobb's building. The jogging warmed him. The lot was empty except for a few cars. He ran towards the building. He was only a few yards from the back door when a familiar voice boomed out of the darkness.

"Hey, Owen, there you are!"

Owen looked towards the sound. Steve O'Toole stepped into the light cast by the lights over the door.

The shock froze Owen in place. "Steve. What are you doing here?"

"Looking for you, Dude." Steve was grinning. In his bulky winter coat he looked huge.

Owen was about to say, "I thought you were dead," but held off. Might make things more awkward than they already were.

But Steve wasn't dead, was he? Obviously not. What was going on? Owen said only, "Good to see you're okay."

Steve said, "We've been worried about you, Dude. Where you been keeping yourself?"

"Here and there," Owen said. Owen was shivering again. He saw vapor rising from Steve's breathing and his own as well.

"Your teeth are rattling out of your head, Dude. We should find you someplace warm."

"I'm okay," Owen said.

"No, you're not," Steve said.

"Have you talked with Mahir?"

"Yes, I have."

Owen asked, "Is he angry?"

"At what?"

"At me."

"Not really," Steve said. "Sad. Disappointed, maybe. But we all know you're new to the struggle. What happened, anyway?"

What to say? Owen gave his least incriminating version a shot. "I went to campus the day before yesterday. I was planning to do it, but Cobb wasn't there. At least, I couldn't find him. So I thought I'd leave for a while and then go back and do it later."

Steve nodded. "I see. So then Tayoub went to do it himself, right?"

"Right."

"And that was part of the plan? If you couldn't find Cobb, then Tayoub would do it? You were going to take turns trying?"

Steve's idea seemed plausible. "Right."

Steve nodded again, accepting the explanation. "So far as we know, Cobb is still alive, right?"

Owen shrugged. "I guess. Far as I know, anyway."

"Far as you know."

"Right."

"You were taking a chance on finding him here in his office tonight?"

What lie to tell next? Owen couldn't tell Steve he himself was hiding. He said, "Something like that. You never know."

"You never know," Steve said. He grinned a big grin. "We've got to get you out of this cold, Dude. Then you can explain all this to Mahir. Naturally, he's upset Tayoub is dead. You know about that, right?"

"Sure," Owen said. Should he know that?

Steve let it slide. "You want to come with me? I'm parked only a block away."

"I can take my own car. It's nearby too."

"Good idea," Steve said. "Separate cars will be okay."

Steve waited. Owen waited too, then he realized Steve expected Owen to start off for his car. Owen did, and Steve began walking along beside him.

Owen glanced at Steve. He didn't seem angry or anything. He caught Owen's glance and grinned back. He put his hand on Owen's shoulder. "No problems, Dude. We'll straighten out all the confusion."

As they walked on, Owen wondered if he should have taken Cobb up on his offer to sell him a gun. But then what? Shoot his friend? Steve hadn't done or said anything that gave Owen any reason for unease.

In fact, Owen was kind of glad he'd run into Steve. Steve would take him to Mahir, and they'd all talk it over and everything would all be straightened out. Steve had no way of knowing every little thing Owen had been up to. Owen might not even have to follow through with the lawyers tomorrow.

Owen spotted his car up ahead in the darkness. He quickened his pace. Steve lagged behind.

A powerful blow struck Owen in the back. Like someone had punched him super hard. A thunderous explosion of sound deafened him. Owen turned around. Steve was holding a Colt revolver like in the old cowboy movies.

What was it with Arizona and all these guns? He never should have left Connecticut.

Steve fired again. Owen's knees buckled under him and he fell face forward onto the concrete of the sidewalk. He rolled over and lay on his back. The ground was so cold. Steve was standing over him. Steve sighted down his huge gun barrel at Owen and said something, but Owen couldn't hear through the ringing in his ears. Steve shook his head once and was gone.

Was there something Allah wanted Owen to say before dying? Owen didn't know much about it. He'd never given a single thought to dying.

But what came to mind wasn't something from Islam. Strangely, it was something he'd learned from an elderly Jew.

Why remember old Henry just now? Henry had been in his nineties, already frail when Owen met him, a kindly presence at the Temple and a Survivor. In Owen's childhood world, survivor always meant Holocaust Survivor and nothing else.

Henry gave a talk once to the entire congregation. In 1939, Henry's parents had smuggled young Heinrich out of Germany to America. Henry told a hair-raising tale of escaping from Dachau with false documents and wearing an SS officer's overcoat, relying on the lucky fact that the young blond Heinrich had looked more Aryan than most Nazis. Some way Owen couldn't remember, Henrich made it across the Atlantic to America, where, not yet even a U.S. citizen, he joined the U.S. Army.

Henry finally took the oath of U.S. citizenship in Italy as part of mass ceremony the Army held for immigrant soldiers like himself. On D-Day Henry helped storm Omaha beach. Henry fought his way across France with the other Americans, using his native German to interrogate German POWs, a task he relished, and not only because he was good at it. For Henry, the war had begun not in 1941, but in 1933, when Hitler took power. The Germans were an enemy he knew.

On March 22, 1945, a big yellow moon lighting the nighttime sky, soldiers of the U.S. XII Corps' 5th Infantry Division began the 3rd Army's Rhine crossing into Germany. American citizen Henry crossed as one of them.

The war against Germany ended less than two months later. Although Henry spent months using all his free time to search, Henry never found his parents or the little sister he had left behind.

Henry had seen a lot of death, and he knew what a Jew ought to say when he was about to die. Henry had heard Jews say it in Dachau and in hospitals and on the battlefield. He taught the American children:

Shma Yisroel, Adoshem Elokeinu, Adoshem Ekhad.

Hear O Israel, the Lord is our God, the Lord is One.

Owen mumbled the phrase now, over and over:

Shma Yisroel, Adoshem Elokeinu, Adoshem Ekhad.

Owen kept repeating until he couldn't anymore, until he saw no light in this world and the gentle cloud of darkness obscured all, which was nothing.

PART

TWO

32 Hack Hacks

If Mr. Lapidos seemed odd to Aviva, his ex-son-in-law Hack Wilder seemed downright peculiar.

Hack was a chunky shorter man with a neat black beard. He radiated an attitude. Not a hostile attitude—he just talked and acted as if he knew what he wanted to do and exactly how to do it.

In that single way and in no other, he reminded her of Mr. Lapidos.

Hack had called her earlier in the evening to set up what he called "the evening's skullduggery." Following their plan, at 2 AM, he picked her up in her apartment building's lot. He drove an ancient red jalopy which he bragged was a genuine original equipment 1973 Audi Fox. As they chugged from her apartment building over to the SWASU campus, Aviva grabbed the handle above the passenger door like her life depended on it, which maybe it did.

He tootled along the Freeway at a sedate fifty miles per hour. None of the car's chorus of rattles and squeaks seemed to bother Hack, so Aviva figured the car would most likely stay intact. She didn't see any obvious rust holes in the floor, the kind she'd seen often in Mexico and even occasionally in Arizona.

She worried more about being rear-ended. He paid no attention to the angry drivers who honked entire horn concertos from the left as they whizzed by at seventy or eighty miles per hour.

"Was this car a recent purchase?" Aviva asked.

"No."

"Did you buy it in Arizona?"

"No, my wife and I drove it from Minnesota."

"How long did that take?"

"About a week. We were in no hurry."

"So did you come here to get away for the winter?" Aviva had only a vague idea where Minnesota was, but it was somewhere near the north pole, and too cold for any sensible person to live there.

"No" he said. "I like winter. I can ski. We're in a country music band called Dudley and Mattie and Friends. Mattie is my wife. She sings, and she's great. Dudley is based here, and he keeps promising he can get us a tour of the Southwest.

"What do you play?"

"Piano and keyboards."

Interesting that he separated the two skills—piano and keyboards. Aviva knew the reason. Her son had studied only classical piano and turned up his nose at electric keyboards.

Someone roared out of the darkness behind them and blared a cascade of honks and swooped past them on the left.

For the next ten minutes, Hack kept on and on about his wife Mattie and what a great singer she was and how she deserved to be famous. Aviva liked it when men admired their wives, which he obviously did.

Aviva didn't know much about American country music, but she loved Mexican music and Moroccan music and her own family's Ladino songs too, for that matter. One more style would just add to the mix.

She asked, "have you worked for Mr. Lapidos for long?"

He said, "We do each other favors, if that's what you mean."

"Nevertheless, I want to thank you for coming out at this hour. I mean, he does pay you, doesn't he?"

"Oh, he pays me. I make sure of that."

"Because if he doesn't, I will," she said.

He glanced at her and smiled. The smile changed his entire face, as if opening a window into a generous soul. She was liking this man a lot.

He said, "He told me about your case. No matter how much you may think you hate these people, believe me when I tell you I hate them more. And I've never even met them."

"Oh, I don't want to hate them. Hate is destructive. It would harm my soul."

"Tell you what," he said. "I'll put my soul on the line and hate them for both of us. We'll keep your soul out of harm's way. Deal?"

She smiled back. "Deal."

Hack exited the freeway and drove a few miles to a street near SWASU. They found an open spot on the street and he parked there. They exited the car and walked in darkness to the campus. She led him directly to the back door of the Latinx Studies building.

As they approached, she said, "You know, they took my keys."

"Sam mentioned it."

"Never hurts to check," he said, and tugged on the handle. Nothing happened. He said, "Are you ready for the skullduggery?"

She said, "Skullduggery is why I am here."

The fixtures over the doorway shone only dim light. Hack took a tiny flashlight out of his pocket and flicked it on and handed it to her. He said, "Shine the light on the lock, please."

She did. He took a thin leather pouch from his coat pocket. It looked about eight inches long. He opened it out like a book and took one of a half dozen metal probes from inside. He inserted the probe into the lock and wiggled it around. After about thirty seconds of jiggling and muttering he pulled the door open. He pulled the probe out of the lock and stuck it in his pouch and put the pouch back in his pocket. He held the door open for her and followed her into her former work place.

"This way," she said, and led him down the back stairs to her office. At the office door, he pulled out the same probe and did the same trick and this time opened the door in only five seconds.

"Cheap lock," he said. He held the door open. She walked in and he followed her.

"I thought you could do what you need to do from a distance," she said. "Over the Internet."

"I tried, but it's not so easy if the computer's turned off and unplugged," he said. He pointed, and her computer indeed sat on her old desk, its plug laying across the keyboard.

He took out his phone and snapped a flash photo of the layout. She wondered why.

"You're doing a great job with the flashlight," he said. He put his phone away. "Keep it up." He reached behind the computer box and found the end of the cord and plugged it into the socket behind the desktop. He turned on the computer.

Aviva held the flashlight, trying to anticipate and follow his movements to give him light where he needed.

Skullduggery was fun. Aviva felt like one of those Israeli spies infiltrating Tehran to track down the nuclear weapons program. She wondered if she would have been a good spy. She was an okay liar. Not many people knew that, which in a way proved that she was pretty good at it. Also, she could keep her mouth shut. She learned that in Morocco. Tight lips count. She spoke several languages. That would help.

Aviva Bond. She suppressed a giggle.

Hack had sat down at the desk chair. He glanced up at her. His dark beard didn't hide his lips. Maybe he'd heard the giggle. A smile played on them. He said, "Flashlight, please?"

"Sorry." She redirected the flashlight to the keyboard.

Did James Bond ever stand by like an underling and hold a flashlight for a more accomplished spy? She didn't recall seeing that in any of the movies.

Hack said, "Someone went to a little trouble here. They changed your password and tried to delete a whole bunch of files the best they could. I don't know why they didn't just throw out the whole machine or at least hammer the hard drive to pieces. It would have been safer for them."

"Why didn't they, do you think?"

"They encrypted the entire hard drive," he said. "Maybe that made them overconfident. And they didn't know about me. Anyway, I can deal with their cute little precautions when I get home."

He took a flash drive out of his pocket and inserted it into a computer port. He keyed a few commands. "This will take a few minutes."

He leaned back in the swivel chair and waited. He began humming something.

"What's that tune?" she asked. "It's pretty."

"Something I'm working on," he said.

"A composition??"

"A song. Mattie's pregnant and she wants a song about it. She says if I don't deliver the song she won't deliver the baby."

"I have given birth. That does not sound like a threat she can keep."

"You haven't met Mattie," he said. "You should see how long she can hold her breath."

"Can you do what she wants? Write a song on demand?"

"That's a question to which we do not yet know the answer." He keyed a few keystrokes into the computer and pulled the flash drive out of its slot and stuck it in his pocket. He turned off the computer and unplugged it and used his photo as a guide to arrange everything back the way they had found it.

He locked the doors behind them and they walked back to his car. He drove her home and parked in a guest space in her apartment building lot. He walked her indoors and up the stairs to her door. Just before she went in, she asked, "Where can I hear you and your wife's music?"

"We play Wednesday through Saturday nights at the Hedgehog Barrel Tavern, near downtown. We played tonight. We play again tomorrow night."

"I'll be there," she said.

33 Hack Gets Extorted

Hack and Mattie shared a bedroom in the back of Dudley's house. When Hack made it home from his skullduggery with Aviva Soriano, Mattie was lying in bed awake. The portable TV on the bench at the end of the bed was blaring.

It was ZNN. The remote control lay on top of the blankets she had pulled up to her neck. At sight of him, she grabbed it with her right hand.

Hack asked, "Why is this on?"

She smirked. "Where's my song?"

"You know I can't stand ZNN."

"Until you come up with that song you promised, it's going to be all ZNN, twenty-four-seven, all day and all night long."

"This is the cruelest and most abusive thing you've ever done. I should report you."

"Report me to who?"

"To the federal agency you report things like this to," he said. "There must be one."

"Didn't Sam order you never to talk to the Feds, no matter what?"

"Even Sam can't foresee every emergency."

"Get in bed."

Hack pulled down his jeans and threw them on a chair. He climbed in under the blankets and sheets and pulled them over himself. He shuffled his body sideway until they were lying side by side up against each other. She slept naked and her warmth was welcome after the cold of the night, especially since the back bedroom in Dudley's old Arizona house was barely insulated.

From the TV, ZNN Legal Analyst Peter Totte was opinionating. "Authorities are looking into spectacular new accusations against controversial lawyer Sam Lapidos. Lapidos is the rogue attorney who just this past week pulled one of his notorious courtroom tricks, derailing the prosecution of killer cop Stanley Latham."

"Please turn this off," Hack said.

Totte was a fat man whose head barely cleared the desk he sat behind. His egg-shaped bald dome shone in the studio lights. In his near-falsetto voice, he said, "A credible witness has come forward to credibly accuse Lapidos of open Islamophobia, homophobia, transphobia and racism against Palestinians."

Hack begged, "At least mute it."

"Where's my song?"

Totte said, "A Muslim man named Mahir Darwish has filed a Complaint with the Arizona State Bar, describing in horrifying detail the conversation he had with Lapidos when he asked Lapidos to represent his local chapter of the Anti Islamophobia League, or AIL, as it is widely known."

Hack rolled over and reached his left hand across her body for the remote. He managed to put a few fingers on it, but she was too quick and too strong and pulled it away. He would have to wrestle her for it, which normally would have been a fine idea, but she was pregnant.

"What would Dudley and the twins think if they saw you trying to overpower me, a helpless pregnant woman?"

"They'd know it was hopeless," he said. "And have you thought about the harm you're doing our baby? ZNN could warp our baby's mind forever."

"Our baby needs to learn to follow the news. That's part of growing up to become a good citizen."

"True news, sure. But believe me, Sam never said the stuff this Mahir Darwish guy claims he said."

"You trust Sam?"

"With my life. Anyway, even from the little I've heard, I already know Darwish is lying. He claims Sam said racist things about Palestinians. Sam never even uses the word 'Palestinian'. Sam thinks Palestinian is an invented nationality. Sam only uses the word 'Arab'. In his mind Syrian Arabs, Jordanian Arabs, and Israeli Arabs are all just Arabs who live under different governments."

"Really?"

"Really. And I looked it up. Until the state of Israel, the word "Palestinian" only meant Jews. The Arabs picked up the word twenty years later, after the Jews started using the word 'Israeli' and dropped the word 'Palestinian' for themselves."

Peter Totte was working himself into high indignation. "I'm exasperated," he squeaked. "I'm in a condition of outrage. I've reached the boiling point with this terrible man Lapidos. When I read Mr. Darwish's complaint, I cried. I'm in a fury."

"He's an unhappy little man, isn't he?" Mattie observed.

"He's definitely miffed," Hack said. "Or in a high dudgeon. Or maybe just a huff."

Undeterred, probably because he couldn't hear them, Totte didn't let up. "This is the time for rage," he squeaked in a homuncular simulacrum of ire.

Mattie said, "Did you know you're thinking out loud?"

"I thought I was just muttering."

"I'm right here. I hear you. And you're using weird words again. Like homuncular."

"I could explain."

"No, I get the idea. And I think it's sexy when you talk like that." She turned and laid her arm across his chest and snuggled closer, belly pressed against his side. Her warm naked skin warmed his own. Her belly warmed him everywhere. A few fine strands of her long brown hair lay across his bare arm. She smelled like vanilla. She touched his cheek with her fingertips.

Hack said, "You won't at least mute the TV?"

"No song, no mute."

He said, "You expect me to make love with that runt ranting?

"Yes," she said, with her serene smile, born of a confidence justified by history. "That's your only option, Soldier. Yes or no?"

Hack plunged his head under their covers and found a warm home beneath, inviting and perfect.

34 Laghdaf Calls The Cops Again

After a light breakfast, Laghdaf walked from the Vauxhall Arms. He stopped in the same park as the night before. At 8 AM, it was only about 40 degrees. He was dressed only in his lawyer's business suit, with no extra overcoat, and the breeze cut through his thin clothing. He felt colder in Arizona than he had ever felt in Minnesota, even in January.

Had the authorities learned more about Tayoub's death? He sat on his favorite bench again. He took his special encrypted burner phone out of his pocket and dialed his trusted law enforcement friend.

The friend answered. "So you already know?"

"Know what?"

"About your client Owen Deutscher."

Laghdaf hadn't known, but now he guessed. "What about him?"

"Ah, then you don't know."

"From what you're saying, I do. What are the details?"

"Someone shot him to death early this morning on a sidewalk near the SWASU campus."

Laghdaf asked, "Do you have any idea who shot him?"

"From what you've said, I can guess. Can't you?"

"Can you prove it?"

"That remains to be seen," the voice said. "How about you? Can you help us?"

"I'll get back to you."

35 Owen's Car

Hack's phone jangled him awake. He grabbed it off the table next to their bed and stabbed the answer button to stop the ringing. Next to him, Mattie groaned and rolled away and pulled a pillow over her head.

It was Sam. Hack said, "Hang on." He got out of bed and went into the hallway and closed the bedroom door behind him. He leaned back against the wall. He said, "You woke me up."

"It's 9 AM," Sam pointed out.

"I work nights, remember?"

"This can't wait."

"What can't wait?" Hack asked.

Sam told Hack about his new client Owen Deutscher being murdered. "I don't see this as a coincidence. Owen comes to Laghdaf and me wanting to inform on a terrorist plot and within a few hours someone kills him."

"Makes sense. But what do you want from me?"

"How did someone know where Owen was? We didn't know ourselves. We made a point of not knowing."

Hack said, "There are a million ways."

"For instance?"

"Did he drive?

"I suppose so. He got to the hotel to meet with us somehow."

Hack said, "So that's simple. There could be a GPS tracker on his car."

"GPS tracker?"

"Just what it sounds like. Someone plants a small device on his car that continually transmits the car's GPS coordinates."

Sam asked, "How do we find out?"

"I look at his car. Where is it?"

"No idea."

Hack asked, "Did you ever see his car?"

"No," Sam said. "I told you. He just showed up at our hotel and spilled his story."

Sam added, "But let's assume as a working hypothesis that the killers did track him via his car. Isn't it likely his car would be near where his body was found?"

"Sure," Hack said. "But if so, wouldn't the cops have found the car?"

"Not necessarily. There could be a lot of cars around where he was found."

"He'd have his keys on him, right?"

"I see what you mean," Sam said. "They could press the door-opening button and see what happens."

"Or identify the car model from the keys and search the area."

"Right," Sam said. "But suppose for whatever reason they didn't find the car."

"Why should we suppose that?"

"Because that gives us something useful to do."

"Gives me something useful to do, you mean." Hack said.

"Perceptive," Sam said.

"Okay," Hack said. "I can just check the auto registrations in Arizona for Owen Deutscher. Stay on the line."

"I'll wait," Sam said.

Hack snuck back into the bedroom. He grabbed up his laptop and snuck out again. He went to Dudley's living room and sat on a sofa with the computer on his lap and booted it up. He logged in and checked the state automobile registration records.

He picked up his phone. "No Owen Deutscher in Arizona," he said.

"He moved here from Boston," Sam said. "Suppose he never registered his car in Arizona?"

"Why not?"

"Maybe his cell leader didn't want him to," Sam said.

Hack checked the Massachusetts state records. He said, "Same result. No Owen Deutscher."

"He grew up in Connecticut."

Hack checked the Connecticut records. "Got it," he said. Year, model, color and license plate."

"You know what to do," Sam said, and hung up.

Hack did know what to do. On the Internet, he found a news article on the murder. The article described the murder scene, including its location.

Hack went back into the bedroom and grabbed up his pants, socks and shoes. He bent over the bed and kissed Mattie on her cheek and said, "Off to SWASU." She moaned and pulled the pillow tighter down.

 He stepped out of the bedroom and was careful again to make no noise shutting the door. He sat on the floor and pulled up his pants. He put on his socks and shoes. He got up and took his jacket out of the front closet. He went out the front door to his Audi, which he'd parked on the street in front.

Hack used his phone to navigate towards the spot identified in the news coverage of the murder.

A few blocks short, he pulled over and parked on the street. He walked towards the murder scene. He kept his eyes peeled for a dark older Toyota Tercel with Connecticut plates, but spotted none.

From about fifty yards away, he saw the yellow police tapes surrounding an empty space on the sidewalk.

From here, what was the most efficient search for Owen's car? It would have to be a sequential search. Hack started walking. He walked one block north, then one block south on the other side of the street, back to his starting place at the murder scene. He saw no Connecticut car. He used the same pattern walking east, then west, then south. No car.

Hack continued walking the area for the next hour. In each phase of his search, he expanded his search area by one block. Then, four blocks out and to the west, there was the dark Toyota Tercel with Connecticut plates. Hack checked the plate number to make sure. This was it.

It was 11 AM on a Thursday. It was a residential area. Close packed houses lined the street. People were out and about.

Hack figured he could count on the general indifference of most people. How would the car's owner act? Hack stood glaring at the car and stroked his chin and shook his head in disgust, as if puzzled by some mechanical problem.

He knelt on the ground behind the rear end. He put on the gloves he carried in his jacket pocket. He felt under the trunk. Nothing. He felt behind the bumper. He pulled out a rectangular gray metal object about half as long as his hand. It included the tracker and the magnet.

A thirty-second search. Nothing subtle going on here.

Hack put the tracker back where he'd found it. He pulled off his gloves and pulled his phone out of his pocket and called Sam. Let Sam figure a way to tell the cops where Owen's car was. Just like Hack, the cops would find the tracker in their first two minutes of working it.

36 Aviva's Story

"I'm sorry I couldn't meet with you yesterday the way we planned," Sam told Aviva Soriano. "Something urgent came up."

The two were sitting in the same Vauxhall Arms conference room Sam and Laghdaf had used the previous day for Owen Deutscher.

Laghdaf had kept Sam up to date on his contacts with the special Arizona law enforcement agency. This morning, he was off pestering the cops about Owen's murder.

Aviva asked Sam, "Was this something urgent connected to SWASU?"

"Yes," Sam said. "Do you know Professor Hans Cobb?"

"Not personally, but he's famous on campus. I have seen him walking around as if he owns the place."

"Does the name Tayoub Abawi mean anything to you?"

"Sure," she said. "He's the rapper I had to make out the check for, the one SWASU paid ten thousand dollars for hating Jews. I told you about him."

"He's dead," Sam said. "Cobb shot him."

"Really?" She face revealed no emotion. She remained composed, as if Sam had told her the day would be cloudy with a chance of rain.

He said, "You didn't see it on the news?"

"I try to stay away from the news. What happened?"

"It seems our friend Tayoub went to Cobb's SWASU office armed with a knife and a nasty plan. Cobb is an old-fashioned desert rat who carries a gun. Things went his way."

Sam kept his eyes on her. She was a slightly rounded woman with round brown eyes. She allowed an elegant streak of white to emphasize the darkness of the obsidian hair which hung down to her back and shoulders.

Sam looked away, down at his hands, and found them intertwined beneath the conference table. He disentangled his fingers and placed his hands palm down on the glass tabletop.

She said, "It's a relief. One less person like that in our world. Has Professor Cobb been arrested?"

Sam shook his head. "Not yet, at least. He claims self-defense."

"Will that work for him?"

"Not my problem." Sam asked, "Does the name Mahir Darwish mean anything to you?"

She narrowed her eyes. "He ran that so-called Israel and Indigenous Peoples Conference. He gave a speech. It was worse than the nasty rap. But I never met him. Why?"

"He dropped into my office yesterday and offered me ten thousand dollars a month to represent him and his anti-Islamophobia bunch. Even if I never did any actual work for them."

Her big black purse sat on the glass tabletop in front of her. She folded her fingers of both hands over the straps. "Should I be worried?"

"About what?"

"That's a lot of money."

"Yes, it is."

She inspected his face. He met her gaze with a bland noncommittal expression.

She said, "You told him no, didn't you?"

He nodded. "To do so without your permission would be a conflict of interest."

"Which you don't have, of course. That reminds me." She opened her purse and reached in and rummaged around. She pulled out a parking stub. She smiled. "You said you validate."

"We do," he said and reached out his right hand. She gave him the stub. He took the stub from her slender brown fingers and grabbed a pen and signed it and handed it back.

"Thank you," she said. She put the stub back in her purse.

Two down, one to go. "Does the name Owen Deutscher mean anything to you?"

"No. Should it?"

"He was my client. He was murdered last night."

This time her face expressed an open sadness. "That's terrible. Do you know why? Or who did it?"

"I'm not yet one hundred percent sure."

"I'm very sorry," she said.

"So am I," he said.

Time to get to the point of their meeting. The original reason for representing her. He asked, "How did they deliver the news of your suspension?"

Aviva told Sam about her grilling by her two bosses and how upset Oliva Escobar was to learn Aviva was Jewish and had a sister living in Israel.

She continued, "They sent me back to sit at my desk while they discussed my 'circumstances', which is what they called it. I went and sat in my cubicle like a little girl waiting to see what the principal was going to do to me and Elia Gomez came and told me she was very sorry, but I had to be suspended."

"Did you ask why?"

"Of course. She refused to say anything specific. She said I would get a letter and there will be a hearing on Friday, which is tomorrow. I asked her why the hurry, but she would not say. She asked for my office keys and I gave them to her and boxed up my stuff and left. I thought about making trouble and refusing to give her the keys, but then I decided that's why I have you." Aviva smiled again. "To make trouble."

Sam nodded. To make trouble. That was as good a description of his job as any he'd heard.

She asked, "Can I sue them?"

"Let's see what happens at the hearing tomorrow," Sam said. "You want me to come with you?"

"I asked Elia if I should bring a lawyer. I didn't mention your name. She said I couldn't bring a lawyer and I wouldn't need one anyway. It would be informal."

Sam had heard this kind of thing before. "She called it a 'hearing' but said it would be informal?"

"Yes."

"Do you believe that?"

"Of course not," Ms. Soriano said. "Should I go?"

"Yes. Do you have a recording app on your phone?"

Ms. Soriano said. "I don't know."

"Don't worry about it. Hack can set it up for you. All you'll have to do is press a button. Go to the hearing, say as little as possible, and record everything."

"Which somehow reminds me," Sam went on. "You left your sunglasses in my office yesterday." He took the sunglasses out of his inside coat pocket and handed them to her. As she took them from him, he noticed once again her slender brown fingers.

Sam looked away again from her hands, down at the table.

She said, "Thanks so much. I was worried. I didn't know where I'd lost them." She put the sunglasses into her purse.

Had he lost his place in the conversation? He asked, "You'll record everything, right?"

"I will do as you say. You're good at these things, aren't you?"

"It's my job. I could probably write out ahead of time most of what will happen at this phony hearing. I've learned to know ahead of time what questions to ask and what the answers will be."

She tilted her head. "What do you do when you have a question and you don't know the answer?"

"I try to avoid that."

"Can you do that every time? Always? Ask questions only when you already know the answer?"

For some reason, her curiosity irritated Sam. He ducked it. "For now, maybe you can give me a little more information about your case."

"How do I know what's important?"

He said, "Tell me everything and I'll pick out the important parts as they go by."

"Okay. I'll start with Saloniki, where I was born. That's in Greece."

Sam hadn't meant for her to start that early. But let the client talk. "I didn't know any Jews there survived the German occupation."

"Sixty thousand didn't. But my father and mother escaped into the mountains and joined the anti-Nazi partisans. They were teenagers. That's how they met. After the war, they came back and had my brother and sisters and me. I'm the youngest."

She added, "But I don't remember much about Saloniki. We left when I was two and moved to Morocco."

"Why Morocco?"

"There wasn't much left for our family in Greece at that time. And my father's brother had a business in Fez. So we moved and we lived there until I was ten."

"How was Morocco?"

"Good and bad. Jews have been there for thousands of years, long before Muslims took over."

"I thought most Moroccan Jews went to Israel," Sam said. "Hundreds of thousands, I think."

"That's right."

Sam said, "Before I lose track, how many languages do you speak?"

"My first language was Ladino. Do you know what that is?"

"Yes."

"So that's one. Then in Morocco I learned to read and write Modern Standard Arabic, which is an official state language of Morocco, and also the everyday Arabic dialect they speak in North Africa, which they call Darija. And in Mexico I learned Spanish, which is an easy jump from Ladino, and English in school. So that's four or five, depending whether you count Arabic and Darija as separate languages or just two different versions of the same one. How about you?"

He was supposed to be interviewing her. But he said, "Hebrew, and of course English."

She cocked her head. "That's good. How well?"

"I get by. I can order lunch in a restaurant or get directions on the street. And like I said, I also speak some Hebrew."

She got his weak joke and flashed a smile. "Well enough to try my case?"

"Only in English. There's too much screaming in Israeli courts."

"Screaming is not your way?"

"I prefer making the other guy scream."

"You going to make Gomez and Escobar scream for me?" She asked.

"We'll give it a shot. How was Mexico?"

"Mexico was a wonderful place to grow up. I faced no problems for Jews in Mexico. I went to school and I had many friends and I got married and I had a son. Then my husband passed away."

"How did you wind up in this country?"

"My son went to a North American University. He studied some hi-tech things he tries to explain to me and I don't understand. They wanted him for the U.S. Army and he served. That is how he became a U.S. citizen."

"You're a citizen?"

"Yes," she said. "My husband passed away and I wanted to be close to my grandchildren. My son got me in as a Permanent Resident, and eventually I became a U.S. citizen. I've lived in four countries. But this is the one I like best."

He asked, "You never considered Israel?"

"I have family there, but my son and my grandchildren are here. He lives here in Phoenix. Do you have any children?"

She kept asking Sam personal questions. "One," he said. "A daughter back in Minnesota."

"What does she do?"

"She's raising my granddaughter and working from home, writing a novel. Trying to follow Danielle Steel's example, I guess."

"Oh, yes. Danielle Steel," Aviva said. "I studied English by reading her novels. I had already read them first in Arabic and then in Spanish, of course. Do you like her writing?"

"I haven't read novels for a long time."

"Too serious, I suppose," she said.

The novels were too serious or Sam was too serious? Not sure. He said, "Anyway, I get along better with my gentile ex-son-in-law than I do with my Jewish daughter Lily. You'll meet Hack soon. He'll set up your phone for recording. I've also asked him to take a look inside your work computer."

"Oh, that's taken care of. We did that part last night."

"You did?"

"He called me and set it up. Then he picked me up in his little red car and drove me to SWASU. He picked all the locks and did some cute things with the computer. I held the flashlight for him. He called it skullduggery. I had fun. It was exciting."

Sam was caught off guard. Should he be angry? At what? That Hack and she had gone ahead and done what he wanted them to do? Without his advance knowledge, but so what? Much as he'd like to, he couldn't control everything and everyone all the time.

She asked, "Are you upset?"

"I'm a little surprised, that's all."

She said, "Why?"

"I thought I'd know about it ahead of time. So I could be in on the planning, or something like that."

"You can't control everything and everyone all the time, Mr. Lapidos."

The woman must be a mind reader.

37 Aviva Ponders Sam

Without warning, right in the middle of questioning Aviva about Hack and her launching their skullduggery without his involvement, Mr. Lapidos stood up and walked out of the conference room.

What did this mean? Had she upset or angered him somehow? At the time, she'd assumed Hack and Mr. Lapidos had worked it all out together. If they didn't, how was that her fault?

She sat with her hands in her lap and waited for him to come back. What a curious man. A hybrid of striking self-confidence and nervous energy, as if he doubted everything coming his way. Which she supposed he had to, given his job. A thin man who made quick movements of hands and eyes, always watching everything around him. But also a man who, when he focused on her, made her feel like she was the sole person in his universe, peering into her soul, seeing everything there, maybe even the dark spots. She shuddered.

After waiting ten minutes without Mr. Lapidos coming back, Aviva picked up her purse and walked out through the lobby. Elegant gentlemen and businesswomen strolled about in business suits and sportswear obviously cut from exquisite fabrics and hand stitched by expert tailors. In Mexico, there had been a time she herself could afford such elegance and went about in pride, probably too much pride.

Aviva passed among the *elegantes* through the immense revolving door to the sidewalk and handed the teenage valet her parking stub. The valet retrieved her car. She checked in her purse and counted out three of her few remaining one-dollar bills for his tip. She got into her car and drove to the apartment building where she rented her efficiency.

As she had listened to herself telling Mr. Lapidos her story, it sounded so boring. First I lived here, then I moved and lived there. Then I moved and I lived another place. I went to school. I got married. I had a son. I moved again.

So what? Had her life been unworthy of the attention of this important man who was famous and even had a movie made about him? No wonder he got up and walked out.

Wasn't she at least as interesting as any other woman? Nothing seemed boring while it was happening to her.

There was so much she hadn't told him.

She hadn't told Mr. Lapidos about Saloniki. She didn't remember Greece, but she remembered listening in the darkness as her mother wept and her father comforted her mother about what happened there, and even a few times when it was her mother comforting her silently weeping father.

She hadn't told Mr. Lapidos about the Arab boy in Fez who called her a name and how she grabbed a crushed aluminum can off the street and hit him and sliced his cheek and the blood flowed, and the boy ran away, and how terrified she was, and how her father whisked them all away to Mexico the very next day.

She hadn't told Mr. Lapidos about growing up in Mexico with no grandparents on either side. In Mexico, the people were nice, though most of the other children had grandparents and little Aviva never had any, not to mention that Aviva was different from all the other children in so many other ways.

But maybe Mr. Lapidos already knew all that. Maybe he didn't need to hear it from her. He knew all the answers to questions before he even asked them. How? From similar experiences of his own family? Or from wisdom? He might be wise. He was *inteligente*, that was sure, but she did not yet know whether this man was also wise.

Mr. Lapidos was also a busy man, with important things on his mind, apparently involving murders, and if he rushed off, it was because he had things much more important to worry about than silly little Aviva Soriano and her petty complaints.

38 Sam At the Hedgehog Barrel

Sam had handled a few Bar complaints like Darwish's, usually from disgruntled clients. There were Disciplinary Board Internet forms to fill out. He spent several hours in his hotel room filling them out. He attached the email he'd sent Darwish the day they met. It came to Sam with a jolt they'd met only the day before. Things were happening fast.

If Darwish had a different version of their meeting, he should have responded to Sam's email with his own version, but he didn't. Sam didn't mention in his filings that he'd recorded the conversation. Let Darwish tell as many lies as he wanted. Sam wanted Darwish to freeze his story. Sam could spring the recording later as necessary.

After clicking the button at the bottom of the screen to file the forms, Sam phoned Ms. Soriano. She answered on the first ring.

"I'm wondering about something," he told her. "We learned today that someone was tracking Owen Deutscher's car. They attached a GPS tracker inside the bumper and knew where it was all the time."

"Who did that?" she asked.

"I guess whoever killed him."

"Do you have any idea who that was?"

"Yes, but I'd rather not say over the phone. Anyway, I'd like to have Hack check your car as well, just in case they're doing the same to you. I can set it up."

"That's handy," she said.

"Why so?"

"I'm at the same place as Hack right now."

"Where's that?"

"The Hedgehog Barrel. That's where he and his wife do their music. Why don't you come here too?"

"Me?"

"Have you eaten?"

"I haven't eaten much today," he said. True. Maybe since his breakfast toast and coffee.

"Eventually, you have to eat. How about now? It's almost eight."

Why not? "Okay."

"Great. Do you know where the Hedgehog Barrel is?"

"Not really."

"Look it up." She hung up.

Sam closed his laptop. Hack had really done a job on it. Everything went twice as fast. Sam changed out of his suit into a pair of black jeans and a black mock turtleneck. For warmth against the cool desert night, he put on a dark blue silk blazer.

The Hedgehog Barrel Bar and Grill turned out to be only a short walk from the Vauxhall Arms. Sam strolled in through old-fashioned saloon-style double swinging doors and past a hardwood bar that stretched along the left front side of the restaurant.

There was a stage on the back right, an empty cube carved out of the Hedgehog Barrel's red brick back wall. The stage was about eight feet high and twelve feet wide and twelve feet deep. The brown planks of its polyurethane-coated hardwood floor gleamed in the light flooding down from its ceiling.

Onstage, Hack sat on a stool behind a keyboard. His hands flew up and down the keys, but no sound came out. Must be warming up with his amplifier off. Between Hack and the heavily bearded drummer stood a heavily bearded bass player who looked just like the drummer. A guitarist stood up front of the others, twanging quiet chords, probably tuning his instrument. He kept leaning over to fiddle with the knobs on his amplifier.

Hack's new wife Mattie sat nearby on a chair watching the band set up. She saw Sam and smiled and waved. He nodded and signaled back with a brisk wave of his own.

The club had an old-west décor, but it was clean and modern and roomy, with high gray metal ceilings, a wide dark brown floor and lots of wooden tables and chairs.

Photos and posters decorated the walls on all sides. Some were old sepia photos of long-dead desert Indians and dusty cavalrymen glaring into the camera. Newer and bigger vivid colorful paintings of wild west scenes hung here and there, cowboys with bright red or green scarves and huge domed hats, roping steers or breaking broncs; grizzled cooks dispensing heaping helpings from chuck wagons; dogged prospectors up to their knees in mountain streams, panning for gold.

Near the front of the big customer area, Aviva Soriano was sitting at a table sipping from a glass of red wine. She saw Sam and stood and offered her right hand. He shook her hand and pulled back a chair. They sat.

"Why here?" he asked.

"Hack is quite an interesting fellow," she said. "He told me he plays in a band and his wife sings. I've always wanted to hear live American country music."

"Hack can be interesting," Sam admitted. He lifted his left hand to signal a waitress. She came towards the table. Before she could ask, he said, "Chumpster, please," and she nodded and went away.

Maybe Aviva had the right idea. A beer or two and some music would be a nice break. And he was starving.

"Have you heard Hack's wife Mattie sing?" Aviva said.

"No," Sam said.

"That's odd," Aviva said. "And maybe sad too."

"Why odd?"

"You've never heard your friend play or his wife sing?"

Sam defended himself. "I've heard Hack play."

"When?" she asked.

"About a year ago," Sam said. "I think. In Minnesota."

"And his wife?"

"No," Sam admitted. "I know her, but I've never heard her sing."

Aviva shook her head slowly.

"I live a crowded life," Sam said.

"I know," she said. "You're important. You do important things."

"Why are you so interested?" he asked. "I mean, in Mattie's singing?"

Aviva smiled, it seemed with a touch of sadness. "I used to sing. Back in Mexico. It's something I miss."

"Maybe I could hear you some time," he said, and wondered why he'd said that.

A loud guitar chord twanged from the stage. The band started up. Sam reached into his jacket pocket and pulled out the ear plugs he had brought along and stuck them in his ears.

Aviva watched him with an amused expression, but she said nothing.

The waitress came back with his beer and they ordered their food and listened while they ate.

Aviva had a burger and fries. Sam ordered the salad.

Aviva frowned. She said, "That's not enough to keep a mouse alive." She offered him a fry. He took it. The salt and grease were delicious. She nodded and he took another. Then another.

The first song ended. The guitar player introduced himself as Dudley and the band as Dudley and Mattie and Friends. Sam's musical taste leaned classical and his taste in pop songs toward Ella Fitzgerald singing Gershwin or Rodgers and Hart, but Sam admitted to himself the band was tight and the players were exceptional.

It turned out Mattie was a heartfelt singer. In the raucous numbers, her voice soared high and strong over the band. On the ballads, she dove down into a low part of her voice that warmed every word.

A crowd flooded in. The big room filled with the clamor of noisy drinkers and dancers. Sam was glad he'd remembered his ear plugs. When the room warmed, he removed his jacket and hung it over the back of his chair.

After an hour or so of thunking and twanging, Dudley called a break. Hack waved at Sam as he filed out through the back door with the rest of the band. Mattie lowered herself down from the stage with care and walked over to Sam and Aviva's table.

Mattie said, "Hi, Sam. I never expected to see you here."

"It was Ms. Soriano's idea. But I'm happy she suggested it. Aviva Soriano, this is Mattie Wilder."

The two women shook hands.

"You sing so beautifully," Aviva said. "I'm so glad I came. Could you please sit with us for a few minutes?"

"It'll be fun," Mattie said. "I haven't talked with Sam for a while." She took a chair and sat. She asked Aviva, "How'd you come to hear about us?"

"Your husband helped me out last night with some computer things."

Mattie said, "Oh, so that's where he was last night."

"He didn't tell you?" Aviva said. "And he just went on and on about how great you are. I had to come hear for myself. And he was right."

"Sometimes he's all cloak and dagger," Mattie said. She looked a question at Sam. "Must be an important case."

Aviva said, "I think all Mr. Lapidos's cases must be extremely important."

"I think you're probably right," Mattie said. "Or at least Mr. Lapidos thinks so. What do you say, Mr. Lapidos?"

Sam had no ready answer. Mattie had a way of throwing him off. A loud guitar chord rescued him.

"We're back," Dudley announced from the stage. The band had assembled again.

"That was a short break," Sam said.

Mattie said, "After a break, they always warm up with a long boring instrumental. Several, now that I'm pregnant."

The instrumental wasn't boring. It was one of Sam's favorites, an old Duke Ellington tune called *It Don't Mean A Thing If It Ain't Got That Swing*. Every player took a solo and every solo was good.

In the quiet moment right after the tune, Aviva said to Mattie, "I had a strange thing happen today."

"What's that?" Mattie asked.

"Well, it concerns Mr. Lapidos. He did something very unusual."

Mattie asked, "He didn't get up and walk out in the middle of your conversation, did he?"

"How did you know?"

"Don't take it personally. He gets distracted and wanders off. He spends all his time in his head. The rest of us are just extras in the big movie extravaganzas playing on the big screen in there."

"I see."

Sam said nothing. When you got nothing, nothing is a good thing to say.

Mattie said to Aviva, "Please don't take me wrong. I love Sam. Sam's actually a very good man. But he's not always a nice man, if you know what I mean."

"I think I do. Too serious, maybe?"

"Maybe."

From the stage, Dudley said, "And now, our very own keyboard player Hack Wilder will perform his own personal song he wrote all by himself, *It Ain't Gamblin' When You Know You're Gonna Lose.*"

"Oh no," Mattie said. "I hate that song."

The band fired up and Hack began to sing. Sam had never heard Hack sing, and after the first few words the reason was obvious. He was worse than Laghdaf.

> "Like a fool you bet the ranch,
> But he's beat you with the aces he's showing.
> Hole cards don't matter,
> You know exactly where this is going.
> > You raise anyway,
> > Just to see what he'll say,
> > And hope you can get him confused—
> But it ain't gamblin' when you know you're gonna lose.
>
> The wrong part of town,
> No earthly idea what you're there for.
> This muscle-bound bozo
> Makes a comment you shouldn't care for.
> > You can act like a clown
> > And simply back down
> > But sometimes you just got to choose—

And it ain't gamblin' when you know you're gonna
lose."

The band shifted to a funkier groove as Hack groaned out
the middle part:

"No, it ain't gamblin'
When there's just no way to win.
He's cocked his fist by his ear
He'll lay it right smack on your chin.
        You've run out of luck
        Don't bother to duck
Just pray it leaves only a bruise—
And it ain't gamblin' when you know you're gonna
lose."

Dudley twanged out a gamy instrumental on his guitar.
Then Hack spun out the final chapter of his melancholy tale:

"You met her in some barroom,
Don't rightly recall all you said there.
She's got a lot of miles on her,
But she's still pretty light on the tread wear.
        You think you know why
        She's got that look in her eye--
Or maybe it's only the booze--
And it ain't gamblin' when you know you're gonna
lose.

No, it ain't gamblin'
When you know you got no chance.
        So long to your pride,
        You're roped up and tied,

And like her puppet you're gonna dance.

She's gonna break your heart
>   And that's just the start
>   Of a lifetime of singin' the blues—
No it ain't gamblin' when you know you're gonna lose,
It ain't gamblin' when you know you're gonna lose."

Hack finished his song to groans, hoots and whistles from the crowd.

"My," Aviva said. "What an unusual song."

"I hate it," Mattie said.

Aviva asked, "Really?"

"He met me in a barroom," Mattie said.

"You think the song is about you?" Sam asked.

"Obviously," Mattie said.

A rare chance for Sam to get back at her. "So you're gonna break his heart and give him a lifetime of singin' the blues?"

"I will if he keeps singing that song," Mattie said.

The band launched into another instrumental, this time a gentle rocking number. A bunch of the couples in the crowd got up and began to dance the two-step.

Aviva stood and walked around the table and leaned her head close to Sam's ear. She said, "Let's dance."

Sam pretended not to hear her over the music.

She said again, "Let's dance."

He shook his head. "I can't."

"You can't?" Aviva asked.

"I can't," Sam said, which was the literal truth, because he was a terrible dancer and always had been, at least since junior high school.

What was more, he couldn't dance with a client, which after all, Aviva was, although now, well into his third Chumpster, that detail was getting fuzzier.

For a moment, Aviva stood stranded, a surprised look on her face. The moment could have been embarrassing, but Mattie stood and said to Aviva, "Sure, let's dance. We'll let this important attorney-at-law gobble your french fries all by himself."

"Good idea," Aviva said.

The two women stepped away to join the crowd on the floor. Mattie glanced back over her shoulder and lasered at Sam with a glare which could have melted the Greenland Glacier.

Sam sat, sad and stupid. Maybe he'd been insensitive, but Aviva had put him on the spot. Whatever feelings he was starting to feel towards Aviva, he couldn't give into them. She was a client. A client was a marble sculpture, an unreachable idol, an untouchable icon. Or something like that. He took another belt of his Chumpster.

Sam looked around the room to see if anyone had noticed the uncomfortable moment. Nobody seemed to be paying attention, except for one man in sunglasses at the back wall, who looked away the instant Sam met his eyes.

It was Mahir Darwish.

39 Mahir

Mahir knew himself to be the model invisible man. He knew how to seem quiet and mild in public. He knew how to act friendly without ever crossing the line to become overbearing. He knew how to be inconspicuous.

Though being inconspicuous required him to dress like a Khaffir, it didn't require him to act like one. He sipped a cola and sat alone at a table by the back wall, watching the Jew lawyer and the woman with him. He didn't recognize her.

The band disgusted him. The woman singer had a seductive voice, and even though she was a little pregnant, she was good looking enough to trouble him. Her name was Mattie. Like all American girls, she knew her own sexual appeal. She wore this knowledge in her face and in her expressive eyes and thirsty lips. Under her tight tee shirt and jeans, this woman did not hide her round breasts, her full buttocks, her shapely thighs and sleek legs. She brandished herself like a weapon.

When the band took its break, she surprised Mahir by coming down from the stage and going over to the Jew lawyer's table. Mahir didn't hear what they said, but it was clear the two knew each another. Was this woman singer also a part of whatever Zionist plot Lapidos was devising?

After a while, the band came back on stage. They played an instrumental. Mattie and the other older woman got up and left the table to dance together in a corner. The light was dim in the corner, and Mahir couldn't see the older woman's face, but he could see her body undulating in a manner just as suggestive as the younger pregnant one's.

Who knew what these women were thinking? In that darkness, who even knew what they were doing?

Lapidos was glancing around the room. His eyes seemed to pass over Mahir's and go by. It did not look as if Lapidos had spotted Mahir. Mahir knew how good he was at being inconspicuous.

Then the leader Dudley sang an ear-piercing song. If anyone needed to know why the Prophet had banned music, this song showed the reason.

No one could pretend there was anything spiritual about what came from these instruments, the way some fools defended Bach and Mozart. It was an assault on the ears, like the racket of big city traffic.

It was noisy and raucous. It broke down all restraints and invaded the listener's soul. It was obviously designed to arouse tumultuous and dangerous emotions. It pulsated with a rhythm which in any normal man demanded a sexual response.

If anything, the words were even worse than the music. This Dudley sang out a catalog of haram activities, one after another, escalating in sinfulness, each one worse than the one before.

In the song, a man and a woman were alone in a car at 3 AM. It was clear they were not married, at least not to each other. They had drunk beer. Not satisfied with beer, they had moved on to the more alcoholically potent whiskey. They had danced together. They had kissed. As if that were not bad enough, now the man was demanding sex from her, singing: "Get out of your clothes or get out of my car."

To match these wicked sounds and sinful words, the vile crowd whooped and whistled, as if the crush of people crammed together were insufficiently depraved to satisfy them, the song enticing them to enlist in and intensify the depravity.

And as the people themselves also drank more whiskey and beer, they sang along with the guitarist, they danced, they took one another's hands, hips swaying, couples touching, sometimes kissing, always body to body, trying their best to incite lust in one another, succeeding unspeakably.

The lights were dim, as if to hide what the people were doing. So maybe they had some sense of shame. But Mahir saw no sign of shame.

The two women from the Jew's table were dancing in their dark corner, in company with the rest of the crowd, but separate, moving their feet and swaying and laughing. Even the older one, who by now in her life should have developed some sense of modesty to go with her advancing age.

And the pregnant woman was smiling at the older one. Who knew what lustful fantasies these women shared? At the sight of their dancing and smiling, Mahir flushed from the sudden heat of his own irrepressible desire.

What did these women do when no men were around? Mahir had heard stories and seen movies. Images flooded his mind. He let them. Then, having himself at least some sense of shame, he tried to repress the visions, but it was hopeless. He looked away, at the wall, but soon found himself unable to stop watching.

He said a prayer asking Allah's forgiveness, though of course, at root, the women were to blame.

Western men allowed their women too much freedom. After America joined the House of Islam that was going to change forever.

40 Aviva

Friday morning, Aviva was walking across the parking lot towards the Latinx Studies building, steeling herself to suffer through her bogus hearing, when she saw Mahir Darwish come out the back door.

She had no doubt. It was the same man who'd chaired the fake Conference on Israel and Indigenous Peoples. It was the same man Sam Lapidos had pointed out to her the previous night at the Hedgehog Barrel. What was he doing at her building?

He was about thirty meters away. She stopped walking and watched Darwish stroll to his car, which turned out to be a dark blue Mercedes AMG E63. There was something insolent in the way he walked and even the way he opened his car door. He was so arrogant, so pleased with himself. He lorded it over all others even in his conspicuous choice of transportation.

Should she go to her fake hearing as planned? She was ready. Hack had shown her how to record any conversation on her phone. Sam had prepped her on what to say and what not to say. Sam expected a report and a recording when she came back.

But here was the man Sam told her might be behind her troubles. He must have chosen the nasty rapper Tayoub to perform. What had this Mahir Darwish been doing in the Latinx Building? Working things out ahead of time with her bosses? Sam had told her how the AIL gang had engineered the expulsion of his previous client, the student Amos Owens.

What if she followed Darwish? She might learn something about him and whatever his AIL gang was up to. She could tell Sam about it afterward. The information could help her case.

The hearing was a joke. A kangaroo court. Sam had told her that. She knew it anyway. What was the point?

She was tired of being pushed around. She could fight back. Like James Bond, or at least James Rockford. That TV detective on the old show was always following people in his car, or they were following him. How hard could it be?

She went back to her own little car and got in and started it. When Darwish pulled out, she pulled out after him.

The thrill of adventure. She was making a break, like when she made a break and moved from Mexico to the U.S., or when her family had moved to Mexico in the first place. Her entire life was an adventure, not a string of boring episodes the way she told it to Sam.

Darwish drove like a Moroccan, which meant like a maniac, swerving around other cars, changing lanes without signaling, creating his own lane when he found space enough, as if he were racing the El Dorado Speedway in Juan Aldama, or the Indianapolis 500.

Twice he ran yellow lights, which meant she herself had to run red lights to keep up. She hoped he didn't spot her doing that behind him.

As soon has he got onto Interstate 10, he pulled left into the HOV lane, the lane for two or more people. If the police pulled her over and ticketed her, she would surely lose him.. She tried to keep up from a lane to his right, but when he sped up past 90, she fell back.

If he had not been driving his fancy conspicuous Mercedes, she would have lost him altogether. He was far ahead of her, but she saw him when he crossed four lanes from the HOV lane to the exit on his right. She was far enough behind to give her time to slide lane by lane over to the right and reach the same exit and follow him off. At the top of the exit ramp, he turned left. She followed him.

He slowed now, and it was easy to trail him down a few residential streets to a house. He pulled into a driveway on the left. She kept driving about a hundred meters past the house and pulled over to the right side. In her left side mirror, she watched him get out of his car and go into a nice-looking stucco house.

She turned off her engine and waited. Nothing happened for about ten minutes. Now what?

Darwish had opened the front door with his own key. This must be where he lived.

41 Again A New Client

Friday morning. Sam was having his breakfast of coffee and dry toast in the Hotel Bistro. To atone for the fries he'd scarfed the night before, Sam had only one piece of toast. The phone rang in his suit pocket. He took it out and answered. "Law office."

"This is Harry Cobb," a man said.

"Okay," Sam said.

"I may need a lawyer."

"I'm right here."

"I think it would be better for both of us if you came to see me," Cobb said.

"Why should I do that?"

"Under current conditions, it would be safer."

"I see," Sam said.

Sam already had too many clients, but even if Sam didn't wind up representing Cobb, it made sense to talk to the man and find out what if anything he knew about Aviva's case or about the larger SWASU picture—not to mention whatever was going on with Mahir Darwish and Tayoub Abawi and Sam's murdered client Owen.

"Tell me where and when," Sam said, and Cobb did.

Sam checked his rental car out of the hotel valet service and followed Cobb's directions out to the desert. The day was sunny, but cool and pleasant.

As instructed, Sam parked near Cobb's "Don't Bother Me" sign. Cobb appeared out of the brush and led Sam on a hike a mile or so across the desert terrain to a low spot between two small hills. Long grass and occasional prickly pear cactus spread across both hills. Occasional saguaro cacti sprouted here and there, most young and small, but one at least thirty feet high.

Good terrain for a private meet. The hills and the brush should hide them from anyone else at low level.

Cobb was dressed for the outdoors. He wore a thick brown wool shirt with a pair of big front pockets, dark blue wool cargo pants and high black boots laced almost up to his knees. A broad-brimmed black safari hat perched on his head. The man had hiked ahead of Sam with vigor and strength, and only now, looking him in the face up close, did Sam see how old he was. His face was rough and rugged as his territory, burnt dark by the sun, corrugated with time-dug ruts.

Sam had brought no outdoor gear from Minnesota. He wore his cloudy blue light wool suit, the bespoke one with the jacket specially tailored to smooth and hide the bulge from the 9 mm Springfield XDM semi-automatic holstered under his left arm.

Sam had checked the gun through airport security in Minnesota, then retrieved it when he arrived at Phoenix Sky Harbor airport. Until this morning he'd kept it locked in his hotel safe. Now Sam had no choice but to pack it.

It was legal: Arizona would recognize Sam's Minnesota Concealed Carry Permit, the license he'd acquired when he took on Stan Latham's defense.

Sam checked his Berluti dress shoes. They were his favorite pair. The desert hike had scuffed the shine. He'd take care of that as soon as he got back to the hotel.

Two waist-high boulders stood a few yards apart. Cobb sat on one. He pointed with open left hand at the other, inviting Sam to take a seat. This must be the man's idea of a conference room.

"Seems like all I've done since I got to Arizona is sit," Sam said. "Thanks, but I'd rather stand."

"It's dry. I cleaned it off for you. Hasn't rained here for months. It's a clean friendly stone, and it won't stain your lawyer suit."

"Nevertheless."

Cobb shrugged.

"You called me out here and I came," Sam said.

"I didn't kill Owen, if that's what you're thinking."

"I wasn't thinking that at all," Sam said, which was true.

"It saddens me, actually. He was a nice kid. He had a good heart. Just naïve."

"I don't disagree," Sam said. And he didn't.

"Good mind too. I could tell right away. Could have become someone. The other bastard I did shoot; I had no choice."

"You mean Tayoub Abawi?"

"Yes." Cobb said. "Since I shot somebody, I'm wondering if I need a lawyer."

"Have any authorities threatened to arrest you?"

"Not yet," Cobb said. "Amazes me. They're getting a lot of political heat from the woke people."

"There are Arizona lawyers who deal in your kind of case," Sam said. "Self-defense shootings and the like. They know Arizona state law upside down and backwards and the judges know them personally. You might be better off with one of those."

"Yes, that's true."

"Then why me?

Cobb crossed his arms. "You sure you don't want to sit?"

Sam realized he'd been pacing. He made a conscious effort to stop. He faced Cobb. "I'm fine as is. Why me?"

Cobb said, "I think this might be bigger than just some local shoot-em-up. With bigger implications. Beyond Arizona. Beyond U.S. borders, maybe."

"What makes you say that?"

Cobb pointed to a distant low hill. "You see that hilltop?"

"Sure." The hill looked to be about a klick away.

"You see anything?"

"I see a hilltop."

Cobb asked, "You know who's up there on that hilltop?"

"I haven't thought about it." Though of course, having been a soldier, Sam had thought about it, as he'd also thought about all the high and low places Cobb had led him through to reach these boulders.

"Traffickers have one of their hands camped up there. From a cartel. He stays about a month at a time, then his replacement shows up and he goes back across the border to his home in Mexico or wherever. These guys take turns. He's got a tent and supplies and solar panels for power and he's got at least one long gun. He could probably shoot us from there any time he takes a notion to."

"Comforting thought," Sam said. He restrained the impulse to pat his suit on the spot under which he'd holstered his pistol, useless against a rifle anyway.

"Traffickers run this desert." Cobb said. "Traffickers of every kind, drugs, money, guns and humans. Some do all at the same time. Smugglers cross my land all night long, going both directions, from Mexico into the U.S. and back again. The Mexican border's only 130 miles from here. It's like the Ho Chi Minh Trail."

"I see." Sam had studied a little military history. The Ho Chi Minh "Trail" was the name for communist smuggling and supply routes in and out of South Vietnam during America's war there. It was not literally a single trail, but a collection of routes. Sam asked, "What has that got to do with me?"

"Stop and think," Cobb said. "Look at what's happening. You've got a new client at SWASU, right?"

"What would you know about that?"

Cobb said, "I've been at SWASU for decades. I practically founded it. I know people there. And I know you've got a new woman client who works there, who's being pushed around because she objected to this nasty so-called Israel and Indigenous Peoples conference they held, and because she's Jewish. Why? Who do you think is behind that?"

Sam said nothing.

"Then we have this little Muslim boy Owen Deutscher being ordered to kill me because I showed some Mohammad cartoons in a class on free speech. Who tells him to do that? And when he bugs out of his mission, another Muslim cowboy shows up with a knife and I have to shoot him. Then someone else shoots Owen. Why?"

Cobb had Sam's full attention.

Cobb said, "And how'd they find Owen in the middle of the night? They must have been following him somehow. And how do you know they aren't following you the same way?"

Of course. The surveillance of Sam's office and computers and who knew what else? And his car? Were they following him now? Again, Sam checked his impulse to take a useless look around.

Cobb said, "Somebody's behind all this, right?"

"Do you know who?" Sam asked.

"I'd say that's obvious. Someone connected with this Tayoub Abawi jackass I shot, or with Owen. I'm guessing you know more about that than I do."

Like Mahir Darwish and probably a few others Sam hadn't yet learned about. All Sam said was, "You can never tell."

"That's true as far as it goes." Cobb said. Cobb eyed Sam, as if he were sizing him up. "You can never tell. Will you take my case?"

Sam saw no conflict of interest. And this Cobb was a fighter. He'd be a fun client. Sam said, "Conditional on my partner Laghdaf's approval, yes."

Sam reached out his hand. Cobb stood and shook it. Sam said, "From now on, don't talk to anyone in law enforcement without me there. Or anyone else for that matter."

"I'll take that advice," Cobb said. "One other thing. This new woman client of yours."

"What about her?"

"Is she safe?"

Sam snuck a sideways glance at the hilltop Cobb had pointed out. It looked no different from any other hill. He refocused on Cobb. Sam wasn't in the habit of worrying about his clients' physical safety. But this was a different situation. He admitted, "I'm not sure."

Cobb said, "She'll be safer out here in the desert. Something to think about."

"That's crazy," Sam said.

"If it's so crazy, why are you packing that pistol under your arm?"

"You're good," Sam said. "My tailor promised no one would suspect a thing."

"What I see, others will see," Cobb said. "But the pistol is smart. I suspect you'll be firing it soon enough."

"I hope not," Sam said. He looked around. "If I did bring her out here, would you have suitable accommodations for her?"

"I may not look it now, but I was married once, and for a long time. Yes. I'll make sure she's very comfortable. And safe."

"It's something to think about. I'll ask her. It's up to her, not me. Are we done here?"

Cobb stood and stretched his arms up and out. He swiveled his head as if to loosen his neck. There was an audible crack. His ancient face broke into a grin which somehow hinted at the young man he'd once been. "I think so. You need me to guide you back to your car?"

"Thanks, but I've been in a desert before," Sam said. "I can find my way back."

"As you say, sir." Cobb snapped a perfect salute and turned and walked away over a small rise. He disappeared.

Sam hiked back towards the "Don't Bother Me" sign and his car. He watched each step he took through the tough terrain, trying to avoid butchering his Berlutis even worse.

Why did Cobb imagine the Army would ever have made Sam an officer?

42 Maria

Aviva used her phone to search for the nearest hardware store. There was a Trixie Hardware in a strip mall only six blocks away. She drove there and parked in its rutted and potholed lot. She went into the store and used her credit card to buy a bucket, a mop, a squeegee, a bag of rags, and different sized containers of every variety of cleaners and cleansers. She came out and stowed her new equipment in her trunk.

There was Press Dress for Less store next to the Trixie. She went in and strolled the aisles with the other Mexican, black, Indian and poor white customers. She found a two-dollar pair of black sweatpants and four-dollar blue sweatshirt. She wasn't sure why the shirt cost twice as much as the pants. She bought both, along with a striped polyester scarf for one additional dollar. She saw a pair of ear buds and on impulse bought them for another dollar. The black sneakers were the most expensive item, at $4.99.

After she maxed out her credit card, she walked back into the store past the cashiers and found a dressing room. She changed out of the nice business suit she had worn for the hearing and into her new work clothes. She folded her good clothes and placed them in the shopping bag.

She left the store and opened the trunk of her car and stowed her Press Dress for Less shopping bag in the trunk. She drove back to Darwish's house. This time she parked directly in front.

She sat for at least five minutes, hands locked on the steering wheel, her knuckles white, her breath coming hard and fast.

Aviva was furious at the lazy ignorant SWASU so-called "professors" and the way they treated her like throwaway garbage. She was disgusted with Darwish and his phony Jew-baiting Conference. After all these decades, she was still outraged at the Germans and their local allies who had made her parent's lives hell back in Greece, long before she was born.

And she realized she was still angry at the Muslim boy in Fez, the boy whose face she had sliced with the can she picked up off the street. The way she felt, if he were standing in front of her right now, she would do it again. This was wrong of her, but it was how she felt.

And she was definitely at least little bit irritated with Mr. Sam Lapidos, a bigshot attorney who was too big a shot to dance with her, herself only a little Jewish Mexican girl from Greece and Morocco, him so famous and spouting off on TV all the time.

Well, that was off the subject. Or was it? What was the subject anyway?

The subject was that she was finally going to do something. She was going to show all these *pendejos* and *pendejas* what she could do. And one of the chief pendejos was right there in that house, not twenty meters away.

There was no reason Darwish should recognize her. How could he? As far as she knew, he had seen her only once or twice, and she should have been just another face in the crowd.

And if he did recognize her, what was the worst he would do? He would just send her away from his door.

She grabbed her purse off the passenger seat and dug out her contact lens case. She popped out the lenses and stored them. She found and put on her glasses—the ugly owly ones she hated and wore only at home in her efficiency apartment, where no one else could see her. She took them off even to stumble downstairs to do her laundry.

She pulled the lever to open her trunk. She got out of her car and went behind it. She took her new cleaning equipment out of the trunk and closed it.

She tied her new cheap polyester scarf around her chin to cover her hair. Dressed in sweatpants, sweatshirt, owly glasses and scarf, she strode to the front door and pressed the doorbell button next to it. She heard the bell ring inside. Two seconds later Darwish opened the door.

Too quick! No fair. She wasn't ready. For an eon or two he stood looking down at her. Did she look ridiculous? Finally, he asked, "Yes?"

In her authentic Mexican accent, she managed to utter the single word "Maria."

Maria should be a good name to go by. There were millions of Marias in Mexico and Central America, distinguished usually by the next name that came afterward, like Maria Elena, or Maria Teresa or Maria Something-or-other. She was going to be just "Maria."

"Maria?" he said.

"Si."

For a moment, Darwish squinted at her as if puzzled. Then he said, "You mean, Maria sent you?"

She managed to choke out, "Si."

"Maria couldn't make it herself?"

"Si."

"And what is your name?"

Bond? Maria Bond? The funny thought relaxed her enough to answer. "My name Maria *tambien*."

"Tambien? Is that your last name?"

"No." This was working! She conjured up a smile. "Tambien is 'also'. I Maria also."

He shrugged and backed away from the door. He said, "Come on in."

His accent in English suggested a familiar melody. But what?

She carried her bucketful of cleaning supplies through the door. Darwish stepped outside to look both ways, then came back in and closed the door behind her.

She was inside.

He said, "I don't know if the other Maria told you, but the other day I had to ask her to leave suddenly, right when she had started her work in the kitchen." He pointed. "The kitchen is that way."

Aviva took a moment to assert control over herself. She had to. She nodded and smiled her most cheerful smile and carried her supplies in the direction he pointed, which was through a short hallway and into the kitchen.

The kitchen was a mess. Dirty glasses piled on food-encrusted plates in the sink. Crumbs and fragments of chips spread all over the little table with its two little chairs. Stains from unrecognizable liquids spotting the floor.

When she had come up with her plan to disguise herself as a cleaning woman, she had not considered that she would have to actually clean. Well, it was not as if this was the first time she would deal with the mess left by a slovenly irresponsible male. She put her ear buds on and stuck the free end of the jack into her pants pocket and set to work.

She spent the next hour in the kitchen, washing and drying the dishes, sweeping and mopping the floor, washing the windows. She even dusted the pantry. If Maria did a good job, Aviva-as-Maria might gain permanent entry into Darwish's house as his regular cleaning woman. She might be able to feed Sam all kinds of information about AIL and what AIL was up to.

Plus, it was just Aviva's way to do a good job on any task. That was how her parents raised her.

When she finished with the kitchen, she came out into the living room. Darwish was sitting in front of a desk in an alcove off to the side. He was doing something with a laptop. He keyed something in and a face appeared on the screen.

She took out her earbuds and called, "Señor Darwish, what next?"

"Just a moment, Abu Jihad," he said to the face in the laptop screen. He turned and pointed again. "The bedroom and then the bathroom."

She put her earbuds back on and headed into the bedroom. The bed was unmade, with blankets and pillows scattered all over. Should she wash the sheets?

From the living room, she could hear Darwish's voice. He was talking with someone, but she couldn't hear the conversation.

She searched the tall bureau for clean sheets and pillowcases. She found them, along with a lot of underwear and socks, as well as some neatly folded sweaters. She stripped the dirty sheets and pillowcases off the bed and replaced them with fresh ones and made the bed. For the moment, she piled the dirty bed linen in a heap in the corner.

She opened the closet door, but all she saw were slacks and shirts in many colors, in the same style he was wearing right now. On the floor were many pairs of shoes and a pair of high black boots, the kind with hooks for the long laces. The shelves above were empty.

She had found nothing that might help Sam in the kitchen or in the bedroom.

She dusted every wooden surface and came out of the bedroom. Darwish was still talking into his computer, using Zoom or Skype or something like that. He was wearing headphones with an attached microphone. She heard only his half of the conversation.

She understood what she heard. He was speaking Darija.

His accent was strange and hard to follow, but she had no doubt he was speaking a version of the Arabic dialect she'd learned as a child in Morocco. He must be from some part of North Africa, though probably not from Morocco. It didn't matter. What mattered was that she understood.

He was talking about some business deal with some "friends" in Mexico. He must have heard her come into the room, because he glanced back at her and gestured with his head towards the bathroom.

She scurried into the bathroom. Now she hurried through her work, eager to get back while Darwish was still talking. She cleaned the toilets and the sink and mopped the floor. When done, she surveyed. All good. She folded the end of the toilet paper roll in the trademark little triangle of domestics everywhere.

She nodded in satisfaction at her final gesture of authenticity. Mr. Elegant James Bond would never have come up with that!

When she came out, Darwish and the man were still talking.

She was carrying a spray can of furniture polish and a soft rag. She began dusting a table. She kept her head down and faced away from his computer screen as much as she could.

She must have passed in view of the laptop camera. Darwish said, "You mean Maria? She's just a friend doing some dusting."

Pause, while the other man said something.

"No, she's not a cleaning woman. She doesn't even speak English." Darwish turned in his chair and asked, "Maria doesn't speak Darija. Do you, Maria?

She pretended not to hear.

Darwish shouted, "Maria!"

She looked up. "Si?"

Darwish asked in Modern Standard Arabic, "Maria, do you speak Arabic?"

Aviva stared at him.

Darwish switched to Darija. "Do you understand me now?"

Aviva smiled her best simpleton smile. "Qué you speak?"

Darwish frowned and shook his head as if he were hearing something over the headphones he didn't want to hear. He said, "Of course not. I follow your orders always."

Then, to Aviva, in English: "Maria, come here." He crooked his index finger at her.

What now? Aviva did as commanded. As she got near, she saw in the laptop screen the face of another older man she didn't recognize. He said something Aviva couldn't hear. She gave Darwish a helpless look.

Darwish pulled his headphone jack out of the laptop port. Through the laptop speaker, Aviva heard the man in the laptop say in Spanish, "Step closer so I can see your face."

She did as told. Darwish stood up from his chair and moved out of her way.

"Sit," the man in the laptop said in Spanish again.

She sat. She took out her ear buds and clutched them in her hands on her lap. She saw an older man with gray hair and a beard and beetle brows. He looked Mediterranean. His eyes seemed to bore into her from the screen.

He said, again in Spanish, "Let's talk for a moment."

"Yes, *Don*—how should I call you?"

"No matter," he said.

"As you wish, Señor. What would you like to talk about?"

He said, "Let's talk about you. How long have you been cleaning houses?"

She glanced up at Darwish. His face was pale, his lips pressed together.

From what she had overheard, she guessed why. She said, "You mean for a living? Oh no, Señor, I don't clean for a living. I am just helping out my neighbor. He has done favors for me, too. I think these domestic tasks are beneath such a distinguished man as he clearly is."

"Really. And what favor did Mr. Darwish for you?"

"You see, there was this big black dog in my yard. With the big teeth and the growling. He even tried to follow me into my house. I was terrified. Mr. Darwish chased him away. Like it was nothing. He was very brave."

"I do see. What do you do for a living?"

"Nothing yet. I arrived a few weeks ago."

"You speak Spanish well. Like a native, in fact."

She laughed. "Why, that is not difficult for me. I am a native. Of Mexico, I mean."

He nodded, as if satisfied. Then he asked in English. "Do you understand what I'm saying now?"

"I think a little," she said, also in English. "But no so good."

In Darija, he shouted, "Lying bitch!" and a string of other even fouler street insults, the kind her mother would have scolded her for understanding.

Aviva looked up at Darwish with a vacant smile and asked in English, "What he say? Sound angry. I do something wrong?"

"Don't worry, Maria," Darwish said. "Thank you very much. Go back to what you were doing."

She smiled her big cheerful smile at both men and put her ear buds back on and stood. Maybe she had built a small bond with Darwish by lying for him. She corrected herself in her mind: Don't trust him.

She felt a tickle on her thigh and looked down. Her unconnected ear bud jack had popped out of her pocket and was dangling loose. She must have pulled it out when she stood. She turned her body away from Darwish and the laptop to block their view. As she walked away from them, she grabbed the jack and stuck it back in her front sweatpants pocket.

Darwish resumed his place on the chair in front of his laptop. He didn't put his headphones back on.

Aviva sprayed some more furniture polish on the table and went back to her dusting.

In Darija, the man in the laptop said, "Mahir, you do recall, I told you to clean your own house yourself. Even I subject myself to this small indignity and do those tasks myself. If I do them, so should you. Do not regard yourself as above such tasks when the jihad demands it."

"I have been cleaning my own house just as you commanded, Abu Jihad. As Maria herself told you, she's just a neighbor and friend."

"Please don't insult my intelligence," Abu Jihad said. "I understand that a healthy young man like you needs a female now and then. And these older ones are often more amenable and can still be adequately juicy. But she can't be staying in your house."

"I promise. She is not staying here. She is just a visiting neighbor."

Abu Jihad's sigh was audible through the laptop speaker. He said, "And about our other matters?"

Darwish said, "The Jewish woman clerk at SWASU is fired. I spoke with her boss professor this morning. She agreed. It is settled."

They are talking about me. Aviva caught herself pushing the dust rag down into the table so hard that the table lamp rattled on its base. She forced herself to ease up and slow down. The longer she dusted, the more she could hear. And she must not look up.

Abu Jihad said, "And this Cobb, the one who murdered our fighter Tayoub?

"I have sent one of our best men to deal with him, the same fighter who took care of Owen Deutscher in so neat a manner. He is a local and knows this desert."

Deal with Cobb? She shuddered at the obvious interpretation. Maybe she was misunderstanding them. The table shone clean in the sunlight streaming through a window. She left it and began dusting a windowsill.

Abu Jihad asked, "We cannot force the authorities to prosecute this Cobb?"

"No, Abu Jihad, at least we have not succeeded so far. Cobb says it was self-defense. And they have Tayoub's knife. It will have Tayoub's fingerprints and DNA on it. These will support Cobb's story."

"One more reason the Khaffir legal system is a blasphemy," Abu Jihad said. "As if this blasphemer had any right to kill one of us in the middle of dealing out justice. *Al-wala' wa'l-bar*—loyalty and enmity. When it comes to our Ummah and the House of War, there is only us and them. I against my brother; I and my brother against my cousin; I and my brother and my cousin against the world."

"Yes, Abu Jihad." Darwish sounded for a moment like Aviva's son, when he had been a teenager, bored with adults and their tedious repetitive lectures.

"And the Jew lawyer? What is he up to?"

Sam?

"I have been thinking, Abu Jihad. I know Owen Al-Amriki met with Lapidos. Owen must have warned Lapidos about the death sentence about to be imposed on Cobb, and Lapidos in turn warned Cobb. Lapidos and Cobb set it up together. Cobb lay in ambush for Tayoub. There is no way Cobb could have defeated our man Tayoub if caught by surprise."

Abu Jihad said, "Cobb did have a gun."

"Cobb is well over 80 years old."

"Still, a gun is a gun."

"Lapidos has helped other enemies of ours before. Remember the Muslim hater Amos Owens."

"I remember," Abu Jihad said.

"Lapidos refused our generous offer of ten thousand dollars a month to do nothing," Darwish said. "Why? For a Jew who is also a lawyer, the money should have been irresistible. And he met with both the Jewish woman clerk and with Owen Deutscher. He must have bigger plans to harm us. With the killing of Tayoub, we now see his scheme unfolding before our eyes."

"What do you propose?"

"We kill Lapidos too."

More than Aviva wanted to know. How could she get out of here?

"Lapidos is famous," Abu Jihad said. "His death may draw unwelcome attention."

"In fact, the attention will be very welcome. Many hate him."

"True," Abu Jihad said. "And the woman clerk?"

"She is no problem. Once Lapidos is gone, she'll be on her own again and won't even be a nuisance."

Not even a nuisance.

Darwish added, "But I suppose we could kill her too if you insist."

"A clean sweep is better," Abu Jihad said. "Which leads me to ask, what about Lapidos's partner, the other lawyer, Laghdaf?"

"I do not consider him. He is only an *abd*, fit for cattle herding. Here Americans have what they call affirmative action for Africans, so they pretend he is a lawyer. Back home, we bought and sold many such as Laghdaf."

"Nonetheless, I said a clean sweep."

"That is true, Abu Jihad."

"I will think about it." With no further word, Abu Jihad's face disappeared off the screen. Darwish closed his laptop. He turned. "Maria, aren't you almost done?"

Aviva had run out of tables and windowsills to dust. She faced him. "I am done now." She scurried back to the bathroom and gathered her rags and her squeegee and her cleansers and stuffed them into her bucket.

Darwish followed her into the bathroom and looked around. He nodded in apparent satisfaction at her work.

When she came out to the living room, she clutched the bucket handle with both hands to suppress the trembling. Darwish followed, an expression on his face she could not read.

She smiled her brightest smile. She exhaled a loud sigh. "Much work," she said. "More houses. Time for me now to go," and headed towards the door, forcing herself to stick to a walking pace.

Aviva had placed her right hand on the doorknob when Darwish called, "Hold it! Not quite yet."

She stopped and turned, hand still on the knob. Darwish got up from his chair and walked towards her.

Aviva froze.

Darwish reached into his pants pocket and felt around. He shook his head. He muttered something. "Wait," he said. He turned and walked back to his desk. He opened a drawer and reached inside and took something out, but his body blocked her view. She could not see. He turned towards her.

He was holding his open wallet. He smiled and reached in. He said, "You did a very good job. How much do I owe you?"

She said, "How much you pay for other Maria?'

He pulled a wad of bills out of his wallet and handed the wad to her. "Come back next week. You did a better job than she ever did. There's a little extra for you."

43 Aviva Reports

A few minutes into Sam's drive back to his hotel, his phone rang. He dug the phone out of his inside jacket pocket. It was Aviva. Trying to keep his eyes on the road, he thumbed the phone to answer. Dammit—he should have connected his phone to the rental's Bluetooth.

"Where are you?" she asked.

"I'm driving to my hotel," he said. He thumbed the phone's speaker on and clamped the phone between his chin and his shoulder.

She said, "You remember when I told you I didn't want you to think I'm just some woman who panics over everything?"

"I never thought that for a second."

"Well, good, because right now I'm terrified," she said.

"What happened at the hearing?"

"Forget the hearing," she said. "I saw Mahir coming out of the Latinx Building and I followed him."

"You did what?"

"I followed him home. In my car."

"You didn't need to do that. There are a lot of safer ways to find out where he lives."

"I didn't just follow him to his house. I followed him into his house."

"He let you in?"

"I disguised myself. It's a long story."

As Sam drove along, at the same time watching for cars and listening to Aviva's story, she told him about her disguising herself and her cleaning Darwish's house and the meeting Darwish had over the computer in Darija with a man called Abu Jihad and everything the two men said, including their decision to kill Sam and Laghdaf and her, and even about the generous tip Darwish gave her. She finished with, "I don't know whether I want to keep the money."

While Aviva talked, Sam said nothing. When she was finished, he was still twenty minutes out from the Vauxhall Arms. He said, "The money? What do you care about the money?"

"His money is tainted."

"I'd say tainted cash is the least of our problems right now. By the way, Abu Jihad is just a title of honor for a big time jihadi."

"I know that. Between the two of us, I am the one who lived in Morocco and speaks Arabic."

"True. Where are you now?"

"I'm sitting on a couch in the Vauxhall Arms lobby," she said. "Trying to calm myself with a cup of herbal tea. I parked with the valet again. I hope you don't mind."

"Of course I don't mind," he said. "Are there a lot of people around you?"

"Yes."

"Good. Whatever happens, stay there. Wait for me. I'll be there in twenty minutes."

"Okay," she said. Sam hung up.

Sam punched the speed dial for Laghdaf. The call went straight to voicemail. At the beep, Sam said, "This is urgent. As soon as you hear this, please drop whatever you're doing and head over to the hotel lobby right away. Aviva Soriano will be sitting there. Please join her and both of you wait for me together. And keep your eyes peeled for trouble."

Sam hung up and punched the speed dial for Hack.

Hack answered, "Here I am. What's up?"

"I need you to inspect my rental car for GPS trackers the way you did Owen's."

"Is this urgent?"

"Yes. Very. And I may need to borrow your car while you're doing that."

"You want to drive my Audi?"

"Depends. Is it clean of trackers and bugs?"

"Of course. After I found the tracker on Owen's car, I scrubbed mine. It's clean."

"You sure?"

"I have the latest electronic detectors. I'm not letting anyone know where I am or what I'm doing. That's part of the reason I drive the Fox. It's got no electronics invented since 1973. Trust me."

"I trust you," Sam said. "When can you look over my rental?"

"This is an absolute emergency?"

"Absolute."

"I'm home at Dudley's place. You borrow my car and I'll check out yours while you're off doing what you're doing."

"Text me Dudley's address," Sam said. "I have to go to my hotel first. I'll be there in an hour or two."

"I'll still be here," Hack said.

When Sam reached the curb in front of the Vauxhall Arms, he handed his keys to the teenage valet and hurried through the big revolving door into the lobby. He spotted Laghdaf and Aviva sitting together on a couch in the middle of the lobby.

Aviva stood out in her dirty black sweatpants, stained blue sweatshirt, and polyester scarf, but she was the most elegant woman there anyway—enough of that! Sam made his way over and said to them both, "Let's go somewhere and talk."

Aviva stood and stepped forward and put her arms around his waist and hugged him. Caught off guard, Sam held back, keeping his arms stiff, out to his sides.

The warmth and softness of her body disturbed. Her dark hair smelled delicious. He glanced over her shoulder at Laghdaf, who stood smiling his irritating mysterious smile. Sam patted her shoulder and for lack of anything better to say, came up with, "It will be okay."

She let go and backed away. She looked up at him. Tears filled her eyes. She said, "You have no idea." She turned and walked back to Laghdaf's side and turned to face Sam as if she and Laghdaf were the team and Laghdaf were her partner instead of Sam's.

Laghdaf said, "Let's walk to a park I know and talk there."

"Let's," Sam said.

Laghdaf led the way. Aviva walked alongside Laghdaf. Sam followed behind. No one spoke. Sam paid no attention to the shops they passed. He kept his eye on Aviva, wondering what next.

They reached the park. Aviva sat on a bench and stared off at some kids playing soccer on the grass. Sam sat on the bench as well, not too close. The smell of her perfume was still strong in his head, despite the sweet outdoor breeze.

Laghdaf stayed standing. He said to Sam, "Aviva filled me in. Have you got anything to add to what she told me?"

Sam said, "I just met with Professor Cobb, and he wants us to represent him."

"Wouldn't that make him our third new client in three days?" Laghdaf said.

"I'm losing track," Sam admitted. "But I think it's four days."

219

"You're right," Laghdaf said. "Aviva was Tuesday, Owen was Wednesday, and this is Friday. And this is your way of relaxing after your tough trial. But I am interested in his situation. I agree."

"I'll let him know," Sam said. "When Aviva and I see him today."

"You and Aviva?" Laghdaf asked.

"Yes. He offered to take her in. He says he can protect her out in the desert."

Laghdaf asked Aviva, "Aviva, what do you want?"

She asked him, "Isn't Professor Cobb the one who shot that nasty rapper Tayoub?"

"Only after Tayoub tried to kill him," Laghdaf said.

"Even better," she said. "This Cobb sounds like a good friend to make. I'll go."

"You don't want to ask about any accommodations he has for you?" Sam asked her.

She kept her eyes on the kids roaming across the field, shouting, laughing, kicking their ball. "You don't know me at all," she said. "I will be fine, whatever his accommodations."

Laghdaf said, "I think I'll take a look at Mahir's house. We should be keeping our eyes on him."

To Sam, Laghdaf said, "If he moves, I will let you know."

"Good idea," Sam said. "Do you have a gun?"

"Certainly," Laghdaf said. "I am an American citizen."

44 Hack Inspects Sam's Car

Hack was standing by his Audi at the curb in front of Dudley's house when Sam drove his rental past him into the driveway.

Hack waited while Sam and Aviva walked up the driveway. The two were coming at the same time, but somehow, they didn't seem to be together. Aviva wore what looked like a studiously neutral expression on her face.

Aviva listened with apparent interest and Sam with apparent resignation as Hack lectured them on the various ways his own special personal transportation was secure against hacking and tracking.

Hack said, "This little red Audi Fox of mine was built in 1973, before they started using computer components. Nowadays they have what they call the Internet of Things. They can hack into your car or your home refrigerator or water heater if they want to. But my Audi is immune to all that. And I inspected it manually myself, top to bottom, inside and out, just the same way I'm going to go over Sam's rental. I also took it out into the desert far from any electronic interference and used two of the current top detectors. It's safe."

Mattie came out of the house and up the driveway carrying a jacket. She handed it to Aviva. "It can get cold around here at night."

"Thank you," Aviva said. She put it on. Then, to Hack, "But what if they're watching Cobb's place. Can't they catch us there?"

"I'll keep an eye out," Sam said.

Hack handed Sam the keys to his car. He said, "Please take care of my precious."

"Have no fear," Sam said, and took the keys and got in on the driver's side.

Aviva gave Mattie a hug and Hack a peck on his cheek and got in on the passenger side.

They drove off.

Hack walked down the driveway past the house on his left. Sam's rental was parked on a concrete extension of the driveway, a short dogleg to the left and behind the house, just big enough for a truck or car.

In this densely populated residential area, Hack didn't bother trying any of his electronic detectors. There was too much interference from wi-fi, blue tooth, cordless phones and all the rest of the electrosmog.

Instead, he began a manual investigation of the outside, including the roof and the door seams, the space between the front windshield and the hood, the tire wells, the grills and the trunk, including spaces like those under the pad and behind the taillights. Of course, Hack checked inside the front bumper, where he'd found the tracker in Owen's car, and under the back bumper as well.

Nothing.

He got into the back seat and checked all around, including inside the pockets on the front seats and under the front seats. He moved to the front seat and checked the glove box and side pockets.

Nothing.

He spent the next hour or two removing and replacing quarter panels and lights. Still nothing.

Hack slid into the front seat again and spent a few minutes unscrewing and pulling out the car stereo. Behind it he found a rectangular gray box about half the size of his palm. On it was a white label. The label bore a bar code and a bunch of numbers. Someone had hooked a little battery to the device.

It was a GPS tracker. It was active.

But was it from Darwish's crew? Or maybe from the rental car agency? They'd want to know where the renter took their car.

Did it matter who put it there? Anyone could take advantage of the tracker's signal with the right information. Hack unhooked and removed the tracker and laid it on the car seat, then replaced the car stereo.

Forty minutes later, he found another tracker under the hood, glued to the frame with industrial strength Velcro. The tracker was smaller than his thumb. A cable connected it to the car battery.

More than one someone wanted to know where Sam drove this car.

45 Laghdaf

Laghdaf hurried back to the hotel. He rode the elevator up to his floor and went to his room. He changed out of his business suit into hiking gear. He retrieved his pistol and below-the-waistband holster from the safe, along with a spare loaded magazine and a box of rounds.

On his way out of the hotel, he stopped off at the shop and bought a box full of cheese-and-cracker snacks, five bottles of water, and a new thermos which he filled with hot coffee from the hotel lobby. He retrieved his car from the hotel valet and drove to the address Aviva had given him for Darwish.

By the time Laghdaf reached the place, it was night. He drove past the house. Lights were on inside. He drove to the end of the block and turned around and came halfway back. He pulled over to the right and parked.

He pulled out his phone and dialed his Arizona LEO friend. When the man answered, Laghdaf said, "Things are happening very fast right now. What are you doing about the situation?"

The man said, "Don't worry. We're good at stopping things before they get out of hand."

Laghdaf said, "So far you have stopped nothing."

"Have things gotten out of hand yet?"

"I would say so. My client is dead. Another client is in danger."

"Sometimes these things have to work themselves out," the man said.

"I don't know what that means."

"We have limited jurisdiction," the man said.

"You intend that to reassure?"

"Have you told us everything yourself? For example, where your client Aviva Soriano is right now?"

"Why should I?"

"In the interests of full disclosure," the man said. "All the facts."

Laghdaf said, "I have told you nothing that was not true."

"Same for me," the man said. He clicked off.

No help there. Might as well have been in Mauritania. Back home, there had been a few incursions Laghdaf and his brothers had dealt with personally. Slavers, for example. That is when Laghdaf learned to use a gun.

Laghdaf was now a respected American attorney, but the notion of relying on the government to deal with what Sam and he faced barely grazed his consciousness. Family, clan, and tribe was what a man counted on, and Sam was family.

Laghdaf took his binocular case out of the glove compartment. He set a water bottle in the cup holder. For comfort, he lowered his seat halfway back. He ate a cheese-and-cracker snack, vigilant to avoid spilling any crumbs. He took a few swallows of coffee from his thermos. He took his expensive infrared binoculars out of their case and focused them on Darwish's house and waited.

46 Act In Haste

Aviva said, "It looks like rain." Sam snuck a glance at her next to him. She was peering up through the windshield at the sky, which looked only slightly cloudy to Sam.

These were the first words she'd spoken since the little planning meeting in the park. On the entire drive from the hotel to Dudley's house she had spoken not a single word.

It didn't look like rain to Sam, but he didn't want to ruin the relative magic of the moment by arguing. She might go silent again, this time forever. He asked, "How can you tell? It's too dark."

"I know this Sonoran desert. We have it in northern Mexico. I only mention the rain because it could be a problem for us. That is the only reason I speak at all."

He didn't say, "As long as you speak." Instead, he said, "Well, I hope you're wrong."

"Pay no attention to me," she added. "I'm just someone who lived my entire early childhood in a desert country."

Her silent treatment had confused him even more than her offer to dance or the surprise hug. Now she was needling him.

Sam didn't care much for Hack's old Audi Fox. The 5-speed stick shift and its laborious gear changes irritated him after years of driving only highly efficient automatic transmissions. Plus, it took him a few miles to figure out what speeds to shift at.

But Gus Dropo must have done a fine job rebuilding the engine and everything else. The engine had a lot of zip, the brakes were quick and decisive and the steering smooth and responsive.

A single raindrop splatted fat against the windshield. Then another. Then a third.

Aviva cleared her throat and made a show of bending her neck to peer upwards through the windshield again. She began to hum. Somehow, her pantomime irritated even more.

In a few minutes, Sam had to turn on the wipers. There was just enough rain to dirty his windshield, but not enough to allow the wipers to clean it. A few more minutes, and that problem was solved, as the sky opened into a torrent that shrank visibility to near zero.

Sam managed to recognize the turnoff that led him to Cobb's "Don't Bother Me" sign before. As he drove down the potholed road, a parked vehicle started up and swung in behind them. The rain made it hard to be sure, but in the mirror it looked like a red pickup truck.

"I think we're being followed," Aviva said.

"Probably a coincidence," Sam said. "I've been paying attention, and no one's been following us, and Mahir Darwish has no way to know we're coming out here."

"Don't mind me. I'm just a woman who gets frightened by every little thing," Aviva said.

"I never said that," Sam said. "In fact, I said the opposite."

"But it's what you think."

The pickup stopped and pulled over to the side of the road. As Sam kept driving, it faded out of sight in his rearview mirror.

"See?" Sam said. "It was just a coincidence. Probably someone who lives in the neighborhood."

"If you say so."

Sam spotted the dead end and the "Don't Bother Me" sign. He pulled over and stopped. They both got out of the car. The rain had eased to a light drizzle.

"Seems like it's letting up," Sam said. "We should be okay."

Aviva said, "I don't think so. The sky is still black. It's going to pick up again."

"I think the rain's over," Sam repeated. "We should be okay. Come on. Let's find Cobb."

"Can you find him in the darkness?"

"I can find an area he favors. Then he will find us," Sam said, with the same bold assurance he'd deployed over so many decades in court. Maybe his bluff would work for him again.

They set off past Cobb's sign, off the pavement onto the desert ground.

Aviva pulled up the hood of the jacket Mattie had lent her. She still wore her sweat suit underneath. Her sneakers gave her some traction, even in the wet sand and mud.

Sam was still wearing his powder blue business suit and his hard-soled Berluti shoes. The summer weight suit jacket gave him little protection and the shoes no traction at all. As soon as he stepped onto the desert, he began slipping and sliding in the wet. They had to slow down.

Twenty minutes later, halfway to Cobb's twin boulders, the rain picked up again. In the next few minutes the rain escalated from drizzle to downpour to deluge. "We need high ground," Aviva shouted.

This time Sam agreed. He scanned through the darkness for a hill and sensed one looming nearby on the right. He turned towards it. Aviva and her sneakers took the lead. As they climbed, he slipped and scrambled in his slick-soled footwear to keep up. Once he fell to one knee and shredded his pants leg on the muddy ground.

Once atop the hill, they stopped and turned to watch the water rise behind them.

A deafening flood burst with a roar down the depression through which they had been hiking. It was a twenty-foot-wide inundation, carrying with it mud and all the debris it was picking up along its path—branches, chunks of cactus, bushes, entire small trees, and even scattered wooden planks from some wrecked shack upstream.

As they watched from a few yards above the flood, Aviva leaned her head against Sam's left shoulder. He put his left arm around her and she leaned her whole body against him.

For some time they stood that way without speaking.

"We just have to wait," Sam shouted over the noise.

She shouted back, "What if the water rises more?"

It was true. The flood seemed to be rising towards them.

"Then we see how long we can tread water," he said.

She laughed at the old joke as if she'd never heard it.

"Aren't you cold?" she asked.

"A little." The instant she said the word "cold," his body began shivering.

"Let me warm you," she said, and leaned closer. She unzipped her jacket and leaned herself against him and put as much as she could of her jacket around him. The warmth of her body flooded him with feelings long dried up forever.

"Well, this proves one thing," he said.

"What's that?"

"In the Book of Job, where God talks about making it rain in the desert where no man is. I guess it really happens."

She murmured, "You're a funny man to be talking religion at this moment."

"If not now, when?"

"And anyway, we ourselves are here," she pointed out. "It's not true that we are in a desert where no man is."

He said, "You're right. There is a man and there is a woman also."

"Yes."

He laid his chin on the top of her head. She pulled herself back a little and looked up at him. He felt the impulse to kiss her, but he didn't dare. It would be like exploiting her vulnerability.

"You think you're the only here knows some religion?" she asked.

"What do you mean?"

"How about in the Talmud, where it says, 'In a place where there is no man, you be the man'?'

"That's an over-simplified translation. It doesn't say, 'You be the man'. It actually says, "Try to be a man'."

"So why don't you give it a try?"

This was a question to which Sam knew the answer. He bent down and kissed her and, miraculously, she kissed him back.

It had been a long time for Sam and a kiss.

47 Sam and Aviva

For another half hour Sam stood with Aviva in intermingled misery and joy, as the flood first rose almost to their feet, and then subsided almost as fast as it had risen.

Thirty minutes later, they were still leaning together. The sky cleared. A billion stars shone in the dark vault of the desert sky. A full moon was up, and its yellow light illumined the dark mud pit below them where the flood had passed.

She asked, "Do you think it's safe to try for Cobb's place now?"

"I think we'll have to wait a little longer."

They stood for another few minutes before they started their hike again.

They chose a path down the hill in the opposite direction from the flood pit. Over on this other side of the hill, the ground was wet, but not so muddy, as if the flood had chosen only one path and left the rest of the desert relatively dry.

But only relatively. They picked their way together, Aviva more surefooted, Sam more careful. He didn't want to fall again.

They heard another roar in the distance.

"It stopped raining," Aviva said. "What is that?"

"Sometimes floods take a while to happen after a rain," Sam said. "Could be another flood."

"It's different from the roar the flood made," Aviva said.

"Nevertheless, let's find another hill."

They climbed a new smaller hill nearby.

Headlights glowed in the darkness from back the way they had come.

It was a pickup truck. It stopped about a hundred yards away.

"Is it Cobb?" Aviva asked.

"I don't think so," Sam said.

She lifted her arms to wave, but Sam gently placed his hand on her arm. He said in a low voice, "Wait."

A quick series of snicking sounds echoed through the damp night air—the closing of the bolt on a rifle. Sam grabbed Aviva and flung her onto the ground and himself on top of her.

From beneath, Aviva tried to shake him off and rise. "What do you think you're doing?"

He looked up and back towards the headlights. From the direction of the headlights came a simultaneous flash and explosion and a thunk in the damp ground a few feet away. A divot of mud flew into the air.

"Someone's shooting at us. Come on." He stood and tugged at her arm to help get her to her feet. As best he could, he started running them away from the noise, pushing her along ahead of him. With her shorter legs, she was slow, so he had to move just as slow to stay between her and the gun.

More gunshots boomed. Muddy divots popped out of the ground all around them.

He found a three-foot high boulder and shoved her down behind it and dove in after her.

Sam cast his memory back to his training. OODA— observe, orient, decide, act. Sam hated acronyms, but this one had stuck with him.

Well, he had observed. But how much? Who was it? How many were there? Little information to go on. Although it seemed possible there was only one attacker, since so far only one rifle had been fired.

The attacker had to observe too. What was the attacker's ability to do that? He would have seen a man and a woman. He couldn't observe the most important things about Sam, that he was a veteran, and even more important, that Sam was armed.

Did the attacker have night vision gear? Not likely, or at least not working for him. Otherwise, why would he have used his headlights?

Of course, at distance, Sam's pistol would be pathetic against a long gun. How get close enough to neutralize the attacker's advantage? Assuming the attacker was alone.

Aviva said, "What are we going to do?"

He said, "We are going to do nothing. There is no we. After I head back towards the truck, you are going count to sixty, then stay low and keep going forward towards Cobb."

"Whoever that is will shoot you."

Sam drew his XDM. "Or I'll shoot him. Agility can beat raw power."

"What agility? You can barely walk ten feet without falling down."

"Please do what I say."

"Because you're the man?"

"Maybe, but more to the point, I trained for this and I have a gun. And my original mission was to deliver you safely to Cobb. After you make sure I succeed in my mission, send Cobb here to help me or find me, whatever the case."

"Just this once, then."

Sam crawled out from behind the boulder. He heard Aviva begin to count.

He had only the ten rounds in his single magazine. A backup magazine would have ruined the lines of his suit.

If he got close enough, reaction speed would be the key. Maybe the attacker wouldn't expect Sam to move towards him. Or maybe he would. Couldn't rely on a guess about what the attacker might expect.

The headlights went out. What did that mean? The attacker was coming his way and wanted to stay dark?

Meet him in the middle. Sam stayed low and crawled towards where the headlights had been. He used his left elbow and shoulder to propel himself through the muck. He held his pistol in his right hand, off the wet ground, finger on the trigger guard.

No one beats Father Time. Despite the years of treadmills and dumbbells, he was in nothing like the shape he'd enjoyed as a hard young soldier. Not even close. The legs he dragged behind him drooped like overcooked spaghetti. His left shoulder was a raging agony. His neck got more and more sore and he had no idea why.

It started to rain again, this time only a light drizzle. A plus for him. Reduced visibility might let Sam get close enough to use his pistol.

Sam was moving as slowly as possible. Movement drew unwelcome attention. It took him something like half an hour to move the first fifty yards or so.

He came to a low cactus. He veered right around it, but a few spines stuck his trailing left calf. He winced from the pain. He suppressed just the beginning of a grunt, but the small noise he made was enough. Three shots rang out. One round blew apart a barrel cactus only a few feet from Sam's head.

Sam still didn't know where his enemy was. He took a chance and lifted himself from his crawl and scrambled to his right, away from where he'd made his blundering grunt. He tensed for the bullet to hit him, but nothing happened. Ten yards later, he sank face first to the ground again, still holding his pistol off the ground in his right hand.

He propped himself on his elbows and lifted his shoulders and head and scanned the area. Nothing to the right. Nothing straight ahead. Then, to the left, a movement. A dim figure. Coming closer. A white man carrying a rifle at ready, his pale face almost luminous in the mist. He cut his hair close to his scalp and sported a big dark beard. He was thickset and barrel-chested.

The man wasn't facing Sam's direction. Ten yards was plenty close enough for a pistol. Sam rose to one knee and raised his pistol to fire.

As he fired, his foot slipped in the mud and he thumped down, elbow first. The kick blew his slick pistol out of his right hand into a puddle two feet away.

The man turned. The man raised his rifle and fired.

Several rounds hit the ground around Sam.

Sam picked his pistol out of the mud. The muddy pistol was slippery in Sam's hand. Sam fired but knew in the instant he had missed.

Mud flew off the pistol into his face. Sam shook himself and his gun like a dog in the rain. He lifted his left hand to steady the pistol below the barrel. Rain dripped into his eyes.

More sounds of bolt action and another explosion as another round came Sam's way.

Sam fired three fast rounds at the blur of a man and fell sideways into the mud.

This time, no answering fire.

Sam couldn't see through the drizzle and the dark. He brushed the mud and water from his eyes with his filthy suit sleeve.

A few yards away, his attacker lay on his back. His arms were splayed out on the ground. He wasn't moving. Not even a twitch of his beard.

Sam lay back in the mud and stared up at the hazy glow of the moon and the sky. He dropped his pistol and rested his hands on his chest. He should be looking for a second attacker but he didn't have what it took.

"Thank you," he said to God. Then he said it again in Hebrew, a longer version.

Sam lay on his back for some unknown time, a long time. The rain stopped. He heard the sucking sound of footsteps in the mud and turned just his head and saw Cobb standing over his attacker's body. Cobb bent down close to the corpse and picked something up.

"Hello, Professor," Sam called.

Cobb walked over and looked down at him. "Are you all right?"

"I haven't been shot, if that's what you're asking. Otherwise, not so good."

Cobb bent down. "You mind if I take a look at your pistol?"

"Go ahead," Sam said.

Cobb picked it up off the ground next to Sam. He took a clean rag out of his pocket and wiped off the barrel. "And this filthy weapon fired?"

"They had videos showing how it would still shoot even if covered with mud. For once, someone wasn't lying."

"You going to get up?"

Sam sat up. "Eventually."

"I guess it's true what Frank Sinatra said."

"What's that?"

"After a gangster named Cohen knocked him flat one day in Las Vegas, he said, 'Never fight a Jew in the desert.'"

Sam said. "It might be a good idea to look around to see if that asswipe brought any partners."

"I already did, and he didn't."

Cobb handed the pistol butt first to Sam, who took it and holstered it.

Cobb took a flashlight from a pocket and held it to the wallet in his hand. "If you're interested, his name was Steven O'Toole."

Sam said, "According to Owen Deutscher, O'Toole was Tayoub Abawi's assistant. Tayoub Abawi told Owen that Steve O'Toole was dead."

"It seems Tayoub was a little ahead of himself. Do you know why he lied?"

"I'd have to guess," Sam said.

"What's your guess?"

"Maybe they sent O'Toole off grid to do some things for them."

"Like what?"

"Like kill people, for starters."

Cobb spat towards the corpse. "Whoever," he said. "You need help standing up? The reason I ask, you're pretty much covered in muck."

"I could use a hand." Sam reached his right hand towards Cobb.

It had been a long time for Sam and a gunfight.

48 There's Got To Be A Morning After

Sam woke up lying on his back, warm and snug in a sleeping bag. The hard ground beneath felt like his best bed in years. He opened his eyes and muttered the blessing for waking up.

Sam had vague recollections of Cobb helping him over the muddy and puddled terrain to a tent nestled under a rock overhang, and then of Aviva hugging Sam, helping Cobb get him into the sleeping bag, and covering his shivering body with a pile of heavy wool blankets.

Sam looked around for Aviva. She was a mound in her own bag nearby, her back to him, apparently asleep. Cobb was sitting in a wood folding chair with his legs crossed, tobacco smoke rising from a giant bulldog pipe. He was reading a book with a cover in Greek.

Sam had no Greek, but he had two years of high school Latin. He pulled his heavy blankets down and sat up and said to Cobb, "Quo vadis?"

"I'm not going anywhere," Cobb said. "How about you?"

"What are you reading?"

"*The Odyssey*. You know it?"

"I read it in school," Sam said. "In English, of course."

"The poetry's hard to translate. A lot of thing don't make it through to English. In Homeric Greek, it's a great read. Almost 3,000 years old. Do you recall the story?"

Sam said, "Sure. It's about a man who spends ten years in a war far from home, then ten more years trying against all odds to get home—or maybe to get back to himself. My professor explained it all as a metaphor, with lots of symbolism."

"Personally, I think that's crap," Cobb said. "Monsters aren't symbols. They're real. It's a great story, I say a story foundational to our civilization. Homer describes Odysseus as skilled in all ways of contending, by which he means that his hero can fight the monsters with words or with trickery or with sword and spear when it comes to that. Whatever it takes."

"Sure," Sam said, although he didn't get the purpose of having a literary discussion just this moment. But you can't stop a literature professor. "What time is it?"

"Ten fifteen in the morning," Cobb said.

"Time to get up," Sam said. He threw off the remaining weight of the blankets and kicked himself out of the sleeping bag. He was wearing someone else's loose blue wool pants and a thick wool sweater. He asked, "Where's my business suit?"

Cobb answered, "When it's safe to get a fire going, the last few shreds of your lawyer costume will make a charming blue flame. Your dress shirt will add some flair. I saved your holster and gun and your shoes and necktie. I like the tie, by the way. I don't think my shoes will fit you, so you'll have to wear the ones you brought. Your socks are gone too, but I can give you some."

Sam rolled over to squat on his knees. He worked his legs under him to stand up. He was a bit shaky. Cobb watched him rise. From the expression Sam saw on Cobb's face, Cobb expected him to fall face first.

Sam didn't. "I'm fine," Sam said. "Do you know which way is east?"

"What's that?"

"Do you know which way is east?"

Cobb pointed.

Sam asked, "Do you have a hat I can borrow? Any hat will do."

Cobb stood and went over to a trunk. He opened it and dug around and came up waving a brown Stetson. He said, "Buffalo leather."

"Perfect," Sam said. He walked over and took the offered hat and put it on. It settled snug on his head, a perfect fit.

He walked to the east side of the tent and stood nose almost touching its inside canvas wall.

He muttered, "I wish I had my tefillin."

"It's Shabbat," Aviva's voice emerged from her mound. "You don't need them on Shabbat."

"This is Saturday?" Sam asked.

"It sure is," Cobb said.

"So I've been in Arizona less than five days?"

No answer from Aviva or Cobb.

Sam knew most of the required Hebrew morning prayers by heart, and he said them now. He did the best he could without his prayer shawl.

When he finished, he felt okay. Stronger, somehow. Refreshed, even. Alive, mostly. He walked back towards his sleeping bag.

Cobb asked Sam, "What were you praying for?"

"I prayed for rain."

Cobb grinned. "We can always use more rain."

Aviva was sitting up, looking at him with sad eyes. He said to her, "Good morning."

She granted him a weak smile.

He said, "Are you all right?"

"Why of course," she said. "Never better." She rolled over away from him and pulled her blanket over her head again.

Naturally, Cobb had a cook stove, but it sat gray and unlit in the tent corner. He offered only a cold breakfast: cheese, flat bread, crackers, peanut butter, bottles of fresh water. "No hot coffee today," he said. "Anyone take it cold?"

Aviva's voice came again from out of her mound. "I do."

Cobb mixed up some instant and Sam took a cup of it to Aviva. She sat up to accept it. She and Cobb drank their coffee while Sam settled for water. He sat on his sleeping bag and gulped down a bottle. He asked for another, which Cobb gave him.

He asked Cobb, "Did you save my phone?"

Cobb shook his head. "Never saw it. You probably lost it last night somewhere in the desert."

"I need to talk to some people," Sam said.

"I'm keeping radio silence," Cobb said. "The desert sun will dry up the ground sooner than you expect. I'll take you both back to your car. You can go talk to everyone in person."

A little after noon, Cobb led Sam and Aviva on a trek across the now-sunny desert to the red Audi, which still sat where they'd left it the night before. On the way, they passed the scene of Sam's gunfight the night before.

Sam asked Cobb, "Where's the pickup?"

Cobb said, "While you snoozed the night away, I drove it to an isolated spot I know and parked it there, far from here. Aviva followed in your snazzy little red speedster and picked me up and brought me back here."

"Aviva? You did that?"

"It was just driving. I can drive a car. You needed your sleep and it was necessary," she said.

Sam asked Cobb, "What about O'Toole's rifle?"

241

Cobb said, "I left it and the rest of his kit with him in his pickup. You only hit him once, and the round passed all the way through him. The cops will test the rifle and find out it was fired, and that will help them reconstruct a story having nothing to do with you or this place."

Cobb shook his head in sadness. "Too bad. It was a nice piece of artillery, a Winchester Model 70 Featherweight, thirty-ought-six."

When they reached the outlet road, Cobb handed Sam his wallet and said, "I'll see you both soon." Aviva stood tip toe to kiss Cobb's cheek. He accepted the kiss with a smile, then winked at Sam. He turned and trudged back into the desert. Then he was gone.

Aviva walked over to the Audi driver's side door and unlocked it and got in.

Sam got in on the passenger side.

"To Dudley's, right?" she asked.

Sam nodded.

She drove them back. Sam laid his head against the passenger window and fell into a drowse. Neither spoke. In about half an hour they pulled up at Dudley's. She stopped the car in front of the house and turned it off. They both got out. They walked up the sidewalk to the front door. She knocked.

Hack opened the door. He said to Sam, "Why are you wearing that sombrero?"

"It's a Stetson," Sam said.

"Where's your lawyer uniform?"

"The rain soaked it through," Sam said. "It's ruined."

"So now you want to grow up to be a cowboy?"

Sam shrugged, too exhausted to engage. "We brought back your car."

Mattie appeared in the doorway. Aviva took off her jacket and handed it to her. "Mattie, thank you so much. I don't know what I would have done."

Mattie said, "Rough night for you, I think. Would you like something hot to drink?"

"That would be wonderful," Aviva said. "Here," Aviva said to Hack. She handed him the keys.

Hack took the keys. Aviva followed Mattie into the house. Sam followed Hack out to the car. Hack began walking around it like a car rental agent inspecting a customer's return, only more thorough.

After fifteen minutes, "I guess the car is actually okay," Hack said to Sam.

"The car is cleaner than when I got it," Sam said. "I bet it's the cleanest it's been in months."

"The rain gets all the credit," Hack said. Then, "Come with me."

Hack led Sam up the driveway. Sam's rental stood there just to the left on a concrete extension of the driveway. Hack opened the front0020passenger door and leaned in and came out with two black boxes, one about palm size and the other thumb sized.

"Guess what these are?" Hack said.

"GPS trackers?"

"Exactly," Hack said. "What do you want me to do with them?"

"Put them back," Sam said.

Hack stroked his trim dark beard with his fingers. "Do you know how long it took me to find and remove these?"

"Please do as I ask."

"Why?"

Sam said nothing.

Hack stroked his beard some more. "Okay. But it'll take an hour or two."

"I'll pay double."

"Double nothing is nothing," Hack pointed out. "But you're the customer."

"Is Dudley around?"

"Sure," Hack said. "I'll get him." He opened the passenger side door and laid the trackers on the seat. He closed the door and went inside the house.

A minute later, Hack came out with Dudley.

Up close in the sunlight, Dudley looked pretty much the way he'd looked onstage two nights ago at the Hedgehog Barrel, gray bearded, potbellied but strong looking, the kind of man who might possess what Sam was after.

Hack introduced them. They shook hands. Sam said to Hack, "The sooner the better, please."

Hack nodded and went back to the rental car and opened the driver side door and reached in. The hood popped open.

Sam said to Dudley, "Let's talk privately, please." He walked into the back yard past Hack, who was already leaning under the rental's hood.

Dudley followed Sam.

After about twenty yards, Sam stopped. He turned and asked Dudley, "How much for an AR15?"

Dudley said, "Depends."

"I'll give you three grand, with carrying case and some ammo."

"That's too much. You in a hurry?"

"Yes."

"How many rounds?"

"Two full magazines should do."

Dudley looked around. "Why the secrecy? There's nothing illegal going on here."

"I know that," Sam said.

Dudley nodded. "That's right. You'd know that. You're the lawyer Hack helps out time to time. His ex-father-in-law. Hack claims you're the smartest guy he knows. Except maybe himself, or so he thinks. I saw you in the crowd at the Hedgehog the other night. But you look different."

"I am different," Sam said.

"You know," Dudley said, "I could offer you a fine hunting rifle instead. Bolt action. Very accurate."

"The AR will do fine," Sam said.

"Okay," Dudley said. Come on."

Sam followed Dudley through the back door into the house. Dudley said, "Wait here," and went upstairs.

Sam wandered into the kitchen. Aviva was sitting at the table with Mattie. They were laughing about something.

When Sam saw Aviva, he felt a pang of regret for the first time this morning. What might he miss out on?

He said to Aviva, "Let's talk, please."

Mattie smiled and pulled out her chair and walked out of the kitchen into the living room.

Aviva stayed put. She looked up at Sam. She said, "I suppose you'll toss me away like all the others, now that you've had your way with me."

He said, "One kiss is having my way?"

"I am a serious person," she said. "A woman of virtue. I don't fool around."

"Neither do I," Sam said. He bent over and put his right hand on her soft left cheek and kissed her. She kissed him back, warm, soft, inviting, promising.

She pulled back. She said, "Well, then."

"I've got an errand to run," he said. "Law stuff."

"Don't start lying to me now," she said.

"You're right," he said. "It's only sort of law stuff. Anyway, you'll be very safe here with my friends."

"My friends too, I think," she said. "See you soon."

Sam left the kitchen and went back to wait at the bottom of the stairs. Dudley came down and handed Sam a soft sided case about a yard long. Sam hefted it. "May I take a look at what I'm buying?"

"Sure thing. Follow me." Dudley led him outdoors across the back lawn into the garage.

A wide metal work bench spanned the back of the garage. Sam placed the case flat on the bench and unzipped it, revealing the rifle. "Nice single point sling," Sam said.

He lifted out the weapon and checked its safety—on.

To confirm there was no round in battery, he used the charging handle to pull the bolt carrier assembly back and caught it open with the bolt's hold-open lever. He eyeballed the chamber and then stuck his little finger inside it. Empty.

Sam had never fired an AR15, but it was built on the same platform as the M16 he'd carried in the Army. It felt natural and comfortable to him.

"Everything you asked for is in the case," Dudley said. "And this weapon's reliable," Dudley said. "I've fired it thousands of times. Not one misfire. It's great for hunting." He looked at Sam as if expecting a response.

"I'm not much for hunting," Sam said.

Dudley nodded.

Sam clicked on the bench's work lamp. He held the barrel under the intense LED light. The small engraving on the top read, "5.56 NATO." The caliber he wanted. "I'd like to make sure of a few things," Sam said.

"Everything you need is right here on the bench," Dudley said.

Sam hit the release lever and loosened and pulled first the takedown pin and then the pivot pin. He separated the rifle into upper and lower receivers.

He broke down the upper receiver and inspected the various parts. He made sure all were sufficiently lubricated. He oiled the lower in a few key points. He reassembled the weapon.

All this took Sam about five minutes. Dudley had watched in silence. Dudley said, "Check out the Bushnell red dot sight. Helps you acquire your target fast. You can keep both eyes open. You don't lose any peripheral vision."

Sam checked the safety again—still on. Sam tried sighting on an oil can on the floor next to the garage door. He found himself looking through an empty metal loop with a red dot in the middle. Easy to center the red dot on the can and to imagine pulling the trigger.

After verifying again no round was in chamber, he flicked the safety from "SAFE" to "FIRE." He sighted on the can and pulled the trigger. A satisfying "snick" sound. He recharged and dryfired again. He repeated the two-step process several more times.

"Nice trigger pull," Sam said. "Good reset point."

He recharged the weapon and reset the safety to "SAFE" and placed the weapon back in its case. He zipped up the case.

He took the two magazines from their pockets on the outside of the case. Both were full, each one holding 30 rounds of 5.56 NATO, the caliber he was after, full metal jacket, in a reliable brand. He replaced the magazines in their pockets on the case and snapped down the pocket flaps.

Sam pulled his wallet out of his pocket and looked inside it. "Turns out I don't have the three grand on me."

Dudley said, "You're good for it."

"I may not make it back here—that soon, I mean."

"Send it through Hack. I see him every day. It won't hurt to have a bigtime lawyer owing me a favor."

"You're right. Call me anytime. I do owe you," Sam said. "By the way, do you have a few nines for my sidearm?"

"Sure thing," Dudley said. He reached up to a shelf and grabbed a cardboard box and laid it on the bench. "Take what you need."

Sam reached into the box and grabbed a handful of rounds. "These should do," he said. They felt cold to the touch as he slipped them one after the other into his right pants pocket.

Sam pointed at a sixpack of bottled water at the corner of the bench. "A couple of bottles would be nice."

"No problem," Dudley said. He grabbed the six pack and tore two bottles out of the plastic retainer and stuck them into pockets on the outside of the case.

"Perfect," Sam said. "Thanks again." They shook hands.

Sam carried the case out into the yard. Dudley stayed behind, "to clean up a few things."

The car's hood was back down. Hack was wiping his hands on a rag. He said, "It turned out putting the trackers back was easy. I knew just how and where. Finished already."

"I misplaced the phone you gave me," Sam said. "You got another?"

"Of course," Hack said. He walked into the house, leaving Sam a few moments to stand and think, which gave him the chance to realize how lousy he felt.

His shaky legs barely held him up. A sharp pain was stabbing him somewhere inside his left shoulder. He'd gotten only a short sleep after a long night. He had to suppress yawn after yawn.

He glanced around at the thin patches of grass and up at the wide blue sky. Somewhere a dog barked. The smell of grass and sweet flowers filled the air. Life was good, and maybe about to get better. It would be a shame to lose it now.

Hack came out holding a soft black bag by its two soft handles. He laid it on the grass and unzipped it and took out a small black phone. He said, "I have to do some setup." He turned on the phone and fiddled with it for a few minutes. He pressed some buttons and showed Sam the little screen. "There's your new number. Got it?"

"I got it," Sam said.

Hack handed Sam the phone. Sam put it in his shirt pocket. He said, "Fob, please?"

Hack handed him the rental car's fob.

Sam stowed the gun case in the trunk and got in the driver's seat. He started the car. As he backed down the driveway, he passed the kitchen window and saw Aviva and Mattie sitting at the table, laughing again about something. He backed into the street and turned the steering wheel to straighten the wheels.

Sam took a last look at the house. Hack was standing in the driveway, watching him. Dudley walked over to Hack and said something. Hack shook his head.

Sam took off. Sam drove back towards the desert. After a few blocks, he pulled over and stopped. He called Laghdaf.

Laghdaf answered, "Law office."

Sam said "It's me. I've got a new phone. Please note the number on your caller ID."

"Noted," Laghdaf said. "Where have you been? I have tried calling you many times."

"Busy," Sam said. "I'll tell you all about it in person. How about you?"

Laghdaf said, "I watched Mahir Darwish's house all night. Early this morning I had to leave for breakfast and a break. Then I came back.

"About sixty seconds ago, a big black SUV drove up and stopped in front. Darwish came out and hopped in and they drove off."

"How many?"

"The driver, Mahir and at least one in the back seat. I couldn't see if there were more. Three is already many."

"A clean sweep is best," Sam said.

Sam glanced down at his mangled Berlutis on the car floor. "Have you got your hiking boots on?"

"Of course," Laghdaf said. "Does Darwish going on the move just this moment have something to do with you?"

"I hope so."

49 Mahir Darwish

Sam pulled back onto the road. Laghdaf was following Darwish. Laghdaf called Sam twice more on the way. Laghdaf wasn't yet certain, but with each minute the odds increased that Sam's and Darwish's destinations were going to intersect.

Sam had no doubt of it.

Laghdaf also reported that Darwish's driver was trying to make himself impossible to follow. "He drives like he owns the road, like the laws don't apply to him, the way they do in Nouakchott back home, except instead of a Mercedes or this weak little car of mine, he is driving a big black SUV, the kind with its wheels elevated for high ground clearance, like he wants to dominate every other driver.

"He swerves all around everyone in his way and pays no attention to pedestrians or bicyclists. He has run two red lights so far. It is an effort to keep up with him. But I am his match."

"I'm sure you are," Sam said, having ridden many times as Laghdaf's passenger.

Sam pulled up in front of Cobb's sign and parked near where he'd parked Hack's Audi Fox the night before. He turned off the car. He reached down and lifted his side arm and shoulder holster out from under the front seat. He pressed the release to drop out the pistol's magazine. He thumbed into the magazine as many nine millimeter rounds as it would take—nineteen, if he counted correctly. He inserted the magazine into the pistol grip and racked the slide to chamber a round. He dropped out the magazine again and thumbed one final round into it. He re-inserted the magazine, giving him twenty rounds before he would need to reload. He shrugged himself into his shoulder holster and holstered his pistol.

Sam got out of the car and walked around to the back. He opened the trunk and took out the rifle case. He slung it over his shoulder and closed the trunk and pressed the fob button. The beep told him he'd locked the car. He walked for the third time past Cobb's sign onto the desert.

His Berlutis seemed to be doing the job today. Maybe all the abuse had broken them in. Their hard leather soles and the iron-reinforced heels shielded his feet from the rocky broken ground.

He hiked along the same path he and Aviva and O'Toole had taken the night before.

Sam had a good idea where he wanted to set up. Last night, between the rain and the dark and the gunfight, there wasn't much chance to scout, but he'd noticed a place where the flood path narrowed as it passed between two slightly elevated granite formations.

Now, though he was still beat and sore, his old-time infantryman's training kicked in. He detached himself from all discomfort or pain or exhaustion and watched himself from some other place, the way he sometimes watched himself spout off in court.

If he moved like an old man, it was only because he was. Or at least old age was closing in, if he made it that far.

After about thirty minutes he found the spot. On two sides, granite boulders were stacked several yards high. The path between them narrowed to about ten yards wide. The flood had cleaned out whatever desert brush had been growing there, leaving only a petrifying but still sticky river of hard packed mud, sprinkled with dark rocks, green plant remnants and other detritus.

Sam climbed the formation on his right. His dress Berlutis gave him poor traction, and twice he slipped. Once he slid down near one of the dozens of prickly pear cacti sprinkled among the rocks and dirt. He avoided a calf stuck full of spines by bracing himself on the ground with his hands and digging his heel into the ground.

About five yards higher he found a flat cubby hole between two standing boulders. For concealment, he built a pile from the flatter stones littered all about. When he'd stacked his makeshift wall about a yard high, he unslung his rifle case and laid it on top. He unzipped the case and took the AR out and propped it on the ground against the stone, barrel pointed skyward.

He removed both magazines from their pockets on the outside of the case and laid them on top of the case. He took his two water bottles out of the pockets on the outside of the case and leaned them against the boulder on his left. He laid the case on the ground directly behind his wall. He knelt on it to cushion his worn out knees as well as he could.

He took out his phone and turned it off and put it back in his pocket.

He picked up his rifle. After verifying the rifle's safety was still on, he checked the ejection port. Open. No round was chambered. He picked up one of the two magazines. The top round was on the right side of the magazine. He inserted the magazine into the rifle's magazine well. He tugged the magazine downward to make sure it was seated. It was.

He pulled the rifle's charging handle to chamber a round. He released the magazine out of the rifle and looked at it. The topmost round was now on the left side of the double stack. His rifle had stripped the previous topmost round from the magazine and chambered it. Sam reinserted the magazine and clicked off the safety.

The weapon was ready to fire.

The first sound Darwish was going to hear was Sam firing on him.

Sam sat on the ground behind his wall and settled down to wait. Sitting there in the cool day reminded Sam of intense moments decades ago, when he'd been young and hard and even severe discomfort a mere inconvenience.

A breeze came up and tugged at his new brown Buffalo Leather Stetson, the hat he was beginning to love. It warmed his head and, better yet, gave shade to his eyes. He pulled the Stetson down tight.

His scheme had gaping holes. For instance, no escape plan. What happens, happens.

Sam waited for what felt like an hour. From time to time, he took sips from his water bottle. Even with the soft sided case as cushion, his ancient knees grumbled about the continuous kneeling. He turned around and sat on his butt. Cradling his weapon, his knees up near his ears, he leaned back against his rock barrier.

What woke Sam was first the racket, then the press of hard stones protruding against his back. He opened his eyes to sunlight which nearly blinded him. He turned around and peered over his rock barricade.

It was an SUV, a great black tarantula, huge as Laghdaf had promised, high wheeled, tires with thick ridged treads, cab elevated over the desert ground, crawling up the path, churning wet dirt and spewing debris behind.

Sam leveled his weapon over his barricade.

From some long-ago Army training session, Sam recalled that the first stage of an ambush was something called "the stopper." Sam had never learned the following stages because he dozed off.

The stopper was just stopping the enemy's movement. This should be easy. Sam was looking down and to his right at an SUV less than fifty yards away.

The windshield was tinted dark, but the driver could be sitting in only one spot. Sam sighted his rifle, putting the red dot on the windshield just off center.

Sam fired. Then again. The explosions rang in his ears. Two neighboring holes appeared in the windshield, each with spiderweb cracks spreading out.

The monster slowed and pulled off to its left and shuddered to a stop.

For a moment, nothing more happened.

Sam fired a half dozen more rounds through the windshield into the darkness inside the SUV, as fast as he could.

Three doors burst open and three men burst out.

Darwish came out of the front passenger's seat and took cover behind the black passenger door.

The man who dragged himself out of the rear passenger side was already bleeding from his thigh. He limped away from the SUV, hunting for cover, but there wasn't any. Sam shot him twice more and he fell.

The man who came out of the rear driver side door began running back the way the SUV had come. Sam let him go and focused on Darwish.

Darwish must have spotted Sam. He began firing. The rifle he fired was an automatic, a true weapon of war. The magazine bore the signature banana curve of an AK47, the Kalashnikov long favored by communists, guerillas and jihadis all over the world.

Bullets clattered around Sam's stone wall. Shards of stone showered the air. Divots sprouted high and behind him. Sam ducked and pulled his rifle down to his chest, hoping his barricade would hold against the big AK rounds. He tried to count shots up to thirty, but the firing came too fast. Besides, the AK could handle bigger magazines than thirty.

The firing paused. Was Darwish out, or just reloading?

Sam raised himself to fire again just in time to see Darwish shove a new magazine into his rifle and raise his weapon.

Sam managed to let fly two rounds at Darwish before ducking down again. Another ear-splitting hail of explosions came his way, ricocheting and popping and whining all around, digging at his barricade.

Laghdaf followed the SUV to the dead end at the edge of Cobb's desert. The SUV drove directly into the desert, right past Sam's rental and the orange pipes with their "DON'T BOTHER ME" sign.

No way Laghdaf's little coupe had the road clearance or drive train to take onto this terrain. He parked it behind Sam's rental and got out to hike.

The SUV's path was easy to follow. It left deep tracks in the soft ground.

About twenty minutes in, Laghdaf heard gunfire far up ahead. He quickened his pace. A man came running away from the gunfire, in Laghdaf's direction. The man carried an AK47.

Laghdaf stopped. He carried his .45 Glock in a below-the-waistband holster behind his right hip. He drew it now. He kept it out of sight behind his hip but touched his finger to the trigger guard.

The man had been looking back over his shoulder a lot as he ran, but he must have seen Laghdaf, because about fifty meters away he stopped. He shouted in English, "Who are you?"

From those first few words, Laghdaf recognized the man's accent. It sang in the speech of one of the northern tribes which used to come south to raid and enslave Laghdaf's people.

Laghdaf said, "I am only a happy man out on this beautiful day for a stroll in the desert. After such a bountiful rain, the flowers bloom thick and fast. And you?"

"You must move out of my way," the man said.

"Of course," Laghdaf said. He stepped off the path.

The man walked forward. When he was about twenty meters away, he stopped. He leveled his rifle at Laghdaf. He said, "You look like someone I can use."

"How so?" Laghdaf asked.

"I need some work done. You will do it for me."

"Of course," Laghdaf said. He flashed his sunniest smile, the one he reserved for irritating white people and slow-witted judges.

The man kept his rifle leveled at Laghdaf and walked towards him.

Seeing the man come so close, Laghdaf's heart filled with joy.

When the man was about ten meters away, Laghdaf raised his pistol and fired. He hit his target. As the man staggered back, he lost control of his weapon, and his flurry of wild shots flew into the air. Laghdaf stood still and aimed two more rounds into the man's torso, both hitting home.

The man crumpled and fell.

Never taking his eyes off the body, Laghdaf approached, keeping his pistol trained on it. He lifted the AK47 away with his left foot and gently moved it away. The man was certainly dead. Laghdaf holstered his pistol and picked up the AK47 and ran towards the distant gunfire.

Another pause in the fire from Darwish. Sam raised his head. Darwish was gone. Now what?

Move or stay in place? Sam scanned the ground all around the SUV and back towards his own position but found Darwish nowhere.

Darwish knew where Sam was, but Sam didn't know where Darwish was. Not good.

Sam was exposed. He sat down behind his wall again, cradling his rifle.

His concealment no longer concealed. All Darwish had to do was get above and behind him and shoot Sam to pieces. But to do that, Darwish would have to climb. If Sam found another spot, maybe he could spot Darwish's climb. Where?

Sam picked up his second magazine and scrambled up and to the right. He needed to get high enough to get a wide-angle view, but the slope of the nearby ground was relatively flat, not steep enough to get Sam quickly to the view he wanted.

His right shoe sole slipped under him. His right knee hit the hard rocky ground.

Never mind. Pain is just pain, a condition of mind. You only feel it if you feel it. The point is, keep your feet under you where they belong.

In a few moments, Sam figured he'd climbed about thirty yards away, but no more than five yards higher. He stopped and looked back down on his former nest and on the ground near it.

Still no Darwish.

Sam's most promising nearby position was a flat rock about a foot high and a yard across. Sam knelt behind it and swapped his second magazine into his weapon. He shoved the old magazine into his left pants pocket. He laid his rifle on the rock and assumed a prone sniper's position behind it and once again settled down to wait.

In the distance, a small flurry of gunshots, from down the path Darwish's fourth gang member had run.

Interesting, but just now, irrelevant.

Sam waited at least another half hour.

A patience contest. Move slower than slow until you need to move, then move as fast as you can. Darwish must have devoted the entire half hour to advancing about eighty yards to a position higher and behind Sam's nest.

What gave Darwish away was a flash of white from his shirt as he popped up behind a small boulder about fifty yards away, on the other side of Sam's old alcove. Darwish leveled his AK, aiming down into Sam's old nest, searching for Sam.

Sam fired twice, then twice more. Darwish's body jerked on the first few impacts, but Sam kept firing, getting off at least another ten rounds around and into the body, which had settled face forward across the boulder. Rocks and dirt flew everywhere. Sam kept firing till he saw the top of Darwish's dark haired head burst red.

That should do it.

Sam picked up all the casings he could find and put them in his left pants pocket. He slipped and slid his way back to his original sniper's nest.

He hunted around for shell casings and picked up all he could find. There were more than he expected; he must have fired more than he realized at the time.

Terror will do that.

Sam slung his case over one shoulder and his rifle on the other and clambered down the outcropping to the level ground below.

He squatted on a small boulder. In the distance, far to the other side of the dead SUV, a figure was trotting Sam's way.

It was Laghdaf. For some reason, he was carrying an AK. When Laghdaf was about ten yards away, Sam said, "I wonder where you got that rifle."

"No matter," Laghdaf said. He looked at the SUV. "I guess you are all right."

"More or less. I'll need some new shoes. I wonder if Cobb heard all the commotion."

"I did indeed," Cobb said. He came walking up from the other direction. None of the men spoke as he walked around the SUV. He looked inside at the driver and shook his head. He walked over and looked down at the other body on the ground.

Cobb pointed up onto the outcropping. "There's one more up there, right?"

Sam said, "Yes."

Laghdaf pointed back the way he had come. "And one more down there."

Cobb shook his head. "This presents a cleanup problem."

"I can imagine," Laghdaf said.

"Lucky for you I know people with experience in these matters," Cobb said. "And I think they'll be happy to accept this fancy hundred-thousand-dollar SUV for their services."

"Really?" Sam asked. Until this moment, he'd assumed he was going to die or spend the rest of his life sitting in prison, itemizing his regrets.

"Really," Cobb answered. He looked first at Laghdaf, then at Sam. He said, "But this has got to be the end of it. You two have bagged your limit for the season."

50 Settling Accounts

Late one night after their Hedgehog Barrel gig, Hack and Mattie were lying in bed watching ZNN. This time it was Hack who insisted on turning it on and Mattie who complained.

Hack said, "I want to see how they cover the dismissal of that Bar complaint against Sam."

Having made it first into the bedroom, Hack had grabbed the remote for himself. Just now, he had the TV on mute. Hack could tell by the closed captioning that Lauren Goodwell was yammering on about something he didn't want to hear about.

Mattie said, "My guess is they won't report it at all."

"Just in case," Hack said. "I don't want to miss it."

Hack had finally finished the song. It took a frank conversation with Mattie over coffee and fresh home baked donuts at Dudley's kitchen table.

"Sometimes I think you know everything about music," she began.

For once he was modest. "Nobody knows everything about music."

"You come close as anyone I know. You took all those lessons as a kid, you practiced all those years, you studied music in college, you've played thousands of gigs, every kind of music, Beethoven and Thelonious Monk and blues too. Everything. You must know every chord there could be."

"No one could know that," he said.

"Ditch the fake modesty. And now I want you to forget all that. Pretend you know almost nothing. I want this to be the simplest song ever. None of your jazz chords or your blues riffs, nothing atonal or chromatic or polyrhythmic or those other words you use for sounds you use to show off. Simple and sweet, with words a baby will understand."

"You want a lullaby?"

"Yes."

"But the baby isn't born yet."

"You think I don't know that?" she said. "And I can't stand all this waiting."

"There isn't much we can do about the waiting, is there?"

"I'll do what I do best. Sing."

"Sing?"

"Yes. Sing to the baby."

"A pre-natal lullaby?"

"Exactly," she said. "A lullaby I can sing to my baby right now."

"You think the baby will understand you?"

"I know it for a fact."

"When you told me about this, I must have missed the point. This isn't a song for you to sing with the band?"

She spoke slowly and distinctly, as if to the upcoming baby instead of Hack. "No, it's not for the band. It's for the baby. For me to sing to the baby. Every day, before I have the baby and afterward too. That's the song I want. The simplest song you ever wrote or could write in your life."

With Mattie's explanation as Hack's starting point, the whole songwriting process cost him less than an hour and one Chumpster in a booth at the Barrel. He played it for her, and for once, she seemed satisfied. He heard her often, humming the tune as she cooked or puttered around the house, or sometimes sat reading one of the dopey celebrity magazines she favored.

She'd been humming the tune just a few minutes ago, in bed with him. Maybe didn't know she was doing it.

"By the way," she asked, "What about Aviva's lawsuit against SWASU?"

"They bought her off last week. I guess the SWASU people didn't relish another go-round with Sam and Laghdaf in court."

"How much?" she asked.

"You'll have to ask her or Sam. I don't know. SWASU pays off these things with taxpayer money. It's not their own money, so they don't care. But shutting up Aviva will keep the federal dollars flowing, which is something they do care about."

"What happened to the flash drive copy you made of her work computer?"

"Laghdaf gave the decrypted version to his Arizona law enforcement contact."

"Will anything come of that?"

"Who knows? Depends on things we can't know."

She said, "It shouldn't depend on anything. What about Aviva's car? Did you check for a tracker?"

"Yes," Hack said. "Nothing there."

On the TV screen, Peter Totte's bald dome and fat jowls replaced Lauren Goodwell's flowing hair and pretty face. Hack unmuted.

"Hans Cobb continues to walk free," Totte squeaked. "A white Christian nationalist and white supremacist who murdered a Muslim man..."

As the runt ranted, Hack fell into a near doze. Laghdaf had filled him in on the Cobb case. Cobb had proved self-defense.

After eight months, Hack was still waiting to hear ZNN mention Hack's own case against them. A year ago, ZNN had crowded their airtime with denunciation and vilification of

Hack as a racist murderer. Laghdaf had sued on Hack's behalf.

At the time, Hack been fired from his job and was running a crappy little computer repair shop in a crappy little town on the edge of nowhere. Hack had not exactly qualified as a public figure, the kind ZNN routinely slimed without legal consequence, relying on gaping holes in the law of slander.

Totte said, "In other legal news, ZNN continues to contend with a meritless nuisance lawsuit from a disgruntled loner and accused murderer. Suffice to say, the nasty little creep should put away any plans he has to retire soon."

"Finally," he said. "They mentioned me. I feel honored. It's gratifying and validating."

"Can ZNN call you that?" Mattie asked. "Disgruntled, and a nasty little creep?"

"According to Sam, they can," Hack said. "I can't sue for mere insults and epithets."

"I could call you a bum and a louse and you can't sue me?"

Hack added, "And he was careful to call me an 'accused' murderer, which is true. Though ZNN itself was the main accuser. But I'll talk to Laghdaf. Maybe what Totte said will help us pry more money out of ZNN."

Finally, Totte got around to Sam. The Bar authorities had dismissed the complaint against Sam. Naturally, Totte was agitated at this "ratification of untrue, hurtful and racist language." Totte made no mention of Sam's audio recording of his entire conversation with Darwish, which Sam had provided ZNN.

Hack clicked off the TV.

Mattie snuggled up close to him. Whenever she did that, something deep inside gave a little hop of joy. Joy and lust. A nice combination.

She said, "You and I and the baby are doing all right. And at least there's a legal system where a person can get justice."

"Yes, there's a legal system where a person can get justice," Hack said. "Sometimes. For now."

51 A Party

The next week Sam asked Aviva a question to which he already knew the answer, and of course that answer was "Yes."

Sitting next to Mattie at the wedding, Hack commented, "Sam went direct from hermit to husband without passing through courtship."

Mattie just patted his hand.

After the ceremony, Sam and Aviva celebrated by renting the small back room at the Hedgehog Barrel for an intimate group of friends and family.

Sam's daughter and Hack's ex-wife Lily flew in from Minnesota with her ten-year-old daughter Sarai.

Sarai's arrival thrilled Hack. Although they texted or spoke on the phone every day, it had been weeks since he'd seen his daughter in person.

Hack's best friend Gus Dropo flew in too. Hack was happy to see his giant bearded partner, one of the few people in Hack's life who ever knew what Hack was talking about.

Laghdaf brought a woman friend named Maryam who was shy and didn't say much, but she radiated sweetness.

Aviva's son David and his wife Miriam came too, along with her two grandchildren Moises and Mariana, who were about the same age as Sarai.

Although invited, Cobb begged off. He sent a note. "I've been to one wedding in my life. My own. That's plenty. Best wishes."

Everyone sat together at one long table. Dudley, Marty and Bob set up their gear to play in the corner. They left an open space in front for anyone who wanted to dance.

It had not been a long time for Hack and a wedding—he'd played about a thousand of them. But he made the most of the free food and the Chumpster and the company.

Hack sat between Mattie and Gus, with Lily across the table from them.

Dudley and Marty and Bob played a few acoustic instrumentals. Aviva and Sarai danced together. Aviva taught Sarai her old style moves. When Aviva sat down to rest, Sarai hustled her grandfather to get up and dance. Since Sam never turned Sarai down for anything, there he was, dancing.

Hack had never seen the Sam-is-dancing phenomenon before. He asked Lily, "You've known your father longer than anyone else here. Have you ever seen him dance?"

"Yes," she said. Her dark eyes misted. "A very long time ago."

Gus said, "He moves with all of the grace of a Prussian drill sergeant."

Hack said, "More like a spastic marionette."

Gus said, "Or maybe one of those little cuckoo figures that pops out of a clock and swivels around and goes back in."

Mattie said, "You two should talk. I've seen you. Gus, you're nothing but one of those circus bears, hopping back and forth on your two big hairy legs."

Lily said, "Hack, you just lean back and forth like a mummy."

The two women exchanged high fives across the table.

Hack needed a way to get back. Hack had noticed that from his place in the corner, Dudley seemed to be aiming a lot of his fancier guitar riffs at Lily. Hack said to his ex-wife, "I think Dudley likes you."

"What do you mean?" Lily said

"I mean, he likes you likes you," Hack said.

Lily glanced over the weather-beaten Dudley and shook her head. "Sarai and I will be out of here tomorrow morning. I have to get back to my novel, and Sarai has to get back to school."

At the start, Sarai and Aviva's two grandchildren had circled one another with the customary caution, but when Sarai heard the other two speaking Spanish, she answered in the same language, which thawed some of the ice.

Sarai was studying Spanish and loved to speak it with real Mexicans, or in this case, real Mexican Americans, who'd learned it from their parents.

When the kids discovered they all studied Hebrew in their Jewish schools, the ice melted. From then on, they spoke only Hebrew with one another.

But Sarai spent most of her time close by her grandfather Sam. He interrogated her about school and books and her Hebrew studies. She answered all his probing questions with cheerful good nature. She knew his style.

About three hours in, after what Hack guessed was at least Aviva's third glass of wine, Aviva stood and announced, "In 1492, the same year Columbus collided by accident with America, Spain expelled all the Jews who wouldn't convert, including my ancestors. But we kept our Spanish language, which we call Ladino. This is a Ladino song I heard my mother sing. It is called *Avrij mi galanika*, which I translate for you as *Open My Beauty*."

Sarai asked Sam, "Grandpa, will you understand the words to her song?"

"I'm happy to listen to her voice," he said. "But it would be nice."

"I'll translate for you," Sarai said.

Starting with hands over her heart, with dramatic gestures, Aviva sang a vigorous song to an almost martial rhythm. Her voice was a little warbly, but low and good, and she hit the notes:

Avrij mi galanika
Que ya v'amanecer
Avrij yo vos avro
Mi lindo amor
La noche yo non durmo
Pensando en vos

Mi padre esta meldando
Se sentira.
Aruvale la ojica
Se durmira

Mi hermano esta excriviendo
Se sentira
Aruvale la pendulica
Se sentira

Mi madre esta
Enfornando
Se sentira
Aruvale la palica
Se sentira.

When Aviva finished, everybody clapped, and Aviva smiled at them and curtsied. She plumped herself down and took another swig of her wine.

Sarai kept her eyes on Aviva throughout the entire song. When Aviva sat down, Sarai said, "Wow."

Hack asked her, "So you understood?"

"Pretty much," Sarai said. "Some words I didn't. That happens to me in Spanish anyway. The song is kind of hot stuff, at least for ancient times."

For Sarai, ancient times meant ten years ago.

"What do you mean?" Lily asked.

Sarai said, "There's this girl in her bedroom. It's almost sunrise, but she hasn't slept because she can't stop thinking about her boyfriend. She wants him to come to her, but he's afraid to do that because her family might hear what they're up to."

Sarai went on. "She tells him, my father is reading, and my brother is writing, and my mother is cooking. But if you steal my father's glasses and my brother's pen and my mother's spoon, they'll all fall asleep."

Sarai shot a brilliant smile around the table. "The rest is left to the listener's imagination."

Gus said, "An early *Let's Get It On*.

Mattie said, "Somehow, in Ladino, it seemed more romantic."

Lily nodded at Mattie. "Very romantic."

Sarai nodded too. *"Muy muy romántico."*

"Spanish does that," Gus said. "It's really no fair."

Being pregnant, Mattie drank no wine. But sobriety never cramped Mattie's style. She stood and announced she was going to sing something new Hack had written especially for her and for their new baby.

Like Aviva, Mattie sang of waiting for someone, but not for a lover. She intertwined the fingers of her two hands, cradling her slightly swelling belly, and sang in their direction a sweet graceful tune. To others, it might have seemed she was singing to herself, but Hack knew otherwise.

Come soon, little stranger,

We can't wait to meet you,
We're longing to see you
And welcome you home.

Come soon, little stranger,
Our arms are so empty,
We need you to fill them,
To make you our own.

You're all we can dream of
We're eager to see you,
To touch you and hold you,
And kiss you for real.

Come soon, little stranger,
My arms are so empty,
Come soon, little stranger,
And make them your home.

Come soon, little stranger,
I can't stand this waiting,
I can't wait forever
To make you my own.

THE END

(FOR THOSE WHO READ MUSIC)

It Ain't Gamblin' When You Know You're Gonna Lose
Words and Music by Joseph Vass

Where There Is No Man

Max Cossack

2

Where There Is No Man

Max Cossack

73 **F**   **f#dim7**   **C**   **C7**

it ain't gam-blin' when you know you got no chance. You're

77 **F**   **f#dim7**   **G7**

roped up and tied and like her pup-pet you're gon-na dance. She'

81 **F**   **f#dim7**   **dm7**   **G7**

gon-na break your heart and that's just the start of a life-time of sin-gin' the blues.

85 **G7**   **C**   **am7**   **F7**   **Gsus**   **E7 am7**

And it ain't gam' blin' when you know you're gon-na lose.

89 **dm7 G7**   **C**   **am7**   **F7**   **Gsus**   **C7**

And it ain't gam-blin' when you know you're gon-na lose.

3

275

Come Soon, Little Stranger

Words and Music By Joseph Vass

make them your home. Come soon, lit-tle stran-ger, I can't stand this wai-ting I

can't wait for - e - ver to make you my own.

277

Made in the USA
Middletown, DE
19 February 2021